"OPEN THE POD . . ."

. . . the larger of the two men ordered.

His subordinate hesitated for a second, then initiated the sequence that opened the double-sealed hatch.

"No!" Wesley screamed helplessly. Strong hands pinned his arms to his sides and stuffed him inside the air-tight container. In the cramped confines, the boy's head struck a solid mass of tubing, dazing him, while his assailants sealed the pod.

When Wesley came to his senses, both men were gone. The ensign screamed and pounded on the smooth convex walls, but not even a whimper could be heard outside the class-zero unit. With horror, he realized that they could have killed him easily by programming the pod for a vacuum. But they had let him live . . .

At least until the air ran out.

Look for STAR TREK Fiction from Pocket Books

STAR TREK: The Original Series

Final Frontier
Strangers from the Sky
Enterprise
Star Trek IV:
    The Voyage Home
Star Trek V:
    The Final Frontier
Spock's World
The Lost Years
#1 Star Trek:
    The Motion Picture
#2 The Entropy Effect
#3 The Klingon Gambit
#4 The Covenant of the Crown
#5 The Prometheus Design
#6 The Abode of Life
#7 Star Trek II:
    The Wrath of Khan
#8 Black Fire
#9 Triangle
#10 Web of the Romulans
#11 Yesterday's Son
#12 Mutiny on the Enterprise
#13 The Wounded Sky
#14 The Trellisane Confrontation
#15 Corona
#16 The Final Reflection
#17 Star Trek III:
    The Search for Spock
#18 My Enemy, My Ally
#19 The Tears of the Singers
#20 The Vulcan Academy Murders
#21 Uhura's Song

#22 Shadow Lord
#23 Ishmael
#24 Killing Time
#25 Dwellers in the Crucible
#26 Pawns and Symbols
#27 Mindshadow
#28 Crisis on Centaurus
#29 Dreadnought!
#30 Demons
#31 Battlestations!
#32 Chain of Attack
#33 Deep Domain
#34 Dreams of the Raven
#35 The Romulan Way
#36 How Much for Just the Planet?
#37 Bloodthirst
#38 The IDIC Epidemic
#39 Time for Yesterday
#40 Timetrap
#41 The Three-Minute Universe
#42 Memory Prime
#43 The Final Nexus
#44 Vulcan's Glory
#45 Double, Double
#46 The Cry of the Onlies
#47 The Kobayashi Maru
#48 Rules of Engagement
#49 The Pandora Principle
#50 Doctor's Orders
#51 Enemy Unseen
#52 Home Is the Hunter
#53 Ghost Walker

STAR TREK: The Next Generation

Metamorphosis
Encounter at Farpoint
#1 Ghost Ship
#2 The Peacekeepers
#3 The Children of Hamlin
#4 Survivors
#5 Strike Zone
#6 Power Hungry
#7 Masks

#8 The Captains' Honor
#9 A Call to Darkness
#10 A Rock and a Hard Place
#11 Gulliver's Fugitives
#12 Doomsday World
#13 The Eyes of the Beholders
#14 Exiles
#15 Fortune's Light
#16 Contamination

#16

STAR TREK®
THE NEXT GENERATION

CONTAMINATION

JOHN VORNHOLT

POCKET BOOKS

New York   London   Toronto   Sydney   Tokyo   Singapore

An *Original* Publication of POCKET BOOKS

POCKET BOOKS, a division of Simon & Schuster
1230 Avenue of the Americas, New York, NY 10020

STAR TREK is a Registered Trademark of
Paramount Pictures.

This book is published by Pocket Books, a division of
Simon & Schuster, under exclusive license from
Paramount Pictures.

ISBN: 0-671-70561-X

First Pocket Books printing March 1991

10 9 8 7 6 5 4 3 2 1

POCKET and colophon are registered trademarks of
Simon & Schuster.

Printed in the U.S.A.

For Nancy,
the captain of my heart

Foreword

More than a few folks wrote me bemoaning the fact that I didn't include a foreword in my first STAR TREK The Next Generation novel, *Masks*. That was my first published novel, and it never occurred to me that people would be interested in me. Plus, *Masks* was written under a much tighter deadline than this work. So, with all this leisure at my disposal, let me unwind and thank a few people.

Contamination could not have been written without the help of two people: Tom Cheyney and Cary Reich. Tom is the managing editor of a very fine trade journal called *Microcontamination*. In fact, it was while perusing an issue of *Microcontamination* that the idea for this novel was born. Cary, besides being an excellent brother-in-law, is an expert in the field of ophthalmic engineering: cornea transplants, semi-permanent contact lenses, and the like. Thanks to them, the mysteries of the cleanroom and ultraclean manufacturing techniques were revealed to me and, I hope, to you.

Speaking of mysteries, let me thank those mystery aficionados who added so much to that element of the book: Steve Robertson, Marilyn Dennis, Susan Williams, Janie Emaus, and Linda Johnstone. Their suggestions and tips were absolutely invaluable, and I have renewed respect for my friends who write mystery novels. Thanks to Peter David, and thanks to Andrea and Kevin Quitt, who must've read every STAR TREK book ever written. Jim Shaun Lyon and Stephen C. Smith are due a debt of gratitude from all of us for the way they promote STAR TREK novels.

I am forever grateful to Dave Stern and Kevin Ryan of Pocket Books for allowing me to start my novel-writing career at the top. Gene Roddenberry has been thanked so profoundly and so often that he probably won't hear my little voice—but thanks anyway, Gene. I would even like to acknowledge an entity that gets more brickbats than thank-yous—Paramount. For a quarter of a century, they have risked their money to support STAR TREK. In the beginning and in resurrecting STAR TREK for the movies, it was hardly a sure thing.

I would love to supply a real address, but I may be moving soon. So please continue to send letters to Pocket Books and please be patient and understanding of the circuitous routing required.

Since this book is about contamination in scientific circles, I want to deliver a stun blast to those "doctors and scientists" who promote pesticide use. Come on, you guys, the writing is on the wall. Cancer pockets in farming communities, DDT-laden fish in Santa Monica and Hudson bays, nerve problems, eye problems—those poisons are killing us! Turn in those comfy salaries and get busy trying to find alternatives. Maybe I'm so irate because I live in California, where the pesticide pimps have repeatedly sprayed my house with Malathion (fighting the medfly, don't you know). Coating schools, houses, and playgrounds in pesticide doesn't do anything but increase the poison levels in our bodies and the food we eat. If we are ever to realize an optimistic future like STAR TREK, we have to get rid of the kill-'em-at-any-cost syndrome. I pray we see a day when all pesticides will be banned and we stop poisoning our planet and ourselves.

John Vornholt
Los Angeles

CONTAMINATION

Chapter One

FEAR. UNCERTAINTY. ANGER. Confusion. Pain. The salvo of emotions struck Deanna Troi with such force that she nearly recoiled from the disheveled woman pacing in front of her. Lynn Costa clawed both hands through brambles of red and silver streaked hair, then tugged violently at the hem of her royal blue tunic. Her thin shoulders—hunched from too many hours bent over a lab bench—shook with rage.

"How dare he put me here!" she shrieked. *"How dare he!"*

"Dr. Milu simply followed procedure," Deanna said calmly, "after you admitted to destroying records. Wouldn't you like to take a moment to explain why you did that?"

"They were *my* records," the woman hissed, "from *my* project! How long do I have to stay here?"

The ship's counselor manufactured a smile. "This isn't a cell—it's only a consultation room."

The woman stopped pacing, and hope glistened in her tired aquamarine eyes. "Then I'm free to leave?"

"Of course," Deanna replied evenly, "but I thought you might want to discuss what's troubling you."

1

"Don't you know? You're a damn Betazoid!" cursed the scientist. "I thought you could read minds, like Dr. Milu."

"I can sense emotions," Deanna admitted, with a trace of self-consciousness. "I'm not a full-blooded Betazoid like Dr. Milu. And even *he* can't read minds, only communicate telepathically."

"Who cares?" shouted the woman, leaning across Deanna's desk and glaring at her. "A two-year-old could read my mind! *I want off this ship!* I can't stand it here any longer!"

Deanna sighed, wondering how much more of this she could stand before she called Dr. Beverly Crusher and had Lynn Costa sedated. She didn't care if the woman was a giant in her field, one of the most revered scientists in the Federation. Dr. Costa needed help, but for the moment she needed to sit down, be quiet, and listen to reason.

And those were the very words she heard herself saying: "Sit down, Dr. Costa, and be quiet."

Miraculously, the scientist sunk down into the chair opposite Deanna Troi and stared at the younger woman. Her disjointed stare lasted only seconds before she buried her face within trembling hands and sobbed. With each wracking sob, the unruly mop of hair obscured more of her delicate features. "He's leaving me!" she sputtered.

Deanna rose from her seat and put a soothing hand on the woman's frail shoulder. "Who's leaving you?"

"Emil."

Lynn Costa looked more like a child than a woman nearing eighty years of age. Deanna could hardly imagine that this was the person—along with her husband, Emil—who had spearheaded the Micro-contamination Project to unheralded heights of achievement. Their marriage was more than a domestic arrangement—it was science's most famous ongoing collaboration.

"How long have you been married?" the counselor asked quietly. She knew she could simply glance at her screen and have the answer, but she wanted to sample Lynn Costa's emotions as she answered aloud.

The woman leaned back, taming a hank of unruly hair with one hand and wiping away tears with the other. "Forty-eight years," she muttered. "Too long to care what happens to him, but I do."

Love, thought Deanna, that most unpredictable of emotions. "Why is he leaving you?"

"He says he wants to retire. To Switzerland," she scoffed. "In the beginning, we worked so hard to get away from Earth and into space, and now he wants to go back."

"I've heard Switzerland is quite beautiful," replied the Betazoid. "Why not retire? You and your husband have earned a rest after all you've accomplished. Just to have perfected the biofilter—"

"Not the damn biofilter!" shrieked Dr. Costa, leaping to her feet and shaking her fists at invisible tormentors. "Why does everyone want to talk about the biofilter? That was a generation ago, and you'd think we hadn't done anything since!"

Instinctively, Deanna reached out for the distraught scientist as she collapsed. The counselor was not a large person, but Lynn Costa felt as small and helpless as a wounded sparrow in her embrace.

"There, there," she whispered, as the frail woman again dissolved into sobs. "You are among friends."

The woman sniffed. "I've never really felt that. It's always been work, work, work. A galaxy full of microcontaminants to categorize, isolate, and learn to

3

avoid. I thought coming to the *Enterprise* would be the crowning achievement of our careers. But instead . . . it's been our downfall."

So seldom had Deanna ever heard anyone speak ill of the *Enterprise* that she was taken aback. But there was nothing in Dr. Costa's wrenching emotions that indicated any real resentment against the ship or its crew. The *Enterprise* was simply the setting for the final act of a distinguished career, and perhaps a marriage.

The counselor didn't think she could prolong Lynn Costa's career, nor was she sure it was a good idea to do so. But she would do everything within her power to salvage a marriage that had endured forty-eight years.

Firmly, Deanna proclaimed, "You and Emil should take a sabbatical together, just the two of you. While you're away from the ship, in a relaxed frame of mind, you can decide what to do with the rest of your lives."

"Yes!" rasped the scientist, suddenly bright-eyed. "We must get off the ship . . . as soon as possible. But where?"

"You're in luck," the Betazoid responded cheerfully. "In a few days, we're due to rendezvous with a new starbase on a giant asteroid called Kayran Rock. I believe the *Enterprise* will only stay for the opening ceremonies, but I'm sure you and Emil could remain longer. This is the first starbase built upon an asteroid, and it must be quite a unique place to visit."

With wraithlike hands, Dr. Costa gripped Deanna's tunic and held on desperately. "Whatever it takes, Counselor, you must get us off this ship. Before . . ."

"Before what?" asked the Betazoid, alarmed by the scientist's overwhelming surge of fear. "What are you afraid of?"

But that emotion was suddenly overshadowed by suspicion. As if she had said too much, Lynn Costa pulled away from the counselor and averted her weary eyes. "I must get back to the lab."

"Please," Deanna pleaded, "don't go yet."

"I must." She darted frightenedly toward the door, which whooshed open at her approach.

Deanna Troi called after her, "Dr. Costa! Let me set up an appointment for both you and your husband!"

The woman stopped briefly in the corridor and turned to Deanna with sad, haunted eyes. "Just get us off this ship."

Counselor Troi rushed after her, but the scientist had already caught a turbolift.

A pair of turbolift doors opened in the underbelly of the ship and Lieutenant Worf rushed out, followed by four security officers. Above their heads, a red light strobed ominously as a siren squawked a deadly warning. The five officers ran stone-faced toward the doors to Engineering, which did not open as expected at their approach.

Worf growled, "Override!"

One woman, a stocky blonde named Kraner, ripped the panel cover off the controls, exposing a mass of circuitry. Her fingers were a blur as she rewired the relays and switches. Worf furrowed his dark Klingon brow and growled under his breath. Actually, he knew he couldn't do any better than Ensign Kraner, but that didn't assuage his impatience one bit.

Finally, after tense seconds that seemed much longer, the door slid open, and the security team barged in. Phasers drawn, they confronted a scattered collection of engineering personnel . . .

Who ignored them.

"Time!" snapped Geordi La Forge from the catwalk overlooking the antimatter reactor. The chief engineer was beaming a smile almost as wide as the apparatus that served as his eyes.

"Two minutes and sixteen-point-two seconds," said the computer noncommittally as the sirens and flashing lights abruptly stopped.

"Excellent!" remarked Geordi, scampering down a circular staircase to Worf's level.

"Terrible!" growled the Klingon, fixing each member of his security team with a baleful glare. "Of course, we would have been under two minutes if the doors had been functioning."

"Did you like that touch?" smiled Geordi. "I thought it added a measure of realism. We've had a number of distinguished and accomplished intruders down here, for example, your Klingon buddies."

Only Geordi could get away with a remark like that, thought Worf. "The conditions of the drill were not the problem," he grumbled. Worf glanced at his party, still tensely clutching their disarmed phasers. "At ease."

"Worf, that was as good as could be expected," insisted the engineer. "How could you improve it, especially coming all the way from the bridge? That's thirty-five decks!"

"Computer?" snarled the security chief. "In the drill just completed, how long were we on the turbolift?"

"One minute and forty-eight-point-three seconds."

"That's inexcusable!" snapped Worf. "Turbolifts should be faster than that."

"The lifts can be programmed to go much faster," admitted Lieutenant Commander La Forge. "But people would be unconscious or pinned to the ceiling after ten or twenty decks. There's the artificial gravity and inertia to worry about. And you forget, Worf, not everyone has the constitution of a Klingon."

The security chief's lip curled disgustedly, even as the bumps on his brow crinkled in thought. "I don't want people to black out going to the Ten-Forward Room, but we need to speed up the turbolifts ten or twenty percent in an emergency. You can do that, can't you?"

Geordi rolled his eyes, secure in the knowledge that no one could see the gesture through his VISOR. "Yes, I can," he conceded, "but we'll need authorization from the captain or Commander Riker. Also, you'd better get a security team with strong stomachs."

Worf nodded with satisfaction. "Let me know how soon we can test it." He nodded to Ensign Kraner and the others. "Dismissed."

The big humanoid followed his personnel out, and Geordi shook his head in amazement. To no one in particular, he remarked, "There's a Klingon who needs a hobby."

"Counselor's log, stardate 44261.3," Deanna Troi said slowly, settling back in her seat and corralling her troubled thoughts. The sparse consultation room was almost eerily quiet now, in comparison to the interview of a few moments ago. In the fifteen minutes since Dr. Lynn Costa had abruptly left, Deanna had finished reading the researcher's file. She found nothing of any help.

"I met with Dr. Lynn Costa for a brief period," she told the invisible recorder, "at the request of her superior, Dr. Karn Milu. According to Dr. Milu, Lynn Costa's work and attitude have been erratic for some weeks, culminating in the willful destruction of com-

puter records and laboratory notes. Luckily, most of
the data was recovered from backup systems. Dr.
Costa has refused to offer any explanation for her
actions, but I can certainly verify that she is troubled
and terribly afraid. Our conversation was too short to
be conclusive, but her intense level of fear and anger
would indicate a paranoiac condition.

"Most likely, this paranoia has been brought on by
the possibility of retirement, at the insistence of her
husband, Emil. She resents the pressure he is putting
on her, and she fears for the future of the
Microcontamination Project if she leaves. According
to Dr. Milu, the project is well staffed and well
equipped and has benefitted greatly from the
resources aboard the *Enterprise.* Lynn and Emil Costa
may have started the project, but all indications are
that it will continue successfully without them."

Deanna sighed and took a sip of the herbal tea she
had all but forgotten. It was lukewarm. "That said,"
she continued, "I must make the observation that Dr.
Costa hardly seems like the same person I have met on
several other occasions. Today, she seemed fearful,
dejected, and disoriented, and there is nothing in her
file to suggest a predisposition to that sort of behavior.
She has always been an immensely confident and
capable woman. I can only hope that this behavior is
temporary and does not indicate a more serious
condition."

The counselor frowned, and her lush red lips tightened. "I don't wish to further erode Dr. Costa's spirits
by having her relieved from her duties," she insisted,
"but it's obvious that she can't continue her work in
this frame of mind. The best course of action would be
to arrange an immediate sabbatical for her and her
husband on Kayran Rock. From there, they can secure

passage to anywhere in the Federation. Perhaps they'll return to work here or elsewhere, or perhaps they'll do as Emil prefers and retire to Earth.

"If a change of scenery doesn't work, or for some reason Dr. Costa refuses the sabbatical, she will have to be relieved from duty to undergo a complete psychological and medical evaluation. That is all. Please send a copy of this entry to Dr. Crusher and Commander Riker."

"Acknowledged," answered the computer dutifully.

Deanna Troi picked up her tea, stood and paced for a few moments. Quite by accident, she found herself staring at the comm panel near the door, and she was reminded that Lynn Costa was probably incapable of making any arrangements for herself at the moment. She needed all the help she could get. "Computer?" asked the counselor. "Is Commander Riker on the bridge?"

"Negative," answered the mother hen of the *Enterprise.* "Commander Riker left the bridge fifteen-point-five minutes ago and is now in the Ten-Forward Room."

The Betazoid nodded, though no one was there to see the silent acknowledgment. She reached up to the comm panel and lightly touched the membrane keypad. "Counselor Troi to Commander Riker?"

"Riker here," replied the cheerful baritone. "Hello, Deanna." His voice still held the sparkle of recent laughter. Or did Will's voice always sound that way?

"You sound like you're having a good time," she observed, annoyed that he didn't know enough to be worried about Lynn Costa. She would change that blissful ignorance soon enough.

"I am. Geordi is here and Guinan is on duty—why don't you come down to Ten-Fore and join us?"

"I appreciate the invitation," replied the Betazoid, forcing a much happier lilt to her voice than she felt. "I will be there shortly."

But Deanna Troi stopped off at her cabin first. It was on her way, she told herself, but she also wanted to catch a glimpse of herself in a mirror. Not that she ever saw much different there: the red-and-black uniform that flowed over most of her body and hugged some parts a little closer than she might like, the silky brunette tresses which tumbled like an ebony waterfall from the crown of her head onto her slim but sturdy shoulders, and the calm olive face they framed.

She wiped a moist cloth across her brow and the crook of her neck, then added a pin to her hair. That was all the preparation she could afford Will Riker on this particular day. Why should she be so nervous? she wondered. All she was going to do was ask him to clear the way for Lynn and Emil Costa to disembark at Kayran Rock. Why should even the most dedicated first officer object to two people—especially two lovers—getting away alone together? Even if he himself never seemed to need that release.

The Betazoid furrowed her lush eyebrows in anger at herself. This wasn't the time or place to interject personal feelings. Propriety was one of the disciplines she had accepted as a condition of serving aboard the *Enterprise,* and that meant considering Will Riker as merely another member of the crew. Still, if the two of them were ever able to escape to a place like Kayran Rock and spend some time alone together . . .

Deanna permitted herself a sigh, placed her cup back into the food slot, and dimmed the lights before she marched out.

Guinan smiled her most enigmatic smile at the distinguished couple seated before her. One was a frequent visitor to the Ten-Forward Room and one was not. She set the large orange juice—freshly squeezed Valencia—in front of Dr. Emil Costa and delivered the large fruit cocktail to the lady. The lady glanced away demurely.

The wizened scientist grumped at Guinan, as was his custom, and scratched his white close-cropped beard as he checked the pulp content of the juice with his spoon. His hair was scarcely longer than his stubbly beard, and his color was pale but not unhealthy looking. Guinan found him interesting, especially when he added his own ingredients to the drinks she served him.

Adding ingredients was strictly against regulations, but Guinan wasn't particularly strict, and she knew grain alcohol when she smelled it. He would have plenty of alcohol around his laboratory, and he didn't need to come to the Ten-Forward Room to drink. The proprietress knew that the lounge was Emil Costa's only recreation, and she didn't want to deprive him of his comforts. He and his wife deserved a little special treatment.

However, the lady with him wasn't his wife. Guinan couldn't immediately place her, so her smile remained enigmatic as her gaze drifted from the self-absorbed scientist to the young blond woman beside him. "I'm Guinan," she said directly, holding out her hand in the best Earth fashion, "I don't believe we've met."

The woman smiled shyly and shook the Listener's hand, her pale skin contrasting with Guinan's much darker pigmentation. "I'm Shana Russel. I always wanted to come here, but . . ."

"She's only been on the ship for six months," grumped Emil Costa, with a trace of a Germanic accent. "And fresh out of school at that. Until she completed her preliminary work-ups, she didn't have time for such as this." His off-handed gesture took in a tastefully lit lounge area that had been furnished both elegantly and simply. All around them, through gigantic windows, glistened the wonders of the firmament —stars without end.

Shana smiled proudly, changing from plain to pretty before Guinan's eyes. "But I'm done with my preliminaries, and here we are!"

"This is a celebration drink," muttered Emil Costa. He was already reaching into the inside pocket of his gown for the tiny blue vial Guinan had glimpsed once or twice before. Apparently, he didn't care to conceal it from her any longer.

"May you have more celebrations and more reasons to come here," she saluted them with a slight bow. "I'll be around if you need anything." Guinan moved on with a wave and a touch of reluctance, having wished to chat further with Shana Russel. A new soul met aboard the *Enterprise* was always an occasion.

But new customers beckoned. Among them was Deanna Troi, who had joined Will Riker and Geordi La Forge at their table. The three familiar faces were a study in contrasts, thought the humanoid. Will— affable, gentlemanly, and one of Guinan's favorites— was patiently explaining something to the recently arrived counselor. Geordi was furiously keying in data on a tricorder, stopping every once in a while to check the readout. Deanna—normally the portrait of calm and reason—was shifting uncomfortably in her chair and bristling several shades of Betazoid bronze at every word Will Riker said.

As she drew closer, Guinan heard the commander's voice go up a notch in volume. "Deanna, I can't do anything about the landing restrictions."

The Betazoid countered. "I can't see how beaming

Lynn and Emil Costa to a starbase will endanger our relations with the Kreel."

"The Kreel are a very proud race," the first officer explained. "They've been at war their entire existence, much of it with the Klingons, and that will give anyone a bad disposition. This is a big step for them, allowing the Federation to build a starbase in their home solar system. We've longed to get a look at that big asteroid, and now we have a foothold there.

"But," he continued, "the Kreel don't have transporter technology, and we refuse to give them any until they can develop the rudiments for themselves. That's why we have these restrictions. The Kreel will have a lot of dignitaries at the opening ceremonies, and to avoid embarrassing them, we've all agreed to arrive by shuttlecraft. For at least twelve hours, landing will be restricted to invited guests."

"Then get them invited," Deanna suggested, nonplussed.

"Forget it, Deanna," said Geordi, showing interest in the topic for the first time. "Only three people have been invited from the *Enterprise,* Captain Picard, Commander Riker, and Data. Even *I* couldn't get an invitation."

"You know how the captain howled," Riker insisted. "He did everything he could to get more invitations. The captain and I are expected to go as standard protocol, and, well . . . you know how everybody always wants to meet Data."

"I know," admitted the chief engineer. "I also know that Kayran Rock isn't a huge planet where a hundred ships can orbit at the same time. There are limits on how long and how many ships can keep station with the asteroid. Sorry, Counselor, but we'll have to forget any R&R on Kayran Rock until the next time we're in the neighborhood."

"It's not for *me*," protested Deanna. "It's for Lynn and Emil Costa. They desperately need it."

Guinan stepped from the tastefully appointed shadows. "Hello, Counselor."

"Hello, Guinan," answered the Betazoid distractedly.

"Did I hear you mention Emil Costa?"

Now Deanna gazed up at the Listener. "Yes, do you know him?"

"He's a regular," the server remarked, collecting some empty glasses. "He's sitting about ten meters behind me."

At once, the three crew members craned their necks to see around Guinan, and she busied herself at the table to conceal their curiosity. Will smiled appreciatively and stroked his beard. "Who is that he's with?"

Deanna shot the handsome first officer a phaser blast of a look, then turned her attention to the young blond woman.

"One of his assistants, I gather," answered Guinan. "Her name is Shana Russel, and she's only been on the ship for six months."

Geordi focused his long-range sensors, his mind translating thermal patterns, X-rays, brain wave activity and other graphical representations of Shana Russel. "Would you say she's pretty, Guinan?" he asked.

"She has potential," the Listener replied. "Some men like that sort of wholesome sweetness."

"Yes, they do," Riker wholeheartedly agreed. "What exactly is the problem with Dr. Costa? He doesn't look desperate to me."

"Not so much him, as his wife," Deanna admitted. She took another, harder look at the young woman sitting beside Emil Costa. Shana Russel was gazing into the older man's eyes and doting on his every word, between large bites of fruit cocktail. Every so often, she would glance excitedly out the window or around the room. She looked like a teenager on her first date, and she even smiled at Deanna's frank stare, embarrassing the counselor for her suspicions.

"Some men are quite stoic," Deanna observed, "and never show when they need something."

Will gave her a peculiar sidelong glance, and the Betazoid returned his gaze. "Couldn't they beam over after the ceremonies? Or before?" she suggested. "They just need to spend some time alone together. Will, you of all people should be able to empathize with that."

Geordi cleared his throat and stood up. "I've got to go, Commander. I think we can speed up selected turbolifts fifteen-point-two percent during red and yellow alerts without ill effects."

"Try it," answered Will, relieved to have another topic for discussion, no matter how briefly. "And when you hold the tests, I'd like to be there. Who's going to ride these souped-up turbolifts?"

"I'm saving a spot for Worf," Geordi grinned. He waved a farewell and strode off.

Guinan was slipping away too. "I'll be back," she assured them.

The commander's smile faded, and he shook his head bemusedly at Deanna. "You're not being very subtle about your feelings today."

"I'm sorry," sighed the Betazoid, lowering her face. Then she looked at him with her wide, dark eyes. "I feel that, after everything the Costas have done for us, we owe them an opportunity to find happiness. The new starbase makes an ideal excuse for them to get away by themselves, and they have much to discuss."

Will Riker averted his eyes, remembering that Deanna could probe his emotions without half trying. Not that she would find many surprises, but it was best to keep the conversation on neutral ground. "The *Enterprise* is not going to maintain course with Kayran Rock for very long," he said stiffly. "Certainly not the whole twelve hours. If we arrive early, I'll see what I can do, but I'm not promising anything."

"Would it help if we talked to Emil Costa?"

"No," snapped Will, glancing in the direction of the famous microbiologist. "I don't want to promise him something I may not be able to deliver."

Deanna's exotic features brightened considerably. "Then again, there are only three of you," she suggested, "and a personnel shuttle seats ten. You have plenty of room."

Riker scowled, "Didn't you listen to Geordi? We're not going to have a hundred ships following one asteroid. We may have to do a certain amount of shuttle-pooling with other ships in the area to get everyone to the ceremony on time." He rose to his feet, shook his head, and finally smiled despite himself. "You're quite a romantic, you know that?"

"I'm counting on you to be."

He squeezed her slim shoulder and let his hand linger there for a moment. "I'll do what I can. Have the Costas officially request shore leave, specifying the next available port. At least the paperwork will be in order."

"Thank you," she smiled, touching his hand. Their eyes met for an instant, and she read all the emotions so familiar within the tall bearded first officer: caring, warmth, and a commitment to his career that precluded any long-term romances. He wanted to be the captain of a starship—preferably *this* starship, the *Enterprise*. Not that there weren't captains who were married and had families, but no starship bearing the name *Enterprise* had ever had one.

Reluctantly, he pulled his hand away. "I've got to get some sleep," he said, "and now's a good time, with nothing going on for the next three days while we're en route. I'll see you on the bridge."

"Good-bye, Will."

He strode off, nodding to various acquaintances as he made his way through the half-filled lounge. Deanna averted her eyes from that pleasant sight to the puzzling one of the two scientists seated nearby. The young blond woman, Shana Russel, was cheerfully babbling away, while Emil Costa was looking forlornly at the dregs of his orange juice. He may not have exhibited any of the disturbed behavior that his wife had, but he didn't appear particularly happy. Deanna rose from her chair and walked over to the table.

"Hello," she greeted them, nodding first to the eminent scientist. "Dr. Costa."

"Hello, Counselor Troi," he muttered, barely looking up. "This is one of our assistants, Dr. Shana Russel."

"Pleased to meet you, Counselor Troi!" she enthused, holding out an eager hand. "This is fun coming here—you meet so many interesting people. Won't you please sit down?" Then she glanced nervously at her superior. "If that's all right, Doctor?"

"It's your celebration," he shrugged.

Deanna smiled and settled into her seat. "How are things down on deck 31?"

"You should know better than I," answered Emil Costa. "Don't you talk regularly with Dr. Milu?"

"Not really," admitted Deanna. "Until recently, I hadn't talked to him for several weeks."

"You're a Betazoid, too!" exclaimed Shana excitedly. "This is so wonderful being aboard the *Enterprise,* with Vulcans and Betazoids and even a Klingon. What is *he* like?"

"Shana," grumbled Dr. Costa, "I think the counselor and I have a private matter to discuss. Why don't you go talk to Guinan at the bar? I think you'll find her more interesting than anyone else on board."

"You may want to inspect the artwork, too," suggested Deanna, motioning to elegant sculptures and paintings scattered throughout the café. "We have pieces from all over the galaxy. I promise not to keep Dr. Costa long."

"That's all right," replied the young woman, rising from the table and peering excitedly around the room. "To tell you the truth, more than anything, I just want to stand at the window and stargaze. In the heart of the ship, we don't have any windows, just a few viewscreens. It's not the same thing." Again, she extended her hand. "Pleased to meet you, Counselor Troi."

"Deanna," the Betazoid corrected her. "The pleasure is mutual."

Shana Russel nodded awkwardly and backed away toward the beckoning field of stars. As soon as she was out of earshot, Emil Costa sighed, "Sorry, but I didn't want her to hear your report. That young woman idolizes my wife."

"I don't really have a report," said Deanna, clasping her hands as she composed her thoughts. "Your wife was too disturbed to talk to me for more than a few minutes, but I gather that you wish to retire, and she doesn't."

"Yes," answered the scientist, gazing distractedly at one of Guinan's assistants, who hurried past with a tray of colorful beverages. "Retirement seemed to be the answer, but I'm not so sure now . . ."

"Do you want to end your marriage?" Deanna asked frankly.

Emil Costa snorted a laugh. "What marriage? We're co-workers and, infrequently, lovers. But we haven't been friends for years."

"How do you account for that?"

The scientist scratched his stubbly white beard. "How does something like that happen? Part of it, I suppose, is our adversarial relationship within the project. My job is to find and nurture the biological intruders needed to test my wife's procedures. If I come up with a submicrobe she can't defeat, then I'm the bad guy. Sometimes, she won't talk to me until she figures out a way to filter it."

That's not enough reason to end a forty-eight-year marriage, thought Deanna, and it didn't answer a more troubling question about Lynn Costa.

"Dr. Costa," she said slowly, "your wife is suffering from a fear so profound that it is crippling her. Do you know what she could be so afraid of?"

The scientist looked abruptly away and tried to hail a passing server. "Over here!" he called. "More orange juice!"

"Doctor?" the Betazoid persisted. "What is Lynn afraid of?"

The microbiologist snarled, "I don't know."

He's lying, thought the ship's counselor, and hiding something.

Guinan arrived a moment later, with a fresh glass of orange juice. "I heard you bellowing clear across the room," she smiled, setting the glass in front of Emil. "What will you have, Counselor?"

"Nothing, thank you," said Deanna, not wishing to remain at the table a moment longer than necessary. Neither one said a word until the proprietress had moved on to other customers.

"I'm sorry," muttered Emil, scratching his short-cropped hair. "My wife is . . . just not herself. She needs retirement more than I do."

"I can't convince her to retire," answered Deanna, "but I have convinced her to go on sabbatical alone with you. With a bit of luck, you can disembark in three days, when we reach the new starbase on Kayran Rock."

The aged scientist stared at her, as if the last thing he had expected was such firm action. "That . . . that is very kind of you," he stammered.

"Then you'll go?"

"Of course!" he exclaimed, his wrinkled face creasing into a smile for the first time. "Yes, that would be the perfect solution."

The same reaction as his wife, mused Deanna; both wanted off the ship very badly. She rose to her feet, adding, "I've already talked to Commander Riker about it, and he says you will have to make an official request, specifying the next available port. Will you and your wife do that?"

"Absolutely," replied the doctor, springing to his feet. He was now grinning, as he eagerly pumped the Betazoid's hand. "Counselor Troi, you have made two people very happy!"

"I hope so," Deanna replied sincerely. "I'll be in touch."

"Thank you, thank you!" he beamed.

Emil Costa may have been happy, but Deanna Troi certainly wasn't as she made her way slowly out of the Ten-Forward Room. The ideal solution, he had said. But the ideal solution to what?

What was Emil Costa hiding?

The Betazoid slept fitfully during her rest period, and she twice dimmed the lights, until it was totally dark in her compact but comfortable quarters. Even in a blackness that rivaled space, she lay awake in her bed, unable to clear her mind.

It had been several hours since she had talked to Lynn and Emil Costa, separately, and she longed to counsel the two of them together. Watching them interact might reveal the basis for Lynn Costa's fears and Emil Costa's deception. Deanna hated to play games, but she had something the two of them wanted —passage off the ship—and she could use that as leverage to convince them to meet with her. There were still three days before they reached the asteroid, more than enough time to help them face their problems.

Having decided upon a course of action, Deanna was finally able to relax. With the wild-eyed and wild-haired image of Lynn Costa in her mind, the Betazoid drifted off to sleep. But it wasn't a peaceful repose. She was troubled by a disturbing yet fascinating dream in which she was completely enclosed in a white suit and white helmet. Her labored breathing echoed in her ears, and the stale scent of reconstituted air assaulted her nostrils. Sweat beaded upon her brow and the back of her neck, as she fought off feelings of claustrophobia.

At first, she thought she must be in a spacesuit, prepared to beam down to a hostile planet. But the suit she was wearing was far too supple and light-weight for a spacesuit, even counting the air hoses which extended from the back of her helmet to a small device on her waist. Also, her view through the transparent visor of the helmet was not of the trans-porter room or an alien vista. What she saw was a sterile white room with a row of oblong pods, each just barely large enough to allow a human to seal himself inside. Through gray-tinted glass, she could see a mass of miniaturized equipment within each pod—beakers, tubes, and sensors. The pods were familiar, yet also vaguely threatening.

Before Deanna could inspect her surroundings further, she was drawn to the closest pod. Something was wrong with it, she knew instinctively. As she peered into the smoky glass, a stream of yellow gas seeped from a valve on the outside of the pod. The moment she saw it, she knew she had to run, but the valve ruptured before she could react. Now the stream was a flood, and noxious fumes invaded her eyes, nose, and mouth. Delicate membranes burned with searing pain, and she gagged uncontrollably. The suit was never intended to keep surrounding air out, and the yellow gas poured in. She struggled to stay on her feet, but the battle was already over.

She was dying.

Deanna bolted upright in her bed, panting for breath. Her hair clung to her sweat-drenched neck and shoulders. She swept her hand over the panel beside her bed, and the lights came on full. She staggered out of bed and rushed to the food slot, where she punched up a large glass of water. She gulped it ravenously, trying to erase the dry burning in her throat. For a dream, that one had been horribly realistic. She consumed another glass of water, then sat on the edge of her bed, wiping sweaty hair away from her face.

She didn't know how long she sat there, reliving the nightmare, until the familiar voice of Dr. Beverly Crusher intruded.

"Crusher to Troi," came the voice over the ship's communicator. "Are you awake, Deanna?"

Deanna took a deep breath and composed herself before answering. "Troi here. Yes, I'm very much awake."

"I'm sorry to interrupt you during your sleep period, but it's about Dr. Lynn Costa."

Profound dread welled within Deanna's soul. "What about Dr. Costa?" she asked. "Did you read my log?"

"Yes," replied the doctor. "Can you please come to sickbay."

"Why?" breathed Deanna.

"Lynn Costa is dead."

Chapter Two

DEANNA TROI dashed from the turbolift into sickbay, where she saw a somber clutch of people gathered around an examination table. Dr. Beverly Crusher was probing the frail body on the table, but without much urgency. A glance at the vivid readouts on the wall told Deanna why—all vital signs were at zero.

Among the onlookers was a gigantic humanoid male who stood close to two-and-a-half meters tall, but Deanna's eyes were drawn to a smaller man, Captain Jean-Luc Picard. His sleek head angled back, and his noble chin jutted angrily in helplessness at the sight of the dead woman. At the sides of his trim body, his hands curled into fists.

"How did it happen?" he demanded.

Beverly Crusher nodded toward the hulking humanoid. "I suggest you ask Dr. Grastow," she replied. "He discovered the body."

Grastow was huge but baby-faced, with smooth pink cheeks and tufts of blond beard on his double chins. His sandy-colored hair was short and stubbly like Emil Costa's, and he also wore the same blue lab coat but many sizes larger. He stared in shock at the body on the table, and Deanna could see moistness welling in his puffy pink eyes.

When the big man seemed incapable of speaking, Beverly continued, "We beamed Dr. Costa directly here, but it was too late. She was wearing an environment suit, but it didn't help her against what was apparently a lethal gas."

It was then that Deanna saw the crumpled white suit on the floor—exactly like the one in her dream, down to the helmet with the air hoses.

Dr. Grastow, who appeared to be light years away with his grief, suddenly blinked at Dr. Crusher. "The suit filters air flowing *out,* not entering," he said softly in a high-pitched voice. "It's a cleanroom suit."

"Is there any danger to anyone else?" Picard asked.

"No," murmured the scientist, "the room's been sealed off, and it's negative-pressurized anyway." He pounded a beefy hand onto his forehead. "Oh, this is terrible! *I can't believe it!*"

As the others waited for the sorrowful giant to compose himself, the doors to sickbay slid open, and Commander Riker, Lieutenant Worf, and Lieutenant Commander Data rushed in. They slowed their urgent pace as they approached the examination table. Worf and Data peered at the slight red-haired body, Data with curiosity and Worf with a tightening of the muscles around his thick jaw.

"Bridge is secure," declared Riker, glancing at the lifeless form. "What happened?"

"First of all," Jean-Luc reiterated, "is that cleanroom completely sealed off?"

"All rooms on deck 31 are self-sealing, Captain," answered the Klingon. "Ship's monitors indicate full containment."

Recovering a measure of authority to his soft voice,

Dr. Grastow added, "The filtration system should have that room cleaned up in about two hours. You can go in then."

"It's important we know what happened," said Worf in his no-nonsense bass voice.

"Of course, Mr. Worf," answered Grastow, now sounding eager to please. "I haven't gone into the room yet, and I can only tell you what I *think* happened. Lynn was working on reactive purification —it was a pet project of hers. She often worked on it after hours. The concept is simple, but the execution is elusive."

"Reactive purification," remarked Data, "the conversion of solid contaminants to a gaseous state for easier removal. A theoretical process."

"I'm afraid so," nodded the massive figure. "If perfected, it could save millions of batches of microchips and tissue replacements that are otherwise discarded for minor contamination. Lynn expected the gas to be dangerous, so she was conducting the experiment in a class zero pod. The way the gas was streaming out, I would have to guess there was a rupture in a valve or seal."

He shook his head, his childlike face pouting to hold back tears. "I was working in an adjacent lab and heard the alarm—the room is monitored by a gas analyzer and a particle counter. When I got to the window, I saw Lynn just lying there . . . and I saw the gas. I knew the negative pressure would contain it, so I called sickbay first. Did I do wrong?"

"Not at all," answered Picard, injecting a note of sympathy into his cultured voice. "No one else was endangered, I take it?"

"No one," muttered the scientist. "I'll be happy to answer more questions later, but just now . . . I would like to go to my cabin."

"Thank you," said Picard. Dr. Grastow nodded to the others and slouched out of the room, ducking through the doorway.

Will Riker glanced after the departing scientist, observing, "They grow them big on Antares IV."

"He would be considered small-to-average for an Antarean," corrected Data.

Captain Picard stepped closer to the examination table and stared down at a face that might once have been beautiful, but was now worn and cold and oddly serene. Death has a way of erasing the care lines, he thought. "Has anyone contacted her husband?" he asked softly.

"No," answered Beverly Crusher, looking down.

Jean-Luc frowned, as if this was a part of the captain's job he hardly relished. "I won't announce her death to the ship's populace until I've talked with Emil Costa first. Beverly, as soon as you're done with the autopsy, notify Commander Riker, so that he can schedule the funeral."

"I will," she answered.

"Mr. Worf," ordered Picard, "I'm counting on you to inspect the cleanroom and the pod thoroughly, as soon as it's safe."

"Yes, sir," snapped the big Klingon.

"Number One, Data, return to your posts," added the captain. "There's nothing else we can do here."

"May I accompany you to see Emil Costa?" asked Deanna.

Jean-Luc managed a weak smile. "I would be most appreciative, Counselor."

"Deck 32," Captain Picard told the computer as the doors of the turbolift hushed shut on himself and Deanna Troi. He shook his head uncomprehendingly. "We take so many precautions aboard this ship—it's incredible an accident like this could happen. What am I going to tell her husband?"

Deanna looked fondly at her superior and remembered how proud Jean-Luc had been the day he had welcomed the Costas aboard. He had been a great admirer of their work and had lobbied hard to have the admiralty approve their assignment to the *Enterprise.* He knew, as they did, that serving on a starship entailed risks that serving at a scientific outpost never would, but the Costas, with grown children and already illustrious careers, were exactly the sort of shipmates he wanted.

Often, Deanna had seen her captain anguish over the fate of all the civilians on board, but children and young families—with their lives ahead of them—were his special agony. They just blithely rode along where he led them, oblivious to the dangers. He preferred adults, like the Costas, who recognized the challenges of space and came of their own free wills.

The Costas were also a venerable married couple, and Deanna knew the esteem in which Jean-Luc held marriage, although he had never sampled the institution himself. Sometimes, she thought, his denial of his natural attraction to Beverly Crusher was in deference to his friendship with her late husband. To Jean-Luc, she would always be Jack Crusher's wife.

Therefore, it was with some reluctance that Deanna reported, "Captain, the Costas' marriage was going very badly. In fact, they were just about to leave the *Enterprise* because of it."

"Really?" he replied with curiosity. "And why wasn't I told about this?"

"I only found out a few hours ago," answered Deanna, "and there was some question as to whether they could leave the ship at Kayran Rock."

"We would have been sorry to see them go," muttered Picard, "but that would have been preferable to *this*."

The door of the turbolift opened, and they found themselves in a central corridor opening onto the game room on deck 32. This wing of the lower secondary hull was devoted to living quarters for a mainly adult community of scientists, most of whom worked on deck 31. The recreation room had more card tables than hologram games, and an old-fashioned pool table that looked well used. At the moment, a three-dimensional chess game was in progress between two women, but otherwise the facility was empty. The women were so engrossed in their game that they didn't notice the rare appearance of the captain on their deck.

It was sleep period for most of the researchers, Deanna reminded herself. By all rights, *she* should still be asleep. Then she remembered her horrendous dream and was glad to be awake. How much, she wondered, should she tell the captain? Not that it wasn't his concern, but she couldn't bother him with every dream she had. And death had somewhat negated the importance of Lynn Costa's mental health. Nevertheless, Deanna had a terrible nagging thought she wished would go away.

"Through here," the captain said softly, leading the counselor away from the recreation room and down a deserted corridor. Doors were plentiful, as were letter/number combinations and hologram portraits of some of the residents. There was an eclectic mixture to the decorations in the hallway, with holographic bulletin boards sharing space with art reproductions and hand-drawn children's murals.

The captain stopped, clearly perplexed. "I hope I

haven't made a wrong turn." He tapped a comm panel. "Computer," the captain ordered, "am I close to Emil Costa's cabin?"

"You are near, sir," answered the android within seconds. "His cabin is B-81, the first on the left after the next bulkhead, and he is present."

"Thank you," said Picard. "Out."

Jean-Luc strode down the hall, and Deanna had to hurry to keep up. True to Data's word, they found a door with a name plaque reading, "The Costas." Chin jutting, Captain Picard put his grief aside and braced himself for his unpleasant duty.

He sounded the entrance chime, but nothing happened. He pressed the button again, but still nothing happened. Determinedly, the captain tapped his communicator badge and announced, "Captain Jean-Luc Picard to Emil Costa. I am standing outside your door, and I need to speak with you."

"Yes, Captain," came a slurry mumble, accompanied by a few grunts and groans. There was a loud belch. "I'm not in any condition to see you, Captain."

"This can't wait," Picard snapped. "It's about your wife."

The door slid open immediately, and a bleary-eyed little gray-haired man stared at them. He looked sick, and there was a smell about his breath which Deanna couldn't immediately place.

When no invitation to enter was forthcoming, Captain Picard took a deep breath and spit out his unfortunate news, "Your wife has suffered a tragic accident. She is dead."

Emil Costa blinked at them, the film slowly eroding from his eyes. Then came the denial, as he insisted, "She's working upstairs in the lab . . . her silly reactive thing."

"That's where the accident happened," said

Deanna. "Dr. Costa was already dead by the time her body was transported to sickbay."

"Wha . . ." muttered Emil Costa. *"No!"* he shrieked a moment later. He slammed the door on them.

Captain Picard glanced at the counselor puzzledly, but Deanna was busy sorting out the emotions she had felt before the slamming of the door. Not surprise —almost acceptance. Fright. Guilt. Extreme sorrow.

"Did you smell alcohol on his breath?" asked Picard, moving away from the door.

"Yes," sighed Deanna. So that was the smell?

Jean-Luc held out a hand to stop her from leaving, then peered into his counselor's eyes. "Enlighten me," he said. "What's going on here?"

Deanna shook her head. "I don't know all of it," she admitted. "Emil Costa is hiding something, and Lynn Costa was terribly troubled and frightened when I saw her just a few hours ago. I don't think we can rule out the possibility of suicide."

"Suicide?" repeated Picard, aghast. "Is this suspicion based on something specific you sensed about her, like a death wish?"

"No, not really," conceded the Betazoid. "I hope I'm wrong—I merely bring it up as a possibility. Historically, humans have a tendency toward suicide when they become extremely depressed. They can even subconsciously fabricate a fatal accident."

"You said she was frightened?" asked Picard. "Of what?"

"I don't know why," Deanna answered, shaking her head glumly. "I tried to determine that, but she wouldn't let me."

"Very well," Jean-Luc said decisively, "you will accompany Worf to the site of the accident, and the two of you will ferret out exactly what happened."

"Yes, Captain," replied Deanna without much enthusiasm. Not only was she feeling guilty about not having done more to prevent Lynn Costa's death, she didn't relish the prospect of working with Worf. But she would never let personal feelings interfere with her duty, nor let the captain know about her discomfort. So Deanna manufactured a smile and started down the corridor.

"Counselor," Picard called after her in a voice that was gentle and sympathetic. "I know you and Worf haven't always seen eye-to-eye, but he's the security chief and must conduct this investigation. You've had recent contact with the dead woman and have some insight into her frame of mind. I want a report from each of you."

"Yes, sir," she agreed. In matters pertaining to his crew, she sometimes wondered if Captain Picard's ESP wasn't the equal of hers.

Again, he tapped his insignia badge. "Picard to Worf."

"Yes, Captain," barked the familiar voice with its total respect for authority. "Worf here."

"Meet me in my ready room," ordered the captain. "I'm assigning Counselor Troi to help you in your investigation of Dr. Costa's death."

"Yes, sir," came Worf's reply, and the Klingon was unable to hide the surprise in his voice.

As she and the captain shot upward in the central turbolift to the bridge, Deanna couldn't help but relive the moment when her antipathy toward Worf had developed. She was pregnant with a child of unknown origin, and he had suggested—in his official capacity of security chief—that the child be aborted. Cooler heads prevailed, and the pregnancy was allowed to come to full, if highly accelerated, term. True, the child had posed a danger to the ship, but it was really just the means for an extraordinary entity to experience being human. Ultimately, the experience had enriched all their lives.

But Worf had wanted to abort it.

Rationally, she excused him without question. Had she been in his position, she might have made the very same recommendation. But that didn't change her emotional response, which would need more than a year or two to soften. It was her body, and she felt *she* should have the final say. The decision to give birth—or not—had rightfully been hers to make.

She was certain that the incident had not impacted Worf's psyche as much as it had hers. He had always addressed her civilly and heeded her advice, but they had never really had to work closely on a project together . . . until today.

Picard and Deanna emerged onto a bridge that had been fully expecting to see the captain in a matter of moments. Everything was ship-shape, with Data at the operations console, Ensign Wesley Crusher manning the conn, and Commander Riker standing over the young helmsman's shoulder.

"Worf is in the ready room," said Riker with a nod to his left.

"Thank you, Number One," Picard answered. He stopped for a second. "Status, Ensign Crusher?"

"Course set to rendezvous with Kayran Rock in the Kreel solar system," answered the teenager matter-of-factly. "Warp three."

"Maintain course and speed," nodded the captain. He turned to Riker and lowered his voice. "Any word yet on the autopsy?"

"None, sir," replied Riker, matching the captain's solemn tone.

Picard nodded and strode toward his ready room. Lieutenant Worf leapt to his feet as soon as they entered the private office. The computer screen on

Picard's desk was filled with high resolution vector diagrams and accompanying text.

Worf nodded to the captain and counselor and moved away from the captain's desk. "I've been studying the maintenance reports of deck 31," he muttered, pointing to the screen, "and I can't understand how a seal or a valve could have malfunctioned so badly."

The captain sighed, "Perhaps it was tampered with."

"What?" growled Worf, his several brows knitting angrily.

Deanna stepped between the two males and delivered a summary of her conversation with Lynn Costa, concluding with the statement, "All I'm suggesting is that the possibility of suicide cannot be ruled out."

"Also, Emil Costa may have been intoxicated on alcohol," .the captain added distastefully. "I don't know what any of this means, but I want both of you to investigate and report to me. How soon can you get into that cleanroom?"

Worf stiffened his shoulders and reported, "Dr. Karn Milu is waiting for me . . . *us* . . . in his office, and he will arrange entry as soon as possible."

"Then," declared Picard, "the two of you are dismissed from all other duty until this investigation is completed. That is all."

The Klingon and the Betazoid glanced briefly at one another, then marched out. Together.

Chapter Three

THE ADMINISTRATIVE OFFICES of the science branch were located in the saucer section, on deck 5. That was some distance from the labs on deck 31, but it was convenient to transporter rooms, the bridge, and the majority of science labs. Therefore, it was a short ride in the turbolift for Lieutenant Worf and Counselor Troi, and Worf wished they had more time to discuss the Costa matter before meeting with the ship's ranking scientist, Karn Milu.

He glanced at the Betazoid, but she was staring dead ahead, lost in her own contemplation. He would have preferred to conduct the investigation himself, but he certainly recognized the unique talents of Deanna Troi. And her recent conversation with the dead woman was disturbing, to say the least. Worf had never dreamt that Lynn Costa—or anyone aboard the *Enterprise*—could contemplate suicide. To a Klingon, the only possible reason for *HoH'egh* was extreme cowardice or humiliating defeat in battle. A failed marriage struck him as a ludicrous reason to end one's life.

"Counselor," he said finally, unable to conceal his disgust any longer, "are humans really so susceptible to depression that they would take their own lives, with such little reason?"

Deanna blinked at him startledly, as if he had summoned her from a faraway place. "I'm afraid so," she admitted. "They have a long history of obsession with death. I believe it stems from their early religions, in which the afterlife was portrayed as being preferable to real life."

"I see," muttered the Klingon. He could comprehend the concept, but he would never understand it. How could someone prefer dying to living?

The turbolift deposited them on deck 5, and they strode out to find a thin Vulcan male waiting for them.

"I am Saduk," he said simply, with a cordial bow—there were no handshakes with a Vulcan. "I work on the Microcontamination Project, and I will show you where Dr. Costa's body was found. But first, Dr. Milu would like to speak briefly with you."

"Proceed," said Worf. He liked dealing with Vulcans—you could speak frankly to them and not have to waste time being tactful, as you had to with humans.

They followed the pointy-eared humanoid into an office that was rather sumptuous, by *Enterprise* standards. The captain's ready room paled by comparison. The walls were festooned with sculpted glass cases containing mounted insects from all over the galaxy. Each case was a handcrafted work of art in its own right, and the various preserved creatures ranged from Earth scorpions, curled to strike, to Centaurian water beetles with multiple webbed heads. Flying insects in one case, segmented worms in another, each lovingly and painstakingly mounted and labeled. Spotting a Klingon cockroach with enormous pincers, Worf was forced to suppress a shudder.

Dominating the cabin was a massive amber desk, a

hunk of petrified resin in which thousands of Beta-zoidan grubs were forever frozen. Four computer screens covered the desk and burned brightly, and a large viewscreen blanketed the back wall.

In comparison, the noted entomologist and administrator was an unprepossessing figure: short, squat, and possessed of dense eyebrows which curled back into a kinky mass of gray hair. "Welcome," he said with a sad smile. "I wish your visit here could be under more pleasant circumstances."

"Nice office," Worf said noncommittally.

Karn Milu nodded, then the venerable Betazoid looked pointedly at Deanna. Imperceptibly, the tiny veins in his temples throbbed, and Worf could see Deanna recoil slightly.

With some annoyance, she cautioned him, "Dr. Milu, I receive your thoughts, but I am unable to respond telepathically. In fairness to Lieutenant Worf, I think we should communicate out loud."

"Of course," replied Karn Milu. "I only wanted to see whether you have been practicing since our last conversation. I see that you have not."

"I've had other things on my mind," she retorted.

"Ah, yes," nodded the administrator, "such a tragic accident. I welcome your full investigation."

"On that matter," said Worf, "what can you tell us about the accident?"

"Nothing," shrugged the scientist. "I was as surprised as anyone. I have always given the Costas complete autonomy on their projects, and they certainly don't need my guidance. I have no idea what happened down there."

Deanna looked puzzled. "But, Dr. Milu, you were the one who alerted me about Lynn Costa's mental condition."

"I was following Starfleet regulations, nothing

more," shrugged the Betazoid. "Willful destruction of official records is a serious breech of security. These weren't her private files she succeeded in erasing—but files that were destined for publication throughout the Federation. Thus far, nobody has gotten a good explanation out of her."

"Now no one will," said Worf sagely. "Dr. Milu, you are a Betazoid. Did you not sense something within Dr. Costa that might explain her actions?"

"In contrast with Deanna," replied the administrator, "I *tune out* the emotions of crew members. In addition to heading the entomology section, I possess the rank of commander in Starfleet. I have four hundred and ninety-three other scientists under my command. I have daily duties, such as scheduling and requisitions, and I don't want to be bothered every time a husband and wife have a spat. Oh, I get involved when it's serious—as it was with Lynn Costa—but I don't meddle in emotional affairs unless I have to. That's why we have a ship's counselor."

Milu smiled at her, and Deanna Troi almost blushed. Why did she feel so damn inferior to him? Was it because he was a full-blooded Betazoid, with powers he didn't even care to use? No, she didn't feel envy, just extreme respect. Deanna decided she was suffering from a mild case of hero-worship, nothing more. She admired Karn Milu so much, without really knowing him very well.

"I'm sorry I can't be more helpful," the scientist shrugged, appealing directly to Worf. "But my office and I will assist you in any way we can."

"Who might know something?" Worf asked bluntly.

Karn Milu motioned to the quiet Vulcan. "Saduk has been with the Microcontamination Project longer than anyone, except the Costas. He'll show you around the laboratory and answer any questions you might have. You should also talk to the two junior assistants, Grastow, the Antarean, and the Earth girl . . ." He snapped his fingers, trying to recall her name.

The Vulcan and the Betazoid answered at once, "Shana Russel." Deanna glanced at Saduk, but he never took his eyes off Karn Milu.

"Shana Russel," repeated the administrator, tapping his head as if making a mental note. With a sweep of his hand, he turned off his computer screens, and the office was darker and less intimidating. "Those are the only people who came in contact with the Costas on a regular basis," he added. "Of course, you will want to talk to Emil."

"Yes," agreed Worf distastefully. He turned to the slight Vulcan and asked, "When can we see the cleanroom?"

"Immediately," nodded Saduk, leading them out the door.

Deck 31 and its accompanying residential decks, 32 and 33, were sandwiched between deuterium reactors above and a mass of environmental support equipment below. This restricted location made deck 31 highly secure and the logical choice for any sort of experiments that were dangerous or classified. On the downside, these lower decks were in the narrow part of the battle section, near the weaponry and the battle bridge. There was no saucer separation for them, mused Deanna Troi, and no evacuation in a sudden combat situation.

The counselor knew that working on deck 31 bestowed a certain mystique among the scientific community aboard the *Enterprise*. She was also reminded, as they wound their way down a nondescript corridor, of what Shana Russel had said about there being no windows in the heart of the ship. Deanna and the bridge crew were lucky enough to live at the edge of the ship, surrounded by stars. Down here, on deck 31, there were vast expanses of featureless beige space.

Lieutenant Worf was doing a good job of keeping Saduk talking, not always an easy task with a Vulcan. "I have always admired your extraordinary results," he remarked with a sweep of his hand. "Certainly, no Klingon ship would have work areas as clean as these."

"The entire *Enterprise* is a class-ten-thousand cleanroom," replied Saduk, "meaning the air contains no more than ten thousand dust particles per square meter. Keeping a breathable atmosphere devoid of contaminants is easy, until you let people in."

"Why can't you use transporter technology to sanitize the workers?" asked Worf.

The Vulcan knitted his eyebrows slightly before answering, "The transporter's greatest strength is its ability to recreate exactly what it finds—warts and all, to use a human expression. The biofilter is not programmed to remove the dirt under your fingernails, the dead skin particles, the mucus in your nostrils . . ."

"Understood," Deanna hastened. "It's not practical to use transporters to clean people."

"No," answered the Vulcan, "and not cost efficient either. Every method has been considered, but biological beings are rife with microorganisms, dust, moisture, every contaminant known. Cleanroom suits remain, after hundreds of years, the best solution. Our suits are not designed to keep the wearer safe from the environment—they are designed to keep the environment safe from the wearer."

"Which is why Lynn Costa's suit didn't help her,"

Deanna observed, thinking of the clammy feeling of the helmet in her dream.

The Vulcan nodded, "Yes. The air *leaving* the suit was highly filtered—but not air entering."

He stopped abruptly in front of another faceless corridor, this one guarded by a voice-activated door. "We're here. How far into the environment do you wish to venture?"

Worf narrowed his eyes. "How far? To the site of the accident, of course."

"The pods are in a class-one cleanroom," declared Saduk. He eyed the big Klingon dubiously. "Special cleanroom suits are required."

"Can we dispense with suits?" asked Worf. "We only want to see the place where Lynn Costa died."

"I'm afraid not," Saduk answered. "In order to reach the class-zero pods, we must pass through class-one-thousand, one-hundred, and class-one cleanrooms. Perhaps you have seen the children's toy that is one egg within another egg, each one smaller in size. That is similar to a cleanroom system."

"I don't care what I have to wear," muttered Worf. "Can I bring my tricorder?"

"We will supply you with a dust-free unit inside," the Vulcan replied. He turned to the voice analyzer beside the door. "Saduk requesting entrance."

"Voice-print confirmed," replied the computer, as the door slid open.

They entered another corridor, but this one had immense windows on either side of it. The laboratory on the left was dark, with the shapes and shadows of strange equipment jutting eerily into the gloom. To her right, Deanna could see white-suited technicians moving like ghosts through a roomful of large metal boxes, each one glowing with ultraviolet quartz tubes.

Within this cleanroom were smaller cleanrooms of transparent aluminum, where robots moved with harmonic ease, shuffling wafers of microchips in and out of reactors and furnaces. Along the walls of the busy cleanroom, tanks, pumps, and piping stretched from floor to ceiling.

"That is semiconductor research and development," explained Saduk matter-of-factly. "The developers have to duplicate manufacturing techniques that are common throughout the Federation."

"What is this darkened room?" Worf asked, pointing to their left.

The Vulcan didn't slow his pace for an instant as he answered, "That is a spare research/manufacturing facility for projects from the other decks. We refer to it as the 'guest room,'" he said without smiling.

Before Deanna had a chance to see more, they moved past a bulkhead and made a left turn into a smaller corridor. The floor under their feet suddenly became a silver grating through which air flowed easily, and they were struck by a gentle breeze.

"Your first air shower," explained Saduk. "Our next will be in the transition room."

Before they got to the transition room, they passed some smaller cleanrooms where anonymous white-suited researchers were gathered around electron microscopes and pinpoint laser devices. Some of them sat at lab benches, hunched over culture dishes, their heads covered by hoods suspended from the ceiling by air tubes. The hoods, Deanna knew, kept the work surfaces even cleaner than the room's atmosphere.

"Biomedical labs," explained the Vulcan. "Emil Costa occasionally works with this section."

"Are all these rooms negative-pressurized?" asked Worf.

"It depends," Saduk replied. "Biomedical labs are

usually negative-pressurized, so that air can only enter and nothing can escape. On the other hand, the transition rooms are positive-pressurized, so that dirtier air cannot come in. Air pressure is our greatest ally in keeping the environment clean."

"In an emergency," added Worf, "I can negative-pressurize sickbay, the transporter rooms, or any part of the ship."

"Yes, I know," replied the Vulcan without the slightest pride, "I designed that system."

Worf glanced at Deanna and raised a droll eyebrow, while Saduk stopped at another voice-activated door, this one marked TRANSITION ROOM 3. In smaller letters were the words CLASS 1000.

"Saduk requesting entrance," the Vulcan announced.

"Voice-print confirmed," replied the computer, as the door brushed open.

The transition room was a sterile cross between a closet and a locker room, with racks of white garments and neatly stacked helmets dressing one wall and lockers and private shower facilities against another. The far wall opened directly onto three gleaming showers of air and ultraviolet rays. Bulbous air nozzles protruded from the walls and ceiling of the chambers, and the quartz lamps gleamed overhead and underfoot. Each chamber was marked by a sign proclaiming its destination: MICROCONTAMINATION, MEDICAL, MANUFACTURING.

"Those are turbolifts," said Deanna with a start.

"Not *just* turbolifts," added the Vulcan. "Once you have changed into protective garments, you will be free to enter the class-one-hundred cleanrooms."

Worf started to take off his Klingon sash. "No need for that, Lieutenant," said Saduk. "I am sure we have something large enough to accommodate all of your clothes." He pressed a button, and a conveyor belt brought him a sheet of filmy white material that looked to Deanna like a parachute she had once seen in an Earth movie.

Worf gathered the material up in his arms, while Saduk searched for a helmet. On her own initiative, Deanna took a garment from the nearest rack and was stunned at the lightness of the material. It was like gossamer.

"You won't even know you are wearing it," remarked Saduk with a perfunctory nod.

The garments flowed over their uniforms like a coating of dust, but the helmets were another matter. Saduk had nimble fingers, and he managed to attach the helmet to Deanna's suit in a matter of seconds, but he was unable to alleviate the claustrophobic feeling of the transparent visor, the headpiece, and the tubes stretching behind her to unseen filters.

The air she breathed was slightly stale, but clean air flowed in from vents in the top of the helmet. The helmet and the gloves served as constant reminders to Deanna that *she* was considered to be a walking source of contamination and a threat to the cleanrooms.

Saduk slipped on his own helmet and secured it with a few snaps. "This way," he said, leading them toward the air shower marked MICROCONTAMINATION.

Even through the suit and helmet, Deanna felt the rapid rush of air over her body as she and Worf entered the shower. They stood on a grating through which she could feel the air rushing out of the chamber. The quartz tubes throbbed over her head and under the white booties covering her feet, and she could feel the slight motion of the specially equipped turbolift moving them laterally.

The door on the other side opened, and they

entered a vast room with smaller self-enclosed cleanrooms dotting its surface like igloos on an Antarctic plain. Saduk strode quickly through the white landscape toward a small door on the other side of the room, where another white-suited denizen waved to them.

"Ensign Singh reporting," he said, saluting Lieutenant Worf.

Deanna heard the security officer as clearly as if he had been in her helmet with her, and she surmised that the helmets were patched into the ship's communication network.

"Thank you, Ensign," replied Worf. "Status?"

"No one has entered the room since Dr. Costa was beamed out," answered the ensign, pointing to a door clearly marked CLASS 1.

"Well done," Worf told his underling. "You are relieved."

As Ensign Singh strode away, Deanna moved to the large window overlooking the room with the pods. It was exactly as she had remembered it from her dream: the white sterility, the row of ominous gray-tinted pods, and the miniature lab equipment and sensors within each pod. Suddenly, the sense of déja vu overwhelmed her, and she gripped the window ledge for support.

"Are you all right?" asked Worf with concern.

"Yes," she breathed, granting the Klingon a smile he couldn't fully see. She turned to Saduk and asked, "Is this the window through which Dr. Grastow saw the body?"

"Yes," nodded the Vulcan. "Shall I send for him?"

"No," answered Deanna, "let him rest. Is it safe for us to enter?"

Saduk checked the readouts on an instrument panel beside the window. "Levels normal," he announced.

"Particle count point-six-two; lethal gas analysis is negative. Relative pressure is at negative twelve percent, and pod number one has been deactivated." He punched a code into the instrument panel, and the door slid open.

Worf entered first. Saduk stood patiently while Deanna walked past him; she was in no hurry. The absolute stillness, the silent gray pods, and the knowledge of recent death all combined to make the laboratory seem like a tomb.

The white room was featureless except for the window and the pods. Deanna counted eight of them, all identical except for the identification screens built into their heavily sealed hatches. Some of the screens were dark, but others bore electronic descriptions like BETELGUESE III—IONIZED ATMOSPHERE, UDRYXAL COMPOUND PROCESS REFINEMENT, and SPACE VACUUM—HOLD FOR GRASTOW.

Pod number one's screen was also dark. Worf studied it somberly for a moment, then turned on the tricorder Saduk had furnished him. "We have to check the integrity of all the seals," he declared.

"Agreed," answered the Vulcan. But his attention was focused upon a small mechanism perched atop the pod. "The regulator valve appears intact."

"What is that for?" asked Deanna, reluctantly edging closer to the gray enclosure.

"Rapid pressure equalization," answered Saduk. "For example, if you were finished with your vacuum experiment and wanted to open the hatch, you would have to equalize the pressure first."

"Can the pressure flow both ways?" asked Worf. "Could the gas have escaped from that valve?"

"Highly unlikely," answered the Vulcan. "Experiments with any sort of risk factor are automatically conducted under negative pressure. Additionally, the valve is computer-controlled and would not be tripped with dangerous gases present."

"Computer-controlled," Deanna repeated, studying the blank screen embedded within the pod's thick hatch. Only days ago, Lynn Costa had alerted her co-workers to her condition by destroying computer records. None of them had listened closely enough then.

"Could someone rewrite the program?" she asked. "Either to ignore the gases or to mistake positive pressure for negative?"

The Vulcan cocked his head slightly. "Yes, theoretically," he replied. "The pods have their own computer subsystems."

Worf continued his scan of all the seals. "I don't detect the slightest wear on these seals," he growled. "The maintenance on this equipment has been excellent. I'm inclined to agree with Counselor Troi that this is a very peculiar *accident.*"

The Vulcan got a determined look on his otherwise emotionless face. "If the regulator valve is at fault, it is easy to prove. Computer?"

"Awaiting instructions, Dr. Saduk," the machine answered.

"Reactivate pod number one," he said, "and run containment diagnostics with full simulation."

"Running diagnostics," the computer confirmed. Almost immediately, the gray interior of the pod became darker and dingier, and messages and codes began to flash on its screen.

"Incorrect air pressure readings," announced the computer.

Seconds later, red smoke began streaming from the regulator valve. Deanna recoiled in fright, but Saduk grabbed her arm with a surprisingly firm grip.

"It's harmless," he assured her. "But it's also unexpected and inexplicable, under normal circumstances."

Worf was measuring the crimson stream with his tricorder. "This flow is more than enough to overcome someone in seconds," he concluded. "And, she didn't expect the gas to be so lethal."

Or did she? wondered Deanna. Looking nervously away from the escaping red gas, she glanced down at the floor and saw a small blue vial. In this bastion of cleanliness, the haphazardly discarded object seemed almost shocking. Deanna reached down with a gloved hand to pick it up.

"End simulation and diagnostics," ordered Saduk, who peered intently at the regulator valve as soon as the smoke had dissipated. "This valve may appear intact, but it's not," he declared. "For a malfunction of this magnitude, two things had to occur. First, as you surmised, Counselor Troi, the pod's programming was altered to give a negative reading when the pressure inside the pod was actually positive. Secondly, the valve failed when the pressure differential became too great. Such catastrophic failure is impossible without substantial alteration."

"The valve and the programming were *both* altered?" Worf asked incredulously.

"Yes," answered the Vulcan dryly. "Lynn Costa's death was no accident. Someone killed her."

Deanna Troi felt like someone had punched her in the stomach. She looked around and saw nowhere to sit, so she braced herself against the deadly pod.

"Will you testify to this at an inquiry?" asked Worf.

"Of course," nodded the Vulcan.

Weakly, Deanna asked, "Would suicide be a possibility?"

"Yes," replied the researcher. "Dr. Costa had as much opportunity to tamper with this equipment as anyone. But she could have ended her life in a variety of simpler and less painful methods."

Thoughtfully, Deanna squeezed the vial in her gloved hand. Should she ask about it? Not at the moment, she decided.

"Do'Ha'!" snarled Worf, slamming a gloved fist into a gloved palm. "A murder on the *Enterprise!* I vow that the killer will be brought to justice!"

"Lynn Costa was afraid," Deanna muttered, more to herself than anyone else. She began to feel worse that she hadn't done more to help Dr. Costa right after their disturbing meeting. "It wasn't paranoia," she concluded.

Before Worf could reply, an electronic bosun's whistle alerted them that a message was about to be relayed to all hands. The whistle was followed by a familiar cultured voice. "Attention all hands," it began, "this is Captain Picard. I wish to relay the grievous news that Dr. Lynn Costa died at approximately zero-four-hundred hours today. The cause of death was the inhalation of a lethal gas.

"A full report will be available to all hands as soon as possible," he continued. "According to Dr. Costa's wishes, she will be granted the funeral of a Starfleet crew member. The funeral is scheduled for eighteen-hundred hours in the ship's theater. Before returning to your regular duties, please join us in a moment of silence for our departed colleague."

Deanna, Worf, and Saduk didn't need to be told to be silent. They not only felt the shared loss of a giant within their midst, but they felt the acute burden of being the only ones who knew that she had been murdered.

Chapter Four

IN THE TRANSITION ROOM, Worf and Deanna gratefully removed their helmets and stripped off the white garments. Worf tried to control his anger and frustration by taking deep breaths. Finally, he removed the regulator valve from his suit's pocket and held it between his thumb and forefinger. He glanced around the room, looking for a container. Finding none, he dropped the valve into one of the gossamer gloves, rolled it into a bundle, and stuffed it under his sash. Then, scowling, the Klingon stuffed the rest of the garment into a receptacle.

Deanna looked at her own piece of evidence, the small blue vial. She held it to her nose and sniffed a pungent odor which was familiar. Recently familiar.

The Vulcan, Saduk, had removed his helmet but left his white jumpsuit on. "Where did you find that?" he asked her.

"Inside," she motioned toward the air shower. "Near the pod."

Worf held out his hand and requested, "May I look at that?"

She handed it to him, almost glad to be rid of the foul-smelling object.

Saduk leaned closer to inspect the vial. "It has a capacity of twenty milliliters," he observed. "Very common around any laboratory, but no one would hand-carry a liquid into a class-one cleanroom."

"Somebody did," remarked Worf. He put the container to his own flared nostrils. "Alcohol," he murmured.

Saduk seemed unperturbed by this discovery. "If you are finished with me, Lieutenant," he nodded cordially, "I shall return to work."

Worf dropped the vial into the big glove and again secured the packet of evidence under his sash. "I have more questions," insisted the Klingon. "First, do you know anyone who would benefit from Lynn Costa's death?"

"Would personal advancement be considered a benefit?" asked the Vulcan.

"Yes."

"Then I know one person with such a motive," the scientist replied evenly. "Myself."

"Why is that?" asked Deanna, peering curiously at the Vulcan.

He returned the Betazoid's gaze with dark unwavering eyes. "Because," he replied, "with Lynn Costa dead and Emil Costa retiring, I will be placed in charge of the Microcontamination Project."

"Is this something you've wanted?" Deanna asked.

The Vulcan nodded, "It is my major ambition in life."

"Anyone else?" demanded Worf.

The Vulcan's angular eyebrows merged for a moment before he answered, "No one comes to mind."

"I've seen the maintenance reports," scowled Worf, "now I want to see the programming logs for that pod."

"Very well," said Saduk, "but I doubt if you will

51

find anything. By long-standing custom, pod number one was reserved for Lynn Costa's use, and she steadfastly refused to keep a programming log."

Worf heaved his big shoulders and tried to suppress his anger. "Who allowed *that* policy?" he demanded.

"Karn Milu," answered the Vulcan. "Although it may have been at the request of the Costas. They were very concerned about security."

"So concerned about security," frowned Worf, "that they virtually set her up to be killed!"

The ship's counselor inserted herself between the two males. "Saduk," she asked earnestly, "when Lynn Costa was caught erasing computer records, what sort of records had she erased?"

"Her actions were very strange," the Vulcan concluded. "Mainly, she erased older records of microbe discoveries made while this ship was in orbit around various planets. For the most part, this was material that had been gathered by her husband. It had already been moved from main memory to archival memory and was awaiting widespread dissemination. We restored most of the data, except for some personal files and notes which were unrecoverable."

"With your lax computer policies," grumbled Worf, "how did you know it was *she* who destroyed the records?"

"Emil caught her in the act," answered Saduk. "It was a premeditated act, and she never showed any remorse. Even if Emil had not caught her, we might have surmised her guilt from her recent behavior."

"How would you describe her recent behavior?" asked the ship's counselor.

The Vulcan considered his answer before replying, "Preoccupied. Odd. Illogical."

"Did she seem afraid of something?" asked Deanna.

Saduk remained expressionless. "Yes."

"What?" begged the counselor.

"I don't know," Saduk admitted. "Lately, my full attention has been directed toward several projects that are behind schedule."

Worf snarled under his breath and headed toward the door leading out of the transition room. "Don't discuss our investigation with your colleagues," he ordered. "I'll be sending down some security people and a team of engineers to go over that pod. I'll contact you later about your deposition."

"Understood," nodded Saduk. "Can you conduct yourselves out?"

"Yes, we can," said Deanna, gracing the lean Vulcan with a slight smile. "Thank you."

A moment later, she and Worf were in the corridor, with the air gushing through the grating at their feet. Worf looked down at Deanna and shook his head, muttering, "I shouldn't blame them for being ill-prepared. Who expects something so barbaric as a murder? Even aboard the old Klingon ships, no one ever got murdered but the captain!"

Deanna bowed her head. "Speaking of the captain," she sighed, "we had better go see him."

"Agreed," said Worf. "While we brief the captain, I'll get Geordi started." He struck his communicator badge, and Deanna was struck by the Klingon's forceful action. She knew that there would be no wasted moments in this investigation.

Jean-Luc Picard paced the length of his ready room, shaking his head in disbelief. "Murdered!" he barked, stiffening to attention. "Are you absolutely certain?"

"No," Worf answered, "not until we verify that both the regulator valve and the programming were tampered with. Commander La Forge has assembled a team of programmers and engineers to inspect every aspect of that pod. Saduk could conceivably be mistaken—or lying."

"No," said Picard, "a Vulcan who lied so brazenly would be considered quite insane."

"Captain," said Deanna hesitantly, "I doubt if I could tell whether Saduk is lying or not. He has an extremely strong and guarded intellect. He has admitted to having a motive, and there is the possibility that we are dealing with someone who behaves normally but *is* insane."

Captain Picard just shook his head in disbelief. "You're right," he sighed, "we can't rule anyone out. But first, we have to rule out all other possible causes for the accident. We can't jump to any conclusions."

"Sir," interjected Worf, "I could ask Environmental Support to review Geordi's data."

The captain nodded approvingly. "Use whatever facilities or personnel you need. I trust you to be thorough about this, Lieutenant."

"Thorough and efficient," the Klingon pledged. "If there's a murderer on board, I will find him."

The captain nodded, then turned to his trusted counselor. "Deanna," he said, "I hate forcing you to be a sort of lie detector, but we haven't got any alternative. Can you accompany the lieutenant when he interrogates the . . ." he grimaced in disgust at the word, "suspects?"

"Yes, sir," replied the Betazoid, lowering her eyes. "I had a chance, perhaps, to prevent Lynn Costa's death if I had taken her fear more seriously. I want very badly to find out what happened to her."

"Make it so," Picard ordered.

They stepped into the turbolift, and Deanna eyed the tall Klingon beside her. Worf appeared calm, but his jaw worked furiously when he spoke. "Deck 32," he growled to the computer.

Then he tapped his insignia badge. "Worf to La Forge."

"Geordi here," came the familiar voice. "Sorry, Worf, but so far we haven't found anything unexpected. Somebody could have changed the programming on that pod by altering just a few bytes in the monitoring system. They didn't go through the main computer, so they may have used a debugger. With no programming log, we'll never know for sure.

"As for the pod itself," the chief engineer continued, "it seems to be in perfect working order *except* for that valve you gave me. The calibration of the o-rings was off just enough to let the pressurized gas escape. Whoever altered those rings knew exactly what he was doing, but I'm not so sure you could *prove* they were altered. Whoever did it must have been wearing gloves, and they worked under conditions that didn't leave the slightest trace."

"Understood," Worf grumbled. "Then I assume you don't need us to come down there?"

"Nope," Geordi replied with sympathy in his voice. "We'll stay here and poke through everything until we're satisfied there's nothing left to learn. I'm afraid, my friend, you're on your own."

"Not exactly," Worf disagreed, glancing down at the dark diminutive figure beside him. "Deanna Troi is helping me." The Betazoid responded with an encouraging wisp of a smile.

The turbolift door opened upon deck 32, and Lieutenant Worf and Counselor Troi stepped out onto the same deck Deanna had visited a few hours earlier with Captain Picard. She vividly recalled their disturbing encounter with Emil Costa, and she wondered how she and Worf would fare this time.

"You know," added Geordi through Worf's communicator, "Karn Milu is already complaining about the time this is taking. He says that the scientists can't get to their experiments in the pods. He's convinced that Dr. Costa's death was an accident and won't hear anything about the 'murder theory,' as he puts it. Objectively, he's right. It was a dangerous experiment, and equipment and computer malfunctions are not unheard of."

"It is a murder," Worf answered evenly. He looked down at the Betazoid. "Wouldn't you agree, Counselor?"

"I would," she answered affirmatively. "Lynn Costa was terribly afraid, and I misdiagnosed it as paranoia. She had reason to be afraid—somebody was stalking her."

"Yeah," agreed the chief engineer, "but I wouldn't blame yourself, Deanna. Whoever pulled this scheme off was very determined and very clever. And they knew the workings of these pods intimately. It looks like an inside job."

"An inside job?" Worf queried, glancing at Deanna.

"An Earth colloquialism," she explained. "It means the crime was planned by somebody with inside knowledge and freedom of movement."

"Exactly," Geordi replied. "I'd concentrate on those folks in the Microcontamination Project."

"We're headed for our first interrogation now," the Klingon replied without much enthusiasm. "Emil Costa."

"Good luck," offered the engineer. "I'll prepare an official report for the inquiry."

"Thank you again, Geordi," replied Deanna.

"Out," barked Worf. He looked around the unfamiliar corridors and the game room beyond. A few people were gathered at one of the card tables, and they spoke in hushed tones as they glanced at the unfamiliar duo. Worf tried to ignore them. "Which way to Emil Costa's cabin?" he asked.

"This way," Deanna answered, moving down the corridor away from the recreation room.

"One second," said Worf, "let's see what they know."

She tried to keep up with the big Klingon as he strode into the recreation room and confronted the gathered residents, who numbered six. Other residents watched them silently from the doorways.

"Dr. Baylak," Worf nodded to a dark-skinned human he recognized. He acknowledged the others with brief nods but was not about to waste any time with introductions. "Do any of you know anything about Lynn Costa's death?"

"What caused it?" asked Baylak with concern. "There's a rumor going around that she was murdered."

Worf replied simply, "Murder appears to be a possibility. We're not ruling anything out at this stage of the investigation. Do any of you know anything?"

A slight woman with dark hair stepped forward. Her eyes were so red and watery that it was evident she had been crying. Deanna's heart went out to her.

"I know one thing," the woman said forcefully, her voice quivering a little, "Lynn Costa would never commit suicide—as someone suggested."

"I made that suggestion," replied Deanna with equal force, "based on her behavior prior to the accident. But that assumption now appears to be false."

"Do any of you know anything?" Worf reiterated.

"Her husband . . ." said a stocky man in the back. But his voice trailed off.

"What about her husband?" asked Worf.

The man lowered his head. "I don't know anything for certain," he mumbled, "only things I overheard."

"Like what?" the Klingon demanded.

"I heard them fighting," the man sighed, shaking his head, "typical husband and wife stuff."

Helplessly, Dr. Baylak held out his hands. "We'd all like to help you, Lieutenant, but we don't know anything. I mean, we all know that Lynn and Emil were not getting along. There was friction between them, but I don't know what caused it. They usually kept to themselves and their own work group."

"Does anyone have more information?" asked Worf.

He was greeted by silence. "Inform your colleagues," ordered the Klingon, "I am available at any time to discuss this matter." He motioned to Deanna Troi and strode off.

Deanna could feel the helpless and frightened eyes on their backs as they left the game room. These people were a community—small and close-knit—and violence against one of their number was violence against all of them. Emotionally, they wanted the security chief to catch Lynn Costa's killer. Psychologically, however, they didn't want to find out that someone in their midst was a murderer.

Worf stopped in the corridor, relieved just to be away from those searching eyes. "Which way?" he muttered.

Deanna motioned to the left. "It's not far. Let me lead."

They found the door with the sign reading THE COSTAS, and the counselor wondered how long the sign would remain in the plural. Worf pressed the electronic door chime and braced himself.

A somber—and sober—Emil Costa greeted them. He looked far more gray and bent than Deanna remembered from their encounter in the Ten-Forward Room only a few hours before. That seemed like light-years ago now. His eyes, then defiant and arrogant, were now wary and haunted. The counselor recalled seeing the same haunted look in Lynn Costa's eyes.

"Hello," he murmured, "I've been expecting you."

"May we come in?" asked Worf.

The scientist nodded, stepped back, and motioned them inside. Nervously, he rubbed his hand over the white stubble on his scalp and glanced at his feet. Deanna noticed that he was still wearing his slippers. The quarters were simple and homey, with cherry wood antiques and quaint Bavarian cuckoo clocks intermingled with minimalist Orion tapestries and standard-issue furniture. The Costas traveled light, Deanna decided, for all these furnishings were readily available from the ship's replicator.

Emil Costa slumped wearily into a sculpted armchair exactly like the one in Deanna's cabin. He motioned to the food slot in the wall. "Would you like something?"

"No," answered Worf resolutely. "We've come to inform you that, apparently, your wife was murdered."

The breath escaped from Emil Costa, and he seemed to shrink deeper into the big chair. Nevertheless, thought Deanna, he exhibited none of the shock at the idea that everyone else had.

"Did *you* kill her?" Worf asked bluntly.

"We're not going to mince a lot of words, are we?" Emil smiled wanly. "No, I didn't."

"Do you know who did?" asked Worf.

"No," mumbled Costa, dropping his chin to his chest.

He's lying, thought Deanna. The only problem was,

which question was he lying about? Secrecy seemed to taint his every response.

Lieutenant Worf moved closer to Emil Costa. "If you can't be positive," he said, "can you make a guess about who might be responsible?"

The Klingon was glaring down at the little man, and Deanna couldn't blame Emil for squirming uncomfortably.

"N-no," he stammered. "Lynn was well liked and respected by everyone."

"That's not the question," Worf pounded away. "The question is, who killed her?"

"I don't know!" squealed Emil Costa, leaping to his feet and moving as far away from them as the small room would allow.

Deanna decided to try a softer approach. "Dr. Costa," she interjected, "if somebody killed your wife, wouldn't you want to see that person brought to justice?"

"Of course," the old man agreed. "But in the end, what good is revenge?" Distractedly, Emil stopped to study one of the cuckoo clocks. Gently, he reset the hands of the antiquated timepiece.

"It's very strange," he mused with a dawning realization, "being alone after so many years. Suddenly, I'm able to go where I want to go, do what I want to do—my life is totally my own again. But, to tell you the truth, I wish *I* was the one who was dead." His shoulders hunched pitifully.

Even Worf was impressed by the depth of the man's grief. "We're sorry to intrude at this time," said the security officer, "but justice cannot wait. Did you change, or in any way alter, the programming or the regulator valve on pod one?"

"Is that how it was done?" sniffed Emil Costa, running a grizzled knuckle over his watery eyes. He turned to look at them, those same eyes pleading for understanding. "I've done a few things in my life I haven't been proud of, but marrying Lynn was not one of them."

That much was the truth, decided Deanna Troi, but it was perhaps the first truthful thing he had said. "Why," she asked, "did Lynn destroy the computer files of *your* microbe discoveries?"

The scientist again turned away from them. "There's nothing else I can tell you," he rasped. "If you will please leave me now, I have to send a message to Starfleet."

"We may request your assistance again," warned Worf.

"You know where to find me," Emil replied, adjusting the hands of another cuckoo clock. "I have resigned from the Microcontamination Project, and I will restrict myself to these quarters."

"That would be helpful," snapped Worf. He swiveled on his heels and marched out.

Deanna followed and caught up with the big Klingon in the middle of the corridor. "He's lying about something," she declared.

"Yes," grunted Worf, "even *I* could see that. He evaded your question about the erased files, and he knows more than he's saying."

"But that won't convict him of murder," added the Betazoid. "He seems genuinely remorseful at the loss of his wife."

Worf growled, "More than one murderer has regretted his actions afterward. Who shall we see next?"

"Grastow," answered Deanna. "He discovered the body."

They stepped down into the cabin of the massive Antarean. Apparently, thought Deanna, the floor of

Grastow's cabin had been lowered to accommodate his extraordinary height. Worf led the way into the room, and it was certainly odd to see the Klingon dwarfed by someone.

Dr. Grastow greeted them warmly, almost effusively. "Hello," he smiled, striding forward. "How may I help you?"

"We believe," said Worf, "that Dr. Costa's death was not an accident. The programming and regulator valve on pod number one had been tampered with."

"I suspected as much," replied the Antarean, screwing his chubby pink face into a thoughtful grimace. "Do you have any suspects?"

Worf was taken aback by Grastow's enthusiasm, and he glanced puzzledly at Deanna.

"To be frank," she replied, "everyone is a suspect, including yourself."

"Me?" exclaimed the scientist. "Why would *I* kill Lynn Costa? I *loved* the woman!"

"Loved?" asked Worf curiously.

Grastow shrugged, "Respected, loved, worshipped. It began when I was a boy. On my home planet, we had a terrible infestation of parasitic microorganisms in our soil, and we were literally starving to death." He rubbed his ample stomach. "Antarean dietary needs can be quite exacting.

"Anyway," he continued, "the Costas devoted a year of their lives to solving the problem. We never fully eradicated the parasites, but they taught us hydroponic farming under ultraclean conditions. That was twenty standard years ago when I was just a lad, but I vowed at the time that I would repay this debt to the Costas. I graduated in the top two percent of my class at the Academy, and I passed over several plum assignments to become their assistant. My classmates said I was crazy, but I have never regretted my decision. That was three years ago."

"Then you came to the *Enterprise* with them," concluded Worf.

"Yes," answered the Antarean. "Only Saduk has been with them longer."

"Excuse me," said Deanna, carefully phrasing her question, "when we saw you in sickbay, you were distraught with grief. Now you seem to have completely adjusted to Lynn Costa's death. What changed your attitude?"

"I rested," shrugged Grastow. "We Antareans have a remarkable mental constitution, if I may say so myself. Rest allows us to block out negative emotions and emerge totally refreshed. It was terribly disturbing to discover Lynn's body, but I am over that now." He grinned broadly. "Now I am ready to assist you in any way I can!"

"Yes," muttered Worf skeptically. "We've already heard your account of how you discovered the body and alerted sickbay. But why weren't you surprised to hear it was murder?"

"Because," answered Grastow, "I am in charge of maintenance on the pods. After thinking clearly about the circumstances of the accident, I couldn't see any other possible explanation. You are fairly certain it was a murder, aren't you?"

"Until we find a better explanation," said Worf. "Can you tell us who did it?"

The Antarean paced thoughtfully around the room, an action which required three or four strides. "The pods," he explained, "are in a cleanroom that is under the jurisdiction of the Microcontamination Project. Although other scientists use those pods, they aren't allowed in there unless one of us accompanies them.

We usually monitor their experiments for them. That would mean the logical suspects are myself, Saduk, Shana, and, of course, Emil."

"So," pressed Worf, "given that assumption, who is most likely to have murdered Lynn Costa?"

"I hate to say it," grimaced the Antarean, "but Emil is the likely choice. During the last few months, the two of them quarreled like you wouldn't believe. A few times, I thought they would come to blows."

"Do you know the cause of these quarrels?" asked Deanna.

"They didn't need a cause," remarked the giant humanoid. "Just being in the same room was cause enough. They tried to avoid each other, and we went out of our way to avoid putting them together, but that wasn't always possible. To be truthful, Lynn was a bit testy with everyone. I used to be able to get a laugh out of her, but not lately." He shook his head sadly.

Deanna Troi furrowed her luxuriant eyebrows before adding, "Emil told us that he was in charge of developing the organisms needed to test Lynn's procedures. Could their differences have been professional?"

"I suppose," the Antarean replied. "But you would think they'd be used to that after forty-odd years. When I joined the project on Earth, they were like lovebirds. I don't know what happened to them. It can't be dissatisfaction with the work—we've made tremendous strides since coming to the *Enterprise*. Maybe it was age. Humans have been known to age badly."

Worf scowled dubiously, then removed the blue vial from under his sash. "Have you ever seen this?" he asked, handing the container to the Antarean. "Counselor Troi found it on the floor, near the pod."

"That's odd," said Grastow, squinting puzzledly at

64

the vial. "Of course, I've seen vials like this—they are very common. But in the cleanroom? Maybe somebody was using it in an experiment in one of the pods."

Grastow shrugged his massive shoulders and handed the container back to Worf, who again tucked it within his sash. "Thank you," said the Klingon, not hiding his disappointment.

"I have one more question," said Deanna. "How do you feel about Saduk taking over the Micro-contamination Project?"

For the first time, the cheery expression faded from the cherubic face. "Is that official?" he asked.

"It will be," answered Worf, "with Emil Costa retiring. He says he has already resigned from the project."

"Oh," the Antarean moaned, plopping into a chair. "I think I'm going to need some more rest."

"What is your objection?" asked Deanna.

Grastow threw up his hands with alarm. "Have you ever worked for a Vulcan? They don't know the meaning of the word 'rest'! I have nothing personal against Saduk, but I may have to review my situation here."

"I see," said Deanna thoughtfully. She looked at Worf, who was already moving toward the door. "Thank you for your cooperation."

"You're welcome," answered the glum Antarean.

A few moments later, Counselor Troi and Lieutenant Worf found themselves back in the unfamiliar corridor. They kept their voices low, because the residents of deck 32 were starting to emerge from their quarters for the first work shift of the day.

"Your reaction?" asked Worf.

The Betazoid shook her head, "I didn't sense he was lying. He seemed sincere about everything he said. Of course," she concluded, "if he can really block out negative thoughts, I might not be able to tell if he's lying."

"Yes," Worf agreed glumly. He was beginning to dislike the course these investigations were taking. Everything was inconclusive, from Geordi's inspection of the pod to the individual interrogations of the so-called suspects. None of them had what could even remotely be called a motive. Even Saduk's "confession" to wanting Lynn Costa's job was hardly noteworthy. The Vulcan would have had the job anyway in due time; he would outlive everyone else on the project by about a hundred years.

Not that Worf expected someone to jump up and admit to killing Lynn Costa. If this had been a Klingon ship, the culprit might come forward of his own volition, and he would have a damn good reason for his crime. Klingons were not proud about killing —not anymore—but they did admit to the necessity when all else failed, when self-preservation was at stake. But who could have felt threatened by an aging reclusive scientist? If Lynn Costa's fame had been threatening to her colleagues, she would have been murdered years ago.

He muttered, "Do you suppose it will do any good to interview Saduk again?"

"I doubt it," replied the Betazoid.

"No," said Worf. "That leaves Shana Russel."

Deanna nodded, remembering the excited young woman she had met in the Ten-Forward Room with Emil Costa. A celebration had been in progress, she recalled, marking the completion of Shana Russel's preliminary work-ups. This meeting was not likely to be so pleasant.

Deanna remarked, "Shana Russel has only been on the ship for six months."

"She had access," said Worf. He slapped his communicator badge. "Computer?"

"Yes, Lieutenant Worf," came the disembodied voice. "How may I assist you?"

"Is Shana Russel in her cabin?"

"No," answered the feminine voice. "She is in the Ten-Forward Room."

"Acknowledged." He looked at Deanna Troi and held out his hand for her to lead the way.

In his ready room, Captain Picard sat stone-faced behind his desk, his anger growing. Not that Dr. Karn Milu's tone of voice was anything less than respectful, nor his words inflammatory. But Jean-Luc Picard was not a man who liked being told how to do his job.

"What happened to Dr. Costa was extremely unfortunate," said the scientist, his bushy eyebrows bristling. "But that is no reason to close down a valuable laboratory for an indefinite period of time. There are security guards posted on every door and engineers crawling all over the class-zero pods. I have no idea if they are taking the proper precautions, because I have been denied entrance."

"Commander La Forge has promised to conduct his inspection as quickly as possible," the captain said evenly. "And I am sure he is taking every proper precaution."

The stocky Betazoid leaned over the captain's desk. "We cannot even monitor the experiments," he claimed, "because programmers from engineering have frozen the subsystems while they go over every line of code. Captain, I was willing to cooperate in every way I could. I ordered Saduk to conduct Lieutenant Worf and Counselor Troi through the cleanrooms as soon as the danger passed. But it's time to mourn Dr. Costa's death and get back to work."

The captain rose to his feet. Though not a tall man, Jean-Luc Picard was impressive when standing at rigid attention, and the Betazoid took a step back from his desk. "Dr. Milu," he snapped, "we are investigating a *murder*. I view this as the most serious transgression that has taken place aboard the *Enterprise* in some time."

"A *possible* murder," Karn Milu countered. "I myself believe the original interpretation was more plausible—that it was an accident. As much as we both admired Lynn Costa, may I remind you that her mental condition was extremely unstable prior to this incident. Plus, her experiments in reactive purification were unauthorized and excessively dangerous."

Jean-Luc bowed his head, forced to admit these points. Could they be overreacting? First it had been an accident, then suicide, and now a murder. In an attempt to explain the unthinkable, were they grasping at straws?

Thoughtfully, he raised a finger and remarked, "I might agree with you, Doctor, except for one thing. We never considered it a murder until your own man, Saduk, made the suggestion."

"An unfortunate suggestion," grumbled the scientist. "They say Vulcans have no emotions, but they do. *You'll* never see them, but *I* can. *I* still haven't seen any proof that it was murder. Have you?"

"The investigation isn't over yet," the captain declared.

"Yes, and that's the problem," insisted Karn Milu, turning on his heel and marching out of the captain's ready room.

Jean-Luc's lips thinned as he watched the Betazoid leave. He reminded himself that if someone were causing a similar disruption to his bridge, he would be equally upset.

He touched his comm panel. "Picard to La Forge."

"Yes, Captain," came the immediate response.

"How much longer are you going to be on deck 31?" Picard asked.

"We're just wrapping up now."

"Good," sighed the captain. "I know you're preparing a report for Lieutenant Worf, and I want to see it as soon as possible."

"Yes, sir," snapped the engineer.

"And tell me, Geordi, is there any indication of murder?"

"Indication?"

"Correction," said Picard. "Is there any *proof?*"

Now the sigh came from the other end. "No, Captain. Nothing conclusive. There's no bullet hole and no smoking gun."

"I see," answered the captain, his jaw tightening. "Get me that report as soon as you can. Out."

Jean-Luc Picard sat back in his chair and turned on his computer screen. Murder or not, he had a eulogy to deliver in a few hours.

Chapter Five

THE TEN-FORWARD ROOM was relatively quiet so early in the day's primary work shift. Deanna Troi and Lieutenant Worf entered the lounge and surveyed the smattering of customers among the mostly empty tables. The hum of conversation died as several pairs of eyes turned in their direction. Wordlessly, a party of three rose from a nearby table and brushed past the Klingon and the Betazoid, glancing at them but unwilling to make direct eye contact.

They know, thought Deanna. *They know we're looking for a murderer.* For the first time, the counselor realized what it felt like to be an agent of law enforcement. Instead of looking for the good in people, as she usually did, she was looking for the evil. The guilty. Even those who were perfectly innocent were made uncomfortable by such scrutiny, and she couldn't blame them for scurrying out of their way.

No doubt the effect was heightened by the presence of Worf. The security chief stood at unyielding attention beside her, his imperial Klingon sash accentuating his massive chest and his eyes glowering under his coarse rippled brow. He looked like the very instrument of justice—a god of vengeance. Suddenly, she was grateful for having such an experienced partner in this lonely duty.

The lithe figure of Guinan padded toward them. "Hello," she said without her customary cheer. "I don't suppose you've come here to relax."

"No," scowled Worf. "We're looking for Shana Russel."

"By the far port," answered Guinan, pointing to a corner of the room where shadows blended into the darkness of space. "She's been sitting there for hours."

They could barely see the hunched blond-haired figure until they drew within a few meters. Even then, the young woman did not look up from her quiet contemplation of the stars.

"Excuse me," said Worf, "we have to speak with you."

"Yes," muttered Shana Russel. She finally looked up, and Worf was surprised by her youthfulness and the depth of incomprehension in her eyes. Her yellow hair matched the paleness of her skin and clung to cheeks dampened by tears. Worf was not a creature given to sympathy, but the distraught condition of this human female softened his manner somewhat.

"May we sit down?" he asked with a bow.

"Yes," nodded Shana Russel, her gaze drifting from the Klingon to the woman with him. "I'm . . . I'm afraid I don't remember your name."

"Deanna Troi," said the Betazoid with a smile she hoped was comforting. "I'm afraid you know why we're here."

"Yes," she rasped, returning her eyes to the window and its unfettered view of the heavens. "I didn't feel like being alone in my room, so I came here. There wasn't any place else to go."

"How much do you know about what happened to Lynn Costa?" asked Worf.

Wiping the errant strands of hair from her cheek, the young woman sat up in her chair. "Grastow came to tell me," she sniffed. "He couldn't believe it, and I couldn't either. We cried in each other's arms."

She cried now and turned to Worf with eyes burning with disbelief. "Since I've been sitting here," she gasped, "I've overheard some people talking. . . . They say it *wasn't an accident!* Is that true?"

"We don't know," he admitted gently. "That's why we're talking to the people who had access to the class-zero pods. Did *you* have any cause to alter the programming or any of the equipment on that pod?"

"On pod one?" asked Shana incredulously. "I wouldn't go near Dr. Costa's experiments unless she asked me to. I can't imagine anyone else would either."

"Someone apparently did," said Deanna.

A realization of the intent of the questioning suddenly dawned on the young scientist, and she bolted upright in her chair. "You think *I* . . . *!*" she shrieked. "You're crazy!"

Worf looked somewhat pained. "We're asking everyone," he explained. "Did you see or hear anything suspicious in the last few days? Do you know of anyone using that pod other than Dr. Costa?"

Shana Russel sank back into her chair and shook her head sadly. Then she covered her eyes with her hands and sobbed softly. Deanna touched Worf's shoulder and cocked her head toward the exit.

Worf nodded and stood. "Sorry to have bothered you," he muttered to the pathetic human. "If you think of anything, please come to see me."

But Shana Russel was beyond hearing his words.

As he and Deanna wound their way between the

empty tables of the Ten-Forward Room, Worf heaved his shoulders with a massive sigh. "She didn't seem to know much."

"No," agreed Deanna glumly. "Nobody does."

"Except for Emil Costa," growled the Klingon, narrowing his eyes. He reached into his sash and pulled out the small blue vial. "I wonder if Shana Russel has seen this before?"

"*I* have," said a voice behind them.

Worf and Deanna turned to see Guinan watching them from behind her saloon-style countertop. "Let me see that," she said, pointing to the vial.

Worf strode immediately to the bar and handed his evidence to the mysterious humanoid. "Do you think you've seen this before?" he asked.

"Or one just like it," she answered. Guinan sniffed the container's narrow opening.

"Where?" demanded the security chief.

"Right here," Guinan replied, motioning around the deserted recreation center. She turned to Deanna. "Emil Costa had it with him when you were last in here and the two of you were talking. He often carried it—to spice up his orange juice."

Slowly, Worf turned to Deanna, and the two of them exchanged looks that confirmed each other's suspicions. After a moment, the Klingon clenched his jaw, pounded his fist on the bar, and stormed out the door. Only by running did Deanna manage to catch up with him.

"Worf!" she called, stopping him before he reached the turbolift. "That's not enough proof. You need more!"

His torso twisted in anger and frustration, and he growled, "I have enough to confront him!"

The Betazoid shook her head firmly. "He would just deny it. And then he would know you had this

73

evidence. Wait until you've got more. Let's build a case against him."

The Klingon's chest heaved a few more times, but he managed to calm himself. "You are right," he groaned. "We can't go to Starfleet with a single piece of circumstantial evidence. And we have to discover a motive—something beyond the stress of marriage and careers. I think the next step is to pore over all the records for the Microcontamination Project and each of its personnel." He gritted his teeth. "Starting with Emil Costa."

Deanna couldn't help it—she was suddenly overwhelmed by a tremendous yawn. "Sorry," she gulped with embarrassment.

Worf smiled, "How much sleep have you gotten in the last twenty hours?"

"Plenty," Deanna lied. "I'm fine."

"You've had perhaps an hour's worth," Worf corrected her. "Collecting data is a job for one person, so why don't you take a few hours to rest? After the funeral, you can help me review the records of Saduk and the other assistants. I want to study Emil Costa's records myself."

"I'm perfectly willing to carry on," the counselor protested.

"I know you are," said Worf. "But I am in charge of this investigation and the allocation of resources. I ask you to rest."

Deanna could see that it was useless to argue. Besides, the weariness of this unpleasant duty was beginning to take its toll on her. She *had* slept for only about an hour, and not too well at that—haunted by her all too realistic dream of Lynn Costa's death. She had misinterpreted Lynn's acceptance of death as a wish for it. Now she knew that Lynn Costa had been

74

stalked by a determined murderer, and that was why the crazed woman had wanted to leave the ship so badly.

"All right," she relented, staring down. "I'll see you at the funeral."

Morosely, Deanna trudged off. Worf, who had never subscribed to the human custom of lavishing praise for praise's sake, called after her, "I welcome your assistance!"

The Betazoid stopped and turned with a smile. For the first time since the incident with her unborn baby, she found herself liking Worf.

Ensign Wesley Crusher tried to amuse himself by watching the statistics whiz by on the console in front of him. Occasionally, he glanced up at the stars careening past on the main viewer. Normally when course adjustments were handled by the computer, the young helmsman still found any number of interesting distractions on the bridge. He would query Data, Riker, or—more rarely—the captain about some topic relevant to their current mission. He read reports about their destination, and he plotted alternate courses for practice. Though it wasn't his specific duty, Wesley would also monitor various ship systems, such as the quantum state reversal unit or the antimatter reactors, just to study their operation.

But the bridge was quieter and far more somber than usual, even for a routine mission like this one. Data was on hand, but he had been given the extra task of dispatching and scheduling the shuttlecraft for the ceremonies at Kayran Rock. The starbase was not fully staffed yet, and a mountain of data had been dumped upon the android by subspace transmission. The data concerned the docking and speed capabilities of various shuttlecraft, the expected arrival and positions of their motherships, the location of other asteroids, and the personal requirements of the participants.

For one thing, Wesley had heard that all Klingon and Kreel delegations had to arrive at different times but be received in exactly the same fashion. Apparently, bad blood still existed between the two races, and the Federation wasn't taking any chances. In addition, few of the ships heading for rendezvous would be allowed to keep station with the asteroid. Kayran Rock was part of a sprawling asteroid belt with some fairly big chunks less than a million kilometers away. With all of these considerations, a substantial amount of shuttle-pooling was proving necessary, and Data was sitting at the ops console, factoring the data into algorithms of his own devising. Wesley knew better than to disturb him.

Commander Riker had been called to sickbay several times by Wesley's mother to discuss the autopsy, and Captain Picard had secluded himself in his ready room. Worf, Deanna, and Geordi were occupied elsewhere by the investigation, so the lad was without his customary companions. The disturbing death of Lynn Costa had cast a pall that had seeped over the entire ship, and the bridge was not immune.

Therefore, he welcomed the message from Lieutenant Worf when it came over the intercom. "Worf to Ensign Crusher," intoned the deep baritone.

"Crusher here," snapped the teenager officiously.

"When your duties allow," said the Klingon, "I would like to see you in my command post."

The teenager tried to control his excitement, guessing that Worf's request must have something to do with the investigation into Lynn Costa's death. "Yes, sir," he snapped. "I'm on bridge duty at the moment."

"There's no hurry," answered Worf. "I'll be here until the funeral at eighteen-hundred hours."

"Acknowledged," Wesley replied. He glanced back at Commander Riker, who had just reclaimed the captain's seat in Picard's absence.

"Go ahead," Riker nodded. "I'll watch the conn until your relief comes."

Wesley punched in a request for relief, then hurried off the bridge. He found himself whistling as he strolled down the corridor, a folk tune he had learned from the farm settlers who had been aboard the ship a year or so ago. The lad quickly suppressed his natural exuberance and put on a somber face. He had to remember that the ship—in fact, the whole Federation—was in mourning. He knew Lynn Costa had been a remarkable woman, but he had always found her distant and inaccessible. He much preferred her husband, Emil, and he was glad nothing had happened to the old man.

His destination was a small command post just off the bridge which Worf occasionally commandeered for his personal use. When he was on the bridge or off duty, a subordinate still manned the post. In this cozy bunker, the Klingon had a full complement of viewscreens for simultaneous visual contact with the shuttle bays, cargo bays, transporter rooms, engineering, and the bridge. Plus, he had his own communications and ops panels, which could be converted at a single command into any subsystem available on the *Enterprise.* All the screens were aglow as Wesley Crusher strode into the cramped confines.

"Have a seat," barked Worf, staring intently at a computer screen which bounced earthy colors off the oils of his dark skin. He was reading as quickly as he could.

"Oh, this is pointless!" he growled, leaning back in

his swivel chair and shaking his massive head. "I could have three or four *lifetimes* and not read all this material."

"Uh, yes," said Wesley with disappointment. "Is that why you've sent for me, to help you read records?"

"No," intoned Worf, leaning forward and flexing his brow to form a bony hood over his black eyes. "I have some undercover work for you."

Wesley scurried forward and slipped into the lone chair opposite Worf's instrument panel. "What is it?" he asked confidentially.

Worf pointed to a screen on his left—it was an electronic datebook. "I see that Emil Costa used to tutor you in microbiology. Do you think that you could reestablish your friendly relationship with him? Keep him company?"

"Right now?" asked Wesley with some horror. "His wife just died!"

The Klingon ground his teeth together for a moment before replying, "I know he is your friend, Ensign, but Emil Costa is the primary suspect in a murder investigation. Perhaps your observation will clear him from suspicion. I told you this was undercover, and I meant it. I want you to stay close to him, watch him, and find out whether he killed his wife. Without letting him know, of course."

"Of course," gulped Wesley, squirming in his seat. "How should I do it . . . just ask him if he killed his wife?"

"Be circumspect," answered Worf. "We Klingons have a saying: A terrible secret cannot be kept. He may admit his crime to you, if he thinks you are his friend."

"But I *am* his friend!" protested the boy.

"Not on this assignment," replied Worf. "You are

78

an investigator, and you are not to tell *anyone*. Is that understood?"

Wesley Crusher mumbled a reply.

"I will inform Captain Picard, Commander Riker, and Counselor Troi. No one else needs to know." Worf stood and stretched. "Remember," he cautioned, "Emil Costa could be a murderer, and you must *never* place yourself in danger. As soon as you uncover any knowledge of his role in Lynn Costa's death, I want you to see me. Is that understood?"

"Yes," answered Wesley.

"You can start to befriend him at the funeral," Worf suggested, returning to his seat. He rubbed his eyes, then peered down at his screens. "Dismissed."

Wesley stood awkwardly and stumbled out the door. In the corridor, he collected oxygen into his lungs and called his brain cells to attention. First, he was staggered that anyone could suspect Emil Costa of causing Lynn's death. Such an idea was preposterous —the man was enraptured of his mate, always had been. He talked about Lynn in reverential tones, even when complaining that she had woken him up in the middle of the night to ask a question she could have looked up on the computer.

The two had seemed ideally paired to Wesley. Both were crusty, not arrogant but watchful of their time and energies; they didn't suffer fools gladly. She had been intense, tightly wound, but he had always seemed kicked-back even with his Prussian underpinnings. Emil looked stern and expected a full day's work and then some, but he had let Wesley explore the submicroscopic world at his own pace. That had been a couple of years ago, before Wes had become an ensign assigned to the bridge, but he remembered Emil Costa as being incredibly kind and patient, for an adult.

Now he could be a murderer, the boy thought glumly. How had his life slipped so much in those few years? Wesley Crusher felt a sudden pang of guilt for not keeping in closer touch with the Costas, but scheduling time with them was difficult, and his bridge duty . . .

No excuses, Wes decided, he should have kept closer tabs on them. But that still didn't explain this bizarre charge against Emil. The boy didn't think for a moment that Emil Costa was capable of killing his wife, unless he was suffering from some horrific mental illness.

The young ensign was suddenly filled with rage, and he wanted to clear his former tutor. But he remembered Worf's stern admonition. No, he couldn't tell Emil Costa why he was coming to see him—he didn't have to. Wes felt truly grieved that the old scientist had lost his wife, and that was reason enough to see and comfort him. Wesley was now grateful for this assignment from Worf, because it gave him a chance to do something he should have done much earlier.

Deciding there was no time to waste in righting this wrong, the ensign tapped his insignia badge. "Ensign Crusher to Dr. Emil Costa," he said, wetting his lips nervously.

"Hello, Wesley," came a voice that sounded very old and very beaten down. "Nice of you to call."

"Doctor," said Wes sadly, "I'm very sorry about what happened to your wife . . ."

"Don't mention it," rasped the doctor. "It was unexpected, but then—these things happen."

"She had a full life," Wesley replied, selecting that phrase from a list of platitudes that didn't come near to expressing what he felt.

"I thank you, Wesley," said a voice too tired to hide the Germanic accent. "You are doing well—I hear about this exploit or that exploit of yours all the time."

"I'm still learning," Wes admitted, "just like when you were tutoring me."

"It's not too late to join the Microcontamination Project," Emil suggested with a glimmer of life in his voice. "There are several openings just now."

The ensign seized upon the opening just presented him. "Yes," he replied, "I was just thinking about that. May I come by, Doctor, and discuss this with you?"

"Well . . ." gulped the voice uneasily.

"I won't stay any longer than you wish," the boy promised. "If you like, I could accompany you to the funeral."

"One step at a time," the old researcher sighed. "You can come by for a few minutes."

"I'm on my way," Wes shot back. "Out."

The teenager nearly bolted down the corridor toward the turbolift.

Chapter Six

DEANNA TROI BOLTED UPRIGHT in her bed, startled by the usually gentle chiming of her doorbell. She had been sleeping deeply, the sleep of the dead, as they say. Even her dreams remained a dull haze of troubled images with no discernible pattern or reason: a glimpse of her home planet in winter, her mother, a smiling Will Riker, Lynn Costa dead on the examination table . . . it all made no sense or too much sense.

The insistent chiming at the door drew her more into waking reality, and she padded out of bed, slipping a robe over her slender shoulders. She tossed her cascade of ebony hair once before opening the door.

It was her countryman, Karn Milu, with his eyebrows beetling angrily. "May I come in?" he asked.

Deanna gripped the collar of her robe, experiencing her usual inferiority complex in the eminent scientist's presence. "I'm not dressed," she protested weakly.

"You are dressed enough," he smiled, eyeing the lingerie that wrapped her completely from head to toe but did little to disguise her supple figure. "I'm sorry, but this is important, and I don't want to go to the captain again."

She nodded, stepped back, and dutifully motioned him in. The door whooshed shut as soon as the stout Betazoid had passed through. He was clearly agitated and spent the first few moments pacing.

"What is troubling you?" asked Deanna with concern.

"Your Lieutenant Worf!" he snarled. "That is what's troubling me. You have no idea the mountain of data he has requested—much of it personal and about half-finished projects. His arrogance has every department of mine in an uproar, especially Microcontamination."

"I apologize," sighed Deanna, "for Worf's exuberance. But he has been given a very difficult task, that of heading a murder investigation."

"*Rapsalak*," muttered Milu, using a common Betazoid expletive. "You show me any proof that this is a murder, and I'll shut down every lab on the ship for him. But I haven't seen anything conclusive at all!"

"Saduk—" Deanna began, but the entomologist wouldn't let her finish.

"Is *wrong!*" he snapped. "And don't tell me a Vulcan always has to be right. That ridiculous pronouncement was a knee-jerk reaction to the shock of finding a serious equipment failure in his lab. Saduk has since then revised his assessment to include the possibility of accident. You can talk to him yourself."

"That doesn't sound like a complete reversal," Deanna observed. "All of us have conceded the possibility of accident." A question popped into her mind, and she wondered if it was related. Matter-of-factly, she asked, "Is Saduk still in line to head the Microcontamination Project?"

Milu blinked at her and raised his bushy eyebrows. "No," he grunted. "This entire incident has led me to question Saduk's leadership abilities. He is an excellent worker, don't get me wrong, but his proclivity for blurting out whatever springs to mind has got to be taken into consideration."

"In other words," replied Deanna, "he's too honest and doesn't have enough of a feel for the politics of the situation. As far as you're concerned, a fatal accident would be unfortunate, but it doesn't leave a splotch on the records that a murder does."

At first, Karn Milu bristled at the suggestion, then he smiled slyly and pointed a finger at her. "You've been practicing your telepathy, Deanna Troi."

Either that, she thought, or you let your guard down, Karn Milu. "Grastow is the choice, isn't he?" she asked.

"That's none of your concern," he answered testily. Then the administrator leveled dark eyes full of warmth and wisdom at her. "There'll never be enough evidence to turn this into a murder case," he insisted, "and that's what you should be concerned about. Thus far, you have nothing more than half-cocked assumptions and insinuations. How would *you* like to lose a mate or an intimate co-worker, then be hit with baseless accusations of murder?"

When she didn't answer, he moved closer to her, cooing, "You and I should be friends, Deanna, not adversaries. I had hoped I could avoid going back to Captain Picard, for Worf's sake. Call off the Klingon and let these people get their lives back in order. We have urgent research that must carry on."

He painted a clear enough picture, Deanna decided—a department wracked by death and insinuation, yearning to put Lynn Costa's death into the past. But she didn't believe it, and she resented the waves of sophisticated charm that were emanating from Karn Milu. He was wooing her in every sense imaginable, intellectually, sensually, emotionally. She was almost reeling from his nearness, and she gripped the food slot for support.

"Stop that!" she ordered, sending an unaccustomed wave of negative emotion right back at him. His eyes widened with surprise, and he stepped back.

"You have no right to try to influence me!" she snapped, sending her fellow Betazoid farther back on his heels. "Lieutenant Worf is in charge of this investigation, and he is conducting it the way he sees fit."

"Yes," countered Karn Milu, dropping all pretense of pleasantry, "but is it best for the ship? I think not, and sooner or later, the captain will agree with me." He turned and stormed out of the room as fast as the automatic door would allow.

Still dazed and angry, Deanna slumped back into her bed. What was going on here? What did Karn Milu's angry reaction mean? Either she was to lose all respect for the only other member of her race aboard the *Enterprise,* or she was to lose faith in her own judgment. Dr. Milu had a point that any proclamation by a Vulcan was automatically held in high esteem. Vulcans weren't infallible, Deanna knew, but she hadn't needed Saduk to tell her that something was wrong with the way Lynn Costa had died.

Deanna had "witnessed" the frail woman's death in her own dream. She knew the *how,* but she was no closer to knowing the *why.* To Karn Milu, it had been simple carelessness. But carelessness was too insubstantial a reason for the fear in both Lynn and Emil's eyes. It didn't explain the certainty in Saduk's voice and the shock among people who knew Lynn Costa.

And carelessness did not come close to explaining Emil Costa's secrecy, the erased computer records, and the hastily discarded blue vial.

If only, Deanna wished, things could be as clear to her as they were to Karn Milu. Unfortunately, for whatever reason, her fellow Betazoid was not seeking the truth. He was seeking peace, a return to normalcy, and a certain measure of collective amnesia. He wanted all the disturbing details of Lynn Costa's death to be swept out to space along with her cold remains. But Deanna Troi couldn't do that. Painfully, she erased the administrator from her mental list of trustworthy allies. Her allegiance was with Worf, who was at least *trying* to find the truth.

The counselor took off her robe and glanced into her wardrobe for something to wear. Better the simple black shift, she decided, in case she didn't have time to change before the funeral. Since she had pledged every available minute to help Worf, she doubted if she would have time for wardrobe changes, or anything else.

On deck 32, Wesley Crusher gently rang the door chime. He waited several moments before hearing the muffled call, "Wesley, is that you?"

The boy tapped his communicator. "Ensign Crusher to Dr. Costa," he announced. "Yes, it's me."

The door opened, and a disheveled Emil Costa gripped Wesley's elbow and dragged him inside. He didn't seem to relax until the door had whooshed safely shut.

"Are you all right, Doctor?" asked Wes with concern.

"Oh, certainly," claimed the scientist, forcing an uneasy smile. "I . . . I don't wish to see just anyone at the moment."

"How are you holding up?" the lad asked.

The microbiologist heaved a sigh, "As well as can be expected. It still hasn't sunk in yet that she's gone, and maybe it never will." His tired expression brightened when he added, "But I have a good portion of my life ahead of me, and I'm very anxious to get off the ship."

"When are you doing that?" asked the ensign with surprise.

"At Kayran Rock," smiled Emil, returning to his bed, where he was stuffing toiletries and personal articles into an unassuming duffel bag. "But I still have enough time to put in a word with both the captain and Karn Milu. I'm sure you would be welcomed into the Microcontamination Project with open arms. You might be able to move very quickly in that department, and you could remain on the *Enterprise,* with all your friends."

"Well, yeah," Wesley stammered, "but I'm not sure I want to give up my position on the bridge. I would prefer something I could do part-time."

The old man shook his head sternly. "Do you think we're playing down here?" he demanded. "This is serious business, the Microcontamination Project. You live in a totally artificial environment, Wesley, and the project is directly responsible for the gases, liquids, and bacteria that are circulating through your body right now! Out here in space, where you are constantly coming in contact with the unknown, microcontamination technology is essential. And, Wesley," he pleaded, "we need brilliant people like you."

Head bowed, Emil corrected himself, *"They* need you. I'm out of it now."

"I could transfer there," the boy replied glumly, "but I still wouldn't make up for the loss of you and Lynn."

The old scientist shook his head dumbfoundedly, then he gazed at a small album of holographic photos, waiting to be packed. He dabbed away a tear with a quivering knuckle, then rubbed his hand over the white stubble on his skull. "Did you ever see pictures of Lynn when she was young?" he murmured.

"No," answered Wesley, stepping forward eagerly. "I'd like to see them."

Emil opened the book of holographic images, and an incredibly young, lithe, almost girlish figure danced before Wesley's eyes. Wesley watched a healthy woman in her early thirties swimming, dancing, and playing tennis. The vivacity and wonder of that red-haired sprite virtually leapt off the pages. Her expression at a tennis ball sailing over Emil's head was joyful. Her stern concentration before diving into a lake was offset in a succeeding photo by her laughter as she struck the water in a belly flop. Her ballroom dancing was enchanting, and the young lad marveled at the images of days gone by, on an Earth he barely knew.

"Wow!" was all he could think to say.

Emil observed, "Pretty far removed from the dour doyenne of the Microcontamination Project."

"What happened to her?" asked Wesley, with the directness of youth.

"In what sense do you mean that?" sighed the old man, gazing forlornly at his past. "Do you mean, what happened to that carefree young woman? What always happens to youth? It fades away into responsibility, duty, obsession. We get old, and we get desperate to pile up the achievements, to top ourselves even when that clearly isn't possible.

"What happens to two people?" the widower continued in hushed tones. "Two people who are joined in so many ways? Who can predict all the twists and turns such a partnership will take? We promised each other it would be a partnership until death, and it was. In that sense, I believe we fulfilled our promise to each other. Although I wish our last months had been happier . . ." His voice trailed away into muffled sobs.

Wesley was mortified. He had not meant to open old wounds and cause his tutor pain. But maybe the tears were cleansing, because the old man did not seem the least bit ashamed of them. Wesley stood quietly and let him cry.

"Thank you, Wesley," he sniffled after a few moments. Emil searched out his handkerchief, coughed into it, then blew his nose. "Of course, you were probably asking if I know who killed her?"

"Uh, yes," stammered the young ensign, stiffening his spine. "Not in so many words, but that is sort of what I was asking."

"Do you think I killed her?"

"No!" Wesley exclaimed, aghast at the idea.

"Then you'd be right," the scientist agreed. He returned to his packing. "I don't mind you sticking with me through the funeral. But I'm getting off this ship tomorrow, and I need a good night's rest."

"Yes, sir, understood," muttered Wes, snapping to uneasy attention. "Is there anything I can do to help you pack?"

"Those cuckoo clocks," said Emil wistfully, pointing to his antiquated prizes on the wall. "I took them apart and put them back together, I don't know how many times, but they never did keep the correct time. I've always thought it was the artificial gravity—those old weights and springs know the difference. I'm afraid I can't take them with me, but would you catalog their i.d. numbers, so that I can have them replicated at my next stop?"

"Where is your next stop?" asked Wes, taking down and inspecting one of the ancient timepieces.

"I don't know," murmured Emil. "At this point, I don't care, as long as it's far away from here."

The silence that followed was sad and oppressive. As if forcing himself out of his doldrums, the microbiologist suddenly clapped his hands and exclaimed, "Wesley, you must let me tell you why you should choose the Microcontamination Project as your next career move!"

He gripped the boy's shoulder and proceeded excitedly, "First of all, excuse me for saying this, but you are being wasted steering the ship. There must be hundreds of officers aboard the *Enterprise* who could fulfill that position as well as you. Most importantly, you can finally round out your education and learn something about inner space. Thirdly, don't forget the recognition and prestige. And the fulfillment of doing something to help everyone in the Federation, not just one lonely ship sailing the hinterlands."

Wesley sat on Emil's bed, forcing a good-natured smile as he listened to Emil's last lecture aboard the *Enterprise.*

Lieutenant Worf groaned as he crashed back into his chair and tried to massage his eyeballs back into his head. His eyes felt like they were dangling on a spit over hot coals somewhere. Even with Deanna Troi's diligent help for the last two hours, they had barely managed to cover all the personal material on Lynn and Emil Costa. Official records of all the other departments and people who used the cleanrooms would have to wait for later. Worf thought about calling in more researchers, but he was in no mood to deliver lengthy explanations on this puzzling case.

Before he had even heard about the counselor's

most recent conversation with Karn Milu, Worf knew they were dangerously close to looking like fools. But he didn't care. To err on the side of zealousness in a just cause was acceptable. Sloth, or anything less than supreme effort, was never acceptable.

The Klingon checked the chronometer in the corner of his current screen. Although his command post was near to the theater, he didn't want to be late for the funeral. He glanced at Deanna Troi, who was correlating information from two biographies written about the Costas. She was concentrating on the public personalities, while he was rummaging through their personal logs, memos, and schedules.

"It's almost eighteen-hundred hours," Worf muttered. "Let's summarize to each other the important matters and leave the objects of curiosity for later. What have you discovered?"

Deanna, too, slumped back in her chair and rubbed her tired eyes. "Early in their careers," she reported, "the Costas engendered their share of enemies and critics within the scientific community. But after they perfected the biofilter, they received support from the highest levels of the Federation, and their critics were no longer paid any attention. The Costas formed the Microcontamination Project and were given carte blanche to pursue whatever research they wanted. The rest, as they say, is history."

She punched up a biographical passage on one of her screens and pointed to a name. "A woman named Megan Terry sued them for scientific plagiarism, claiming that *she* perfected the biofilter while all three of them were co-workers. But Megan Terry lost her suit twenty-five years ago, and she's been dead for three years." Deanna scanned another page of data, adding, "They were forced to resign from a research project on Epsilon IV, but that was *thirty* years ago."

"Why were they forced to resign?" asked Worf.

"They rode roughshod over the administration," replied the Betazoid. "That seems to be a recurring story wherever they were assigned, at least early on. For the last twenty-five years, nobody has dared to stand in their way. To their credit, they've performed an amazing number of altruistic acts, such as bringing clean farming and manufacturing to impoverished planets. They've never taken any payment for any of their discoveries, even assigning the royalties from their patents to a plague relief fund.

"In short," she concluded, "they're almost perfect."

"Not quite," said Worf, squinting his massive brow at his screen. "They have two grown children with whom they have no contact. The children were left with relatives on Earth almost from the day of their births. They have lived in dozens of different places, laying down no roots. They have few friends and no discernible hobbies, outside of Emil's fondness for cuckoo clocks and alcohol. One might say the Costas have been selfish and single-minded in the pursuit of their careers."

Deanna shrugged, "I could name many people on this vessel who fit that description."

"But I must disagree with you," admitted Worf. "Emil has often devoted himself to others. He has tutored Wesley Crusher and several of the young people on the ship, as well as making himself accessible to researchers from other projects. Lynn Costa, on the other hand, was always more secretive and suspicious of others—I could hardly locate any of her personal notes or memos."

"Maybe those were the records she destroyed," suggested Deanna.

"Undoubtedly," Worf grumbled. "Both Costas are well versed in the art of secrecy. I've also discovered that only the *official* records of Emil's microbe discoveries are available. Much of the raw data he collected whenever the *Enterprise* was in orbit around a planet is missing, and so is the testing that was done afterward."

"So what have we got for all our work?" yawned the Betazoid.

"Very stiff necks," snarled Worf. The Klingon lumbered to his feet and gratefully stretched his taut muscles. "I assigned Wesley Crusher an undercover task," he remarked, "and I would like to assign one to you, too."

"Yes?" Deanna replied, somewhat warily.

"At the funeral, can you befriend Saduk and see if he has learned anything new?"

Deanna nodded firmly, "I was already planning to do exactly that."

The theater was crammed to capacity, with every seat filled and people milling in the aisles. The overflow crowd stood outside in the corridor or stopped wherever they were to listen to the service on the ship's intercom. Through a viewport, the stars gently blurred past at warp three, but everyone's attention was on the elegant silver casket in the center of the stage. The sphere was aimed like a missile at the starswept heavens beyond.

Lines of somber faces gazed down at the white-shrouded body of Lynn Costa. Her tiny frame was dwarfed by streams of red and silver hair, festooned with green orchids. The once dynamic face was now peaceful, bland, and rouged with more color than it possessed when she was alive. In the background, a harpist gently stroked her instrument.

Commander William Riker took the podium and looked out on the solemn faces—familiar, unfamiliar, and vaguely familiar. Deanna was talking with a Vulcan who was in the vague category. Wesley Crusher stood next to Emil Costa, whose eyes never moved far from his hands clasped stiffly at his waist. From the Microcontamination Project, the big Antarean and the attractive blond woman stood together. The captain was talking in low tones to Doctors Milu and Baylak, and Worf was prowling through the crowd, his bony forehead sticking out like a shark's fin over the top of the other heads.

It was gatherings like this that reminded Will that the bridge and the occasional away mission were only two of the ingredients that constituted life aboard the *Enterprise*. It was home for a diverse, iconoclastic lot pulled from the farthest reaches of the Federation. Students and apprentices shared duties with the greatest deans of their professions. There was little time for theory—it was all hands-on. In some ways, the *Enterprise* was like a floating academy, with everyone living in one big dormitory.

Except for living in that dormitory, Will marveled at how little he had in common with most of these people. While he explored the buildings and beings of an alien culture, many of them were exploring the world inside a thimbleful of air or water. The one thing they all had in common, Will decided, was a desire to learn what is out there. Certainly, Lynn Costa had that.

The voices had nearly died down now, acknowledging the first officer's presence at the podium. He swallowed hard before he began, "Thank you for attending this memorial service for Dr. Lynn Costa. We are holding it here in the theater instead of a holodeck, because Dr. Costa requested a simple crew member's funeral as prescribed by Starfleet regulations. For that reason, only Captain Picard and I will speak."

He nodded toward the still form in the glass case. "It doesn't strike me as unusual that Lynn Costa should choose to remain in space, because she devoted her life to understanding it. It's the same mystery on the microscopic level as it is on the cosmic level. Dr. Costa actually did something about the space around us, finding ingenious ways to keep it clean and usable. But the real reason she came to the *Enterprise*, I understand, was to make sure we were keeping up the biofilters."

Quiet chuckles graced his last remark, and Will cleared his throat before continuing, "It is my lasting regret—and I'm sure I speak for many of us—that we didn't get to know her better. It wasn't because we didn't want to, but we knew that every minute we stole of Dr. Costa's time was depriving the Federation of her remarkable genius." He turned back to the casket and smiled, "Lynn, we'll miss you, but we'll see you every day in your legacy."

Commander Riker stepped down from the podium to murmured approval, and Captain Picard took his place. The large room and even the corridors throughout the ship hushed to an abnormal silence.

"Normally in these affairs," began a stern Jean-Luc Picard, "the captain is supposed to be reverential, pleasant, and say something comforting. I am certainly glad that Commander Riker was so eloquent, because now I don't have to be pleasant and comforting. I am very *discomforted* by the circumstances surrounding Lynn Costa's death."

Not even breathing could be heard now, and Wesley Crusher glanced at Emil Costa beside him. The scientist's lower lip was trembling, and his eyes looked glassy within the sunken cavities of a sagging face. Wes started to ask him if he was all right, but Captain Picard was speaking again.

"I know," Jean-Luc continued, "this is a sad enough occasion without injecting a specter that none of us wants to acknowledge. Nevertheless, Lynn Costa's death remains an enigma, an accident that shouldn't have happened. So," he pleaded with outstretched hands, "if anyone has any information regarding the tragedy which befell Dr. Costa, please contact Lieutenant Worf, Counselor Troi, or myself."

As the audience shifted uneasily, Picard looked down at the body and shook his head. "We think people like Lynn Costa will live forever, because their impact on our society is as great as the sun's impact on a planet. But we are mistaken. So let's treasure all life while it lasts, because it *is* so fragile."

Jean-Luc tapped on his insignia. "Picard to O'Brien."

"Yes, sir," answered the transporter operator.

"Energize," uttered the captain.

"Acknowledged."

In an aurora of phosphorescent lights from every color of the spectrum, the silver casket dematerialized. Instinctively, most eyes in the room turned to the observation window and the vast starfield beyond, where Lynn Costa's molecules had been forever scattered.

Wesley finally released his breath after the drama of Captain Picard's speech and Lynn Costa's departure. He turned back to see Emil's reaction, but the white-haired scientist was gone.

Desperately, Wes tried to make his way to the door, but the entire crowd was jostling its way in the same direction. Without shoving people out of the way, the teenager could never catch up, so he settled into the general flow and cursed himself for not paying closer attention. As far as Ensign Crusher was concerned, surveillance of Emil Costa was *his* job, and he wasn't about to let Worf down. He had momentarily failed, but Wes was determined to pick up the scent.

Near the podium, Captain Picard exchanged cordial words with several people who stopped to tell him that they didn't know anything about Lynn Costa's death, but wished they did. Picard craned his neck, peering over their shoulders for the person with whom he really wanted to speak. Spying Lieutenant Worf, he motioned the security officer to his side.

"Yes, Captain?" answered Worf attentively.

"Lieutenant," said Picard, lowering his voice, "I wish to talk privately with you in my ready room in fifteen minutes."

"Yes, Captain," Worf acknowledged with a hard swallow.

The Klingon straightened up and watched the captain as he sliced his way through the knot of people. Worf was not the type to second-guess himself, but he began to wonder if he had made the right assumptions, gone to the right sources, and otherwise conducted this investigation in the most expedient way possible. His superior should not have had to make a shipwide appeal for assistance.

In the doorway of the theater, he saw Deanna Troi and Dr. Saduk patiently filing out with the others. At least Deanna's mission to win the Vulcan's confidence had apparently been successful. Worf had to admit his disappointment in not turning up more physical evidence regarding the alleged crime. But, like most Klingons, he was a great believer in the power of subterfuge and the inevitability of loose tongues.

"Lieutenant Worf?" said a soft voice, breaking into his reverie.

He turned to look down at the comely face and figure of Shana Russel. The human female was petite, but her voluminous blond hair gave her extra height. She gazed up at him with eyes that were a lovely shade of blue but were a bit too helpless for Worf's taste.

"Yes?" he answered, with only a hint of politeness.

"I'm sorry," she replied, averting her eyes. "I wasn't very friendly to you and Counselor Troi. Of course, you were just doing your jobs, and it's not your fault if everyone is a suspect. But," she breathed, looking around to make sure no one was listening, "I once heard someone threaten to kill Dr. Costa."

"Who?" asked the security chief, expecting to hear Emil Costa incriminated once again.

"Karn Milu," she hissed.

The Klingon blinked at Shana Russel and the ridges of his brow rippled. "You heard this yourself?" he asked.

She nodded forlornly, "I wish I hadn't."

"Under what circumstances?"

The young assistant glanced around nervously. "I don't really feel like talking here. Can we meet later . . . someplace private?"

"My command post . . ." Worf began.

"More private than that," whispered Shana. "Come to my quarters on deck 32. My cabin is number B-49."

She turned to go, and Worf caught her shoulder in his firm grasp. She managed a nervous smile as he pulled his hand away.

"I may be delayed," Worf told her. "Shall I send an assistant to take your statement?"

"No," breathed Shana with alarm. "Come alone. I don't feel right about this, and I could be stepping on toes. Whatever happens, I don't want to be transferred off the *Enterprise* so soon."

"Understood," Worf nodded.

She squeezed his arm, adding, "Any time is all right, but come alone."

With that final admonition, Shana Russel hurried out the door, which was now clear of traffic. Worf heaved his thick shoulders, wondering what would happen next, and strode out after her.

In the captain's ready room, Jean-Luc Picard stared at his screen, with Data hovering over his shoulder, pointing to a remarkable simulation of shuttle traffic at a giant asteroid.

"So you see, Captain," explained the android, "the docking procedure and disembarkation consumes approximately sixteen-and-a-half minutes, perhaps more if the greetings are prolonged. We would need to allow half-an-hour to be on the safe side. I propose assigning two or more parties to arrive in each craft, resulting in an average of eight passengers per craft instead of four."

"How do you propose we accomplish this?" asked Picard.

Data replied, "The *Enterprise* can set a precedent. By speeding up our arrival in time to meet the Kreel flagship, the *Tolumu*, we can request that their admiralty join us. It is my assumption that the Kreel representatives will welcome a tour of the *Enterprise* and a chance to ride in our shuttlecraft. They are quite curious about our technology. We then have the benefit of controlling their transportation and making sure they don't arrive at the same time as the Klingons. We can delay the Klingons by asking *them* to rendezvous with the *Manchester*."

Picard nodded thoughtfully, remembering how ill-mannered the Kreel could be. Like their archenemy, the Klingons, they hadn't been civilized for very long—some would say they still weren't. "How many are there in the Kreel delegation?" he asked.

"Six," said Data. "With our party of three, that will leave one empty seat on the shuttlecraft."

"Correction," snapped Picard. "In all likelihood, we will have a party of four, and there will be *no* empty seats."

Data cocked his head puzzledly and straightened up, as the door to Picard's office opened. Lieutenant Worf darkened the doorway and intoned, "Permission to enter, Captain."

"Come," said Picard, motioning the Klingon in. "This following bit of news concerns both of you."

Approaching the captain's desk, Worf glanced at Data, but the android shrugged his eyebrows, admitting he didn't know what was coming next.

"At the direct order of Starfleet," muttered Picard, "Emil Costa has been granted permission to disembark at Kayran Rock at the earliest opportunity. He is leaving the ship permanently."

"Captain—" began Worf with concern.

Picard silenced him with a raised hand. "Let me dispense with Commander Data's assignment, then we will discuss yours." He turned back to the android. "We have to increase speed, I presume, to rendezvous with the Kreel."

The android nodded, "Warp four will be sufficient."

"Make it so," ordered the captain. "I have no changes to your proposed schedule and course settings. You may transmit your report to Starfleet with my recommendation."

"Yes, sir," answered the lieutenant commander, heading immediately for the door.

"Data!" called Worf, stopping the android in his tracks. "How long before the shuttlecraft departs?"

"Four hours at the earliest," came the reply. "I'll have a more accurate estimate after I contact the Kreel vessel."

"Thank you," grumbled Worf, and the android was gone.

Captain Picard turned off his screen and clasped his hands in front of him. He looked frankly at his security officer. "I know you're not happy about this latest development," he remarked. "Neither am I. But the fact of the matter is, Emil Costa has a great deal of influence, and we have no right to keep him here."

"Captain," barked Worf, "I'm sure we're about to uncover something. Both Counselor Troi and Ensign Crusher are working on different angles, and we have some physical evidence, a vial discovered on the floor by the pod. Guinan has identified it as being exactly like a vial Emil Costa was carrying earlier."

Jean-Luc slapped his palms on his desk and stood. "You may have evidence," he countered, "but you don't have a crime. I've read Geordi's report, and there's no conclusive proof that Lynn Costa's death was anything but an accident."

"There is instinct," Worf intoned.

Shaking his head glumly, Picard circled his desk and confronted Worf face-to-face. "I sympathize with you," he admitted. "Just now, you heard me ask the ship's populace for help. I have defended you against a very prominent scientist who claims you are disrupting the work of the entire science branch. I have listened to all the theories, read all the data, and I have looked in vain for a suitable explanation."

Worf bowed his head and murmured, "I have failed."

"Nonsense," replied Picard, momentarily gripping the Klingon's brawny forearm. "I assigned this investigation to you and Counselor Troi, and I know you have done all you could. What I didn't realize—what no one could realize—was that the task would be so difficult. Quite possibly, Lynn Costa's death will always remain a mystery. We have to accept the possibility that it will eventually be classified as an accident."

"Captain," Worf grimaced, barely controlling his frustration, "both Troi and I are convinced it's murder."

Picard shook his head and reiterated, "You can't take suspicions and gut instincts to a tribunal. In addition, we need you and the ship's counselor back at your regular duties, and we need to get deck 31 functioning normally again."

Worf grasped at the only available opening. "Captain," he pleaded, "grant me the next four hours until Emil Costa leaves the ship. I promise that if we haven't got enough material to charge him by then, we will conclude the investigation."

Picard shrugged, "Very well, pursue it until then. I wish it could be different, Lieutenant. I wish you could take as much time as you needed, but we have to be realistic."

"Understood," the Klingon nodded. He turned to leave.

The captain called after him, "Try to get some sleep when this is over, Lieutenant. Commander La Forge will need you on the bridge while Data, Riker, and I are off the ship."

"Aye, sir," replied Worf, slumping out the door.

His lips thinned, and Jean-Luc Picard angrily rapped his knuckles on his desk. Anyone who thought the job of a starship captain was wonderful should stand in his shoes at a moment like this. As captain, he was given great latitude, but he could never forget the limitations.

Chapter Seven

ON HIS MISSION to catch up with Emil Costa, Wesley Crusher hurried down the corridor of deck 32. Passing a pair of residents, he smiled cordially and slowed his walk to an easy gait, trying not to look suspicious while he scanned the doors for Emil's cabin. He didn't know why, but Emil's sudden disappearance at his wife's funeral greatly disturbed the boy. Captain Picard's words, though blunt and unexpected, had not been aimed at Emil, as far as Wesley could tell. It had been an appeal for help to everyone on the ship.

The ensign felt he hadn't intruded upon Emil's privacy. He hadn't pressed him for information and had done everything he could to be good company in his time of grief. Now the old man had deserted him. If, as Wes was certain, Emil had nothing to do with his wife's death, why was he acting so guilty?

His eyes suddenly blinked on the sign reading simply THE COSTAS. Wes stopped, straightened his tunic, and chimed to enter.

The door opened as expected, but it wasn't the stooped old scientist who met him. The severe haircut was the same, but it graced the skull of an Antarean who stood at least a meter taller than the teenager.

Wesley Crusher stepped back, then stiffened to attention. "I am Ensign Wesley Crusher," he announced. "Please tell Dr. Costa that I would like to see him for a moment."

The giant Antarean ducked through the portal and stood blocking its entrance. "I am Grastow," he said, his soft voice in direct contrast to his menacing size. "Dr. Costa is seeing no one now. He is resting until his departure on the shuttlecraft."

"Let me pass," demanded Wesley with false bravado. "I was just with Dr. Costa at the funeral, and we have something important to discuss."

Wesley took a step forward, and, before he could react, two monstrous hands grabbed him by his jersey and pushed him firmly against the bulkhead. The air shot out of his lungs, and his head and buttocks stung with the impact. Then the hands let go, and he slid down the smooth wall, landing in a wheezing heap on the floor of deck 32.

The hulking Antarean leaned over him. "By Dr. Costa's direct order," he warned, *"no one* is to see him."

Wesley groaned and struggled to sit up. "I remember you now," he gasped, pointing a wavering finger at Grastow. "You're even bigger *outside* your cleanroom suit!"

The cherubic face scowled down, then the immense body turned and marched back into the Costa quarters. The door whooshed shut with finality behind Grastow.

Ensign Crusher staggered to his feet and took several more painful breaths before his lungs were functioning normally again. So, he mused, Emil Costa had gotten himself some sort of protection.

He could perform his surveillance duties out here. At least he knew where Emil Costa was, stuck in-

side his cabin. Stiffly, Wesley took several strides
down the corridor and positioned himself where he
would have an unobstructed view of Emil Costa's
doorway, without being obtrusive.

And he waited.

Following the funeral, the elegant tables of the
Ten-Forward Room were filling up. Deanna Troi,
seated in the center of the lounge, recognized many of
the patrons from the services. Many more would
come before this night was over to make one last toast
to Lynn Costa. She had been a hero to most of them
and an idol to more than a few. Even to her detractors,
her life and career were monumental achievements.
Her like might not be seen again for generations.

Deanna turned her attention back to her escort, the
tall slender Vulcan, Saduk. He, too, was quietly sur-
veying the crowded café. Deanna had been somewhat
surprised when he had accepted her invitation to join
her in the lounge. She could scarcely remember when,
if ever, she had seen him here before. But on this sad
occasion, even the taciturn Vulcan had apparently not
wanted to be alone.

They sat quietly for a long stretch of time, saying
barely a word, sipping two different types of herbal
tea. Oddly, thought Deanna, she was not in the least
bit uncomfortable at this lack of conversation, and
neither was he. Of course, a Vulcan would never
expect someone to try to make small talk with him,
and it would never occur to him that two companions
should try to amuse each other. They scarcely knew
one another, and their only frame of reference at the
moment was Lynn Costa's death. So the two sat in
silence, occasionally glancing at each other.

Deanna couldn't help but wonder what it would be
like to be romantically involved with a Vulcan, specif-

ically *this* Vulcan. Quiet evenings around the hearth would be the rule, she imagined. Long-term interaction would probably result in a certain amount of telepathic communication that would confound their acquaintances. With Saduk, there would be no arguments, jealousy, or unfounded accusations. Lovemaking would be leisurely, gentle, and spiritual. Vulcans, she knew, had great stamina but little passion, and she would have to compensate with a deeper well of her own passion.

On the downside, they probably couldn't have children without substantial medical intervention. Her one abrupt experience with pregnancy had left her anxious to experience it again someday, naturally. More importantly, she wondered if a Vulcan could ever open up to her, share his innermost dreams and desires. She doubted it. With Saduk, she might never know what feelings he wasn't revealing, what emotions he was keeping bottled up inside. She would have to be content with never really knowing him.

Deanna had all but discounted the idea of ever getting interested in Saduk, when he turned to her suddenly and said, "You are very beautiful."

She blinked at him and blushed, "Why, thank you."

"I did not mean to be forward," he replied politely. "I have been looking at all the females in this room, and I believe you are the most attractive."

"Thank you again," she gulped, sitting back in her chair and blinking at him with amazement. "If you're trying to make sure we have tea again sometime, I would be delighted."

"I have no ulterior motive," he shrugged, taking a sip of the brackish brew made from the bark of a Vulcan tree. "I am celibate."

"Is that because of a vow?" asked Deanna with a

tinge of disappointment. She knew Vulcans took their personal vows very seriously.

"No," he replied, gazing away. "Vulcans remain celibate until they choose a bond mate, and I have chosen to devote all my attention to my work. Domestic entanglements would be a detriment."

"Domestic entanglements," the Betazoid mused aloud. "Did you, by chance, base this decision on your observation of the Costas?"

"Partly," the Vulcan answered with typical honesty. "Mostly, I based this decision on my own past experiences."

Deanna would have liked to explore this topic further, but she had a more important job at hand. "Speaking of the project," she remarked coolly, "how do you feel about being passed over to be its new head?"

The Vulcan raised an eyebrow. "Logically," he observed, "I would be the preferable choice to lead the project. I have more experience, training, and ability, although Grastow can be counted upon to follow the aims and dictums of the Costas explicitly. Perhaps Grastow will be an able administrator, which is something we have lacked."

"Yes," replied Deanna, "I have noticed in our investigation that Karn Milu pretty much let the Costas do whatever they wanted, and the Costas were hardly sticklers for correct procedures."

"Agreed," Saduk nodded. "I believe this murder would not have happened if procedures had been tighter. In that respect, your Lieutenant Worf was absolutely right."

"You said murder," Deanna pointed out. "Karn Milu told me that you had accepted the idea of it being an accident."

Saduk fixed her with piercing onyx eyes. "I always accepted the possibility of accident," he replied, "pending evidence to the contrary. However, my own personal hypothesis has not changed from the moment we first inspected the pod—I believe it was murder."

"Yes," Deanna answered solemnly. "But who?"

Without warning, Saduk stood and lowered his head in a formal bow. "This has been a very pleasant interlude," he remarked, "but I must return to work. We have finally received clearance to return to the cleanrooms."

Deanna fixed him with her own dark eyes. "If you know who did it, tell me."

"I'm not certain," he answered. "Please remember, Deanna, I am devoting every waking moment to saving the project and the various experiments already under way. The dead do not concern me."

With that, the slim Vulcan swiveled gracefully on his heel and marched out.

Deanna was still shaking her head when Guinan strolled past, wearing a broad-brimmed gray chapeau. "He would be a tough catch," she drawled, scooping up the Vulcan's tea cup, "for any woman."

"He's very single-minded," agreed Deanna, "and stubborn. He knows more than he's telling." She exploded with frustration, "*Everyone* knows more than they're telling!"

Deanna glanced around the room, and those who had noticed her outburst politely turned away. "I'm sorry, Guinan," she muttered. "We're no closer to knowing what happened to Dr. Costa. We're at a total standstill."

"Can I be of some help?" asked the Listener.

"Perhaps," Deanna replied, hope brightening her lovely face. "You overhear much of what is spoken in this room. Have you heard any information about Lynn Costa's death?"

"Her husband is the most popular suspect," confided the proprietress. "Others say that Lynn Costa hasn't been herself for over a year, so your idea of suicide hasn't been totally discounted."

"In other words," sighed the Betazoid, "none of them knows anything more than we do."

Guinan frowned, "That wasn't much help, was it? What about the blue vial?"

"Circumstantial," shrugged Deanna. "It might be useful if we had something else, but we don't." She rose slowly from her seat. "I've got more records to go over, but I'll try to check back with you later. Please keep your ears open."

"Always," smiled Guinan.

Lieutenant Worf took his time making his way down to deck 32 and Shana Russel's cabin. He was still replaying in his mind his conversation with Captain Picard. It had been painful for the captain, more painful than for him. In truth, the four-hour time limit weighed more heavily than Captain Picard's lack of confidence in his investigation. The captain had many concerns, but Worf had only one— to find Lynn Costa's killer.

What if it wasn't Emil Costa? What if most of their efforts and suspicions until now had been wasted? Worf knew the business of the *Enterprise* was not police work, but he hated to end the investigation so soon, so inconclusively, merely because the main suspect was leaving the ship. Worse yet, if Emil Costa wasn't the murderer, the murderer would still be aboard the *Enterprise*.

Before he realized it, he had walked past Shana Russel's cabin and had to retrace his steps. The

Klingon gritted his teeth and cursed under his breath; he was getting careless. What if, during this investigation, he had missed more than a few numbers on a door? Worf couldn't remember the last time he had slept, but he wasn't using that as an excuse. He vowed to himself to be sharper, do better.

Worf wondered if, psychologically, he was cut out for the plodding cerebral work of a detective. He wanted action! He wanted to wrap his hands around the killer's neck, not glare at a computer screen for another four hours or ask another round of questions. But he had to follow up every possibility, especially a report that Karn Milu had threatened Lynn Costa's life. Worf chimed at the door, it brushed open, and Shana Russel hurriedly grabbed his hand and ushered him in.

"Good," breathed the young woman excitedly, "you came alone!"

She was wearing a floor-length chiffon nightgown which set off her blond hair strikingly but did little to hide her youthful figure. It was quite inappropriate dress to receive a visitor, thought the Klingon, until he remembered that she had probably been sleeping. But, as he watched Shana Russel nervously pacing the confines of her small cabin, he didn't think she had been sleeping at all.

"I don't know what to do," she moaned, clenching her hands. "I'm afraid I'm getting to be a bit of a wreck." She turned to him with earnest blue eyes. "My whole world's been turned upside down by this. I don't know what to think anymore!"

"Calm down," said Worf in a voice he hoped was soothing. "The way to rest easier is to help us solve this mystery. Now, what is it you wanted to tell me about Karn Milu threatening Lynn Costa?"

"Oh, *that?*" she sighed, running a hand through her

golden hair. It tumbled becomingly around the smooth white skin of her neck and shoulders. "It was in the transition room right after Lynn did whatever she did to the computer records. I don't think they were paying any attention to me—they hardly ever do—and he screamed at her."

Worf asked patiently, "What exactly did he say?"

Shana Russel stopped pacing and deliberately collected her memories. "He said very clearly, 'If you botch this opportunity, I'll kill you.' "

Worf narrowed his eyes. "What opportunity?"

Shana shook her head in frustration. "I have no idea," she groaned. "All I know is he was very mad at her."

"Evidently," grumbled Worf. "But you don't know what he was referring to?"

"No," she answered, staring at him with round, frightened eyes. "What does any of it mean? What's happening to us?"

Before Worf could react, the young woman gripped him around the chest and hung on tightly.

"I'm so afraid," she murmured, nuzzling her face into his chest. "Please stay with me."

Worf gently held her at arm's length. "You're upset," he said hoarsely. "Perhaps, if you talked to Counselor Troi . . ."

"I don't want Counselor Troi," she breathed, fighting past his hands and hugging him tighter. "I want *you*." She looked up at him with eyes that begged for him to comfort her, eyes that promised more than comfort in return. "I realize you don't know me very well," she whispered, "but I really feel alone now. I've got no one."

"I cannot become *involved* at this time," Worf said forcefully, pushing her away again and stepping back.

Shana turned away with embarrassment. "What you must think of me . . ." she sputtered.

"Nonsense," the Klingon answered sympathetically. "This is a trying time for all of us. But it's not a time to seek false consolation. I believe there's a murderer on board this ship, and none of us can rest until he is brought to justice."

"Of course," muttered the girl. "I'm being selfish." She turned back to him, managing a slight smile.

The Klingon cleared his throat and returned to the subject at hand. "Can you tell me anything else about this threat?" he asked.

"No," shrugged the researcher, "only that it made quite an impression upon me. But I never mentioned it to anyone."

"Did anyone else hear it?"

Forlornly, Shana Russel shook her head. "It probably isn't much help, is it?"

"I cannot say," answered the security chief, moving toward the door. "Thank you."

The young blonde smiled hopefully, "Maybe, Worf, when this is all over, we could have dinner together, take a walk on the holodeck . . ."

"When this is all over," muttered the Klingon, "I plan to sleep for at least two shifts. Good-bye."

"Good-bye," Shana Russel answered weakly as her door slid shut.

For almost three hours, Wesley Crusher had stationed himself in a corridor on deck 32 and watched people pay their respects to Emil Costa. Or rather, *try* to pay their respects to Emil, because so far the eminent scientist had refused to see anyone. This, too, struck the teenager as being odd, considering that Emil would soon be leaving the ship and his colleagues forever.

Wes could understand the widower not wanting to see *him*, having already spent several hours with the teenager. But how could he refuse to see old friends, like Dr. Baylak? So far, no one had answered Emil's door except for the big Antarean, who listened to many plaintive pleas but steadfastly turned everyone away. The young ensign was beginning to get suspicious.

In fact, he wondered whether Dr. Costa was in that room at all. Wesley knew that, as a rule, Dr. Costa didn't wear a communicator, so Wesley couldn't simply ask the computer to verify his whereabouts.

There was one way to find out, decided the teenager, and all he needed was a tricorder. The boy left his self-appointed post to search the hallway for an emergency first-aid kit. He knew the hatches on emergency equipment were never locked, and there was always a medical tricorder among the hypos, tourniquets, and bandages. As expected, he located the small red-striped locker at eye level near an intersection with another corridor.

Stealthily, Wesley opened the hatch and pried the tricorder from its mount. He knew the ship's computer was making a note of this somewhere and that somebody from sickbay would probably investigate to see where the instrument had gone and if it needed replacing, but Wesley felt he could explain taking it. He could explain everything—he was on special duty, wasn't he?

Returning to Emil Costa's cabin, Wesley was relieved to find the door shut and no callers around. He aimed the tricorder with its special medical peripheral at the door and searched for all indications of life within a six-meter radius. Inside the cabin, there was only one life form—a large one, to be sure—but only one living being.

So intently was Wesley studying the big Antarean's vital signs that he didn't see the door slide open and the giant himself step out. Suddenly a shadow darkened the tiny screen, and a meaty pink hand swiped the scanner from his grasp.

"What are you doing?" hissed Grastow.

Wesley didn't feel like getting involved in a discussion of the finer arts of tricorder operation, so he walked away. Let Grastow explain the borrowed tricorder!

From the corridor outside Worf's command post, Karn Milu glared with bristling eyebrows at the Klingon and Deanna Troi, both of whom gazed up at him wearily from a bank of display screens. "What can be so important," demanded the Betazoid, "to summon me here at this hour?"

Deanna glanced at Worf, whose jaws were already tightening, and she gave him a confident smile that told him to let her handle this. Worf relaxed slightly and leaned back in his seat. In the last few hours, they had gone over every shred of evidence many times, including Shana Russel's death threat account. Like Worf, Deanna was becoming annoyed with Milu's unseemly lack of cooperation, an attitude which bordered on obstruction, she felt. As shocking as Shana Russel's accusation had been, it could explain what Karn Milu had been hiding.

"We're sorry to have summoned you so abruptly, Dr. Milu," she smiled. "Won't you please step inside?"

Scowling irritably, the administrator finally relented and stepped across the threshhold, allowing the door to close behind him.

"It's not that I mind cooperating," he insisted,

"but I've told you all I can. I've delivered every record, every lab report, every maintenance schedule, and I've shut down the cleanrooms for an unconscionable length of time. What more can you want from me?"

Deanna Troi looked at the entomologist with eyes as cold as those of his petrified beetles. "We want to know," she said calmly, "whether there is any truth to a report that you once threatened to kill Lynn Costa."

The scientist blinked at her, and his face reddened considerably. "Who told you that?" he demanded.

"Never mind," growled Worf. "The exact words you are described as saying are, 'If you botch this opportunity, I'll kill you.'"

Karn Milu burst out laughing, a little too loudly, then remarked, "The only one crazy enough to have said *that* is dead."

"Do you deny saying it?" asked Deanna, her smile gone and her lips unaccustomedly thin.

"Yes," Milu answered with pained dignity. "Somebody is being melodramatic at my expense. I had my disagreements with Lynn Costa, and I was certainly distraught when she erased those records. *But kill her?* The most prestigious scientist under my command? I didn't work with her on a daily basis—I could avoid seeing her quite easily. Even with all her . . . peculiarities of late, she was still a tremendous asset to this ship. And I miss her."

Deanna sat back in her chair, surprised. Somewhere in that convoluted answer, she sensed the truth. But then she reminded herself that Karn Milu had extraordinary mental abilities, powers that far eclipsed hers. She was susceptible to his telepathic thoughts, and he knew how to exert his will very subtly.

"Dr. Milu," she warned, cordially but with steel in

her voice, "if it is ever proved that you have been lying to us, I will personally see that you are prosecuted fully under Starfleet regulations."

"Don't worry," countered the Betazoid. "Like Emil Costa, my service to Starfleet will soon be coming to an end. Am I free to leave?"

"You may go," intoned Worf.

Milu turned his stocky back to them and marched out; even his walk looked indignant.

Leaning back in her chair, Deanna shook her head puzzledly. "I don't understand his attitude," she sighed, "but I apologize for it."

"His attitude is not so remarkable," said the security chief. "He wants to believe the best of his people. For that reason, if no other, he refuses to condone our investigation."

"But," Deanna whispered, "do you think he is capable of threatening someone's life? Even taking a life?"

Worf gazed at her with dark eyes hooded by bony protuberances. "Betazoids are not pacifists," he remarked. "In fact, you take extreme pride in your love of emotions. He is a very proud man, but could he ever become angry enough to kill Lynn Costa?" Worf shrugged doubtfully at his own rhetorical question and punched up another screenful of cleanroom schedules.

Then Deanna wondered aloud, "What did he mean about ending his service to Starfleet?"

But Worf had evidently had enough of unanswerable questions and was poring over the data on his screen. Trying to clear her mind of thoughts that were more disturbing than constructive, Deanna returned to her own screen of raw laboratory records. At the moment, they were searching for the names of everyone who had any contact with the deadly pod, however fleeting. Thus far, their exhaustive search had only widened the list of persons who had access to the cleanroom. Narrowing the list was proving impossible.

"Data to Worf," came the familiar clipped tones of Starfleet's only android officer.

Worf touched his comm panel, responding, "Worf here."

"We are now maintaining course and station with Kayran Rock," said Data. "Per your request, I have the latest estimate of the departure time of the shuttlecraft. We will rendezvous with the Kreel flagship in approximately nineteen minutes. Allowing time for a brief tour of the ship, I estimate shuttlecraft departure in approximately forty minutes."

Worf and Deanna exchanged troubled glances. Neither one of them wanted to admit defeat, but the prospect was staring them in the face, just forty minutes away.

"Thank you, Data," Worf replied. "Out."

With exasperation, Deanna pushed herself away from the console and stood. "With your permission," she groaned, arching a stiff back, "I would like to see if Guinan has overheard anything else."

"Good luck," grumbled Worf, delving back into the morass of statistics on his computer screen.

Deanna hurried out of the command room. She actually had little hope that Guinan would prove to be useful; in truth, she just could not bear to look at the expression of defeat on the proud Klingon's face.

Putting two and two together had always been Wesley Crusher's strong point, and he quickly surmised that if Grastow was alone in Emil Costa's cabin, perhaps Emil was hiding out in Grastow's cabin. A few inquiries later, and he had found out that the Antarean also kept quarters on deck 32. As Wesley made his way through the quiet residential section, he shook his head in bewilderment at this odd state of affairs. Why on earth was Emil hiding out in someone else's cabin, just hours before leaving the ship? It didn't make any sense, unless . . .

Unless Emil was afraid of something.

Now the young ensign had a powerful motivating force stirring him on, the desire to help someone he greatly admired. Upon reaching Grastow's quarters, Wes didn't fool with formalities; he banged on the door and called out in a loud voice, "Dr. Costa, let me in! I know you're in there!"

Wesley was counting on the microbiologist wishing to keep this news somewhat quiet. He was about to yell again, when the door whooshed open, and a hand dragged him inside.

Looking haggard, pale, and closer to a hundred than eighty years of age, Emil Costa sank into an armchair. "Did you have to yell like that?" he cursed. "Haven't you any sense?"

"What about you, sir?" Wesley barked, stiffening to attention. He was always uneasy about questioning authority figures, but he was determined to help his friend. "Why are you in hiding?"

The old scientist bobbed his head wearily. "The story is too long and painful to go into now, Wesley," he sighed. "And besides, I am putting an end to this affair tonight, before I leave the ship. I am resolving it once and for all."

"Your wife's death, too?" asked the boy. "Do you know who killed her?"

Emil Costa gripped the sides of his head and grimaced in pain, as if this was the one question he couldn't bear to hear. "No!" he shrieked. "Demons! Demons from the past or demons from the future—it

118

doesn't matter which. We brought it upon ourselves!"
The old man dissolved into tears.

Wesley swallowed hard and stumbled around the
room, looking for a chair. He sat, profoundly embarrassed and saddened. How could a man as famous and
accomplished as Emil Costa have these kinds of
problems? And what could be done to help the poor
man? Wesley felt totally inadequate to the situation,
and he wished Deanna Troi was there to take over.

"Dr. Costa," he stammered, "would you like to talk
to someone, like Counselor Troi?"

"No!" rasped the old man, staring at Wes with
hollow eyes. "Don't call any of your friends. Like I
told you, I will end this affair tonight, once and for all.
You must trust me, Wesley, and do nothing to interfere."

The teenager countered, "What about your old
friends, like Dr. Baylak? Do you know that Grastow is
lying to all of them?"

"Yes," Emil sighed, smiling sadly. "I wish I could
see them, but the good times are past. And don't
blame Grastow for what he is doing—he is only
following my orders. You must understand, Grastow
would do *anything* for me."

Wesley swallowed hard again, wondering if "anything" really meant anything.

The door suddenly brushed open, and the mammoth Antarean entered his own quarters. Wesley
nearly leapt from his chair, but Grastow hardly paid
the ensign any attention as he rushed to Emil Costa's
side.

"Doctor, are you all right?" asked the high-pitched
voice with concern.

"Yes," smiled Emil, patting his assistant's beefy
shoulder. "You have done well, even if our young
friend was a bit too clever."

Grastow glanced at the teenager, looking as embarrassed as Wesley felt. "I'm sorry," he muttered. "I hope I didn't hurt you."

"Oh, no," Wesley shrugged, wondering if his tailbone would ever stop aching. "I wish there was something *I* could do."

"There is," replied Emil, forcing himself to his feet and straightening his bent frame. "Please don't attempt to follow me."

"Where are you going?" asked Wesley with alarm.

"I must find out," Emil said grimly, walking over to the comm panel by the door and touching it with a trembling hand. "Emil Costa to Karn Milu."

"Milu speaking," replied the Betazoid. "Have you decided to talk?"

"I have," Emil nodded determinedly. "Where are you?"

"I'll meet you in the pod room. We'll have more privacy there."

"Very well," the microbiologist agreed, his lower chin quivering. "Out."

Wesley Crusher rose to his feet and clapped his hands with false cheer. "If you're going, Doctor," he grinned nervously, "I guess I will, too."

"No," said Emil, nodding to his hulking assistant, "I want you and Grastow to stay here."

On this subtle command, the huge Antarean wrapped his arms around Wesley and plunked him back into his chair. The ensign reached instinctively for his communicator badge, but Grastow was swift as well as strong. He wrapped a massive fist around the tiny badge and ripped it off Wesley's chest, taking several centimeters of red cloth with it.

"No, no!" Wesley protested, clawing the giant hands for the communicator. "Give that back!"

But the boy's attention was diverted from the giant

humanoid by the sight of Emil Costa taking a small phaser from a drawer by his bed. "Dr. Costa!" he shouted. "Where are you going with *that?*"

"Merely for safety's sake," the scientist smiled wanly, his drawn face looking like a death's-head. "One cannot be too careful." As the door opened, Emil Costa concealed the phaser in his waistband.

"No!" screamed Wesley Crusher. But one huge hand was already covering his mouth, as another one gripped his neck, brutally pressing him into the chair and holding him there.

Chapter Eight

IN THE MAIN SHUTTLE BAY, Commander Riker watched as the Kreel disembarked from their beat-up shuttlecraft. By human standards, they had to be one of the homeliest races in the galaxy, he thought. The Kreel had gangly bodies with muscular upper torsos that didn't look as if they could be supported by their spindly misshapen legs. They wore almost no clothes over their reddish skin, and coarse hair covered the most unlikely spots while exposing cracked sunburnt flesh that would be far more palatable hidden. Their heads looked to be all jaw and no neck, and strong sinewy arms acted as balancing poles. Instead of walking, the Kreel shuffled menacingly with a slight side-to-side rocking motion.

"Greetings!" Riker called with all the cheer he could muster. "I am Commander William T. Riker, first officer of the *Enterprise*. Welcome aboard."

The delegation of six came to a disorganized stop, and all but one of the Kreel continued gaping about the immense shuttle bay. Two Kreel ignored him completely and shuffled over to inspect the Federation shuttlecraft they would soon be boarding, the

Ericksen. Nevertheless, one of the Kreel made an ungainly bow.

"I am Kwalrak," she cooed in a voice that was unmistakably feminine, even if matted black hair obscured any more obvious feminine characteristics. "First assistant to Admiral Ulree of the Kreel Empire."

One of the visitors inspecting the personnel shuttle lifted an arm that was like a giant crane and waved lazily to Riker. "I am Ulree," he growled. "There are no Klingons aboard, are there?"

Will paused thoughtfully before answering, "One of our bridge officers is a Klingon. But he has been assigned other duties today."

"Cleaning the latrines!" laughed a third Kreel, and his fellows joined him in the uproarious joke.

Riker set his jaw firmly and endeavored to take command of the situation. "I regret that we have such little time to conduct a tour of the ship," he said, "but if you wish to see more than this shuttle bay, please accompany me now."

He strode off impatiently and was about to glance over his shoulder to see if the Kreel were following when he heard the telltale scuffling of their ungainly forms.

Wesley tried to sit still long enough for the Antarean to loosen his grasp, but he was afraid he would black out before that happened. "Say," he croaked, struggling to give Grastow a friendly smile, "Dr. Costa said we should stay here, but he didn't say you should strangle me!"

"You won't try to escape?" Grastow asked suspiciously. His stranglehold loosened a little.

Wes shook his head emphatically. "No way," he

promised. "You think I want to chase a man with a phaser? I don't care where he's going. I'll sit quietly . . . please!"

Looking unconvinced, the baby-faced Antarean finally released the ensign and strode to the door. He stationed himself with one broad shoulder in front of the exit and the other in front of the comm panel, then folded his arms and glowered expectantly at the teenager.

After coughing a few times, Wesley wiped his watery eyes and tried to compose himself. He rubbed his chest where skin poked through instead of the customary communicator badge. He felt naked without it. "You know," said Wes, forcing a bravado to his voice he didn't feel, "you could get into a lot of trouble for keeping me here against my will."

Grastow shrugged, "What happens to me is not important. All that counts is Emil Costa, his happiness, and his safety."

"He doesn't seem very safe to me," Wesley observed. "What is he so afraid of? What does Dr. Milu have to do with it?"

Grastow shook his head. "I don't know. But it isn't important that I know. Or that *you* know."

Wes could tell it was pointless to argue. He shifted uneasily in his seat and scoured the room for anything that could help him out of this predicament. Grastow's quarters were almost impersonally bare: rust-colored standard issue furnishings and a food slot. The lighting had been augmented with extra track lights, and Wesley surmised that Grastow liked, perhaps needed, lots of light. The sensor panel that controlled the lighting and other environmental settings was by the bed, which was barely a meter from Wesley. Grastow was at least four strides away. Although Grastow could protect the comm panel, he couldn't guard every panel in the room, the teenager decided.

Closing his eyes and pretending to massage a stiff neck, the young ensign planned his moves in his head. Like a chess game, he took Grastow's planned actions into account as well. First, a lunge for the sensor panel to plunge the room into darkness. Grastow, he felt, would come right after him, ignoring the door, and Wes would have to stay at the panel an extra split-second to open the door. Just in case, he needed something to slow Grastow down a step. The chair he was sitting in—he could drag it behind him, tip it over, and leave it in Grastow's darkened path.

Wesley's heart began to hammer with anticipation, and he could feel the adrenaline churning uncomfortably in his stomach. He glanced at the big Antarean to see if he was at all suspicious, but Grastow was barely stifling a yawn. He was now leaning against the door rather than blocking it. Well, thought Wesley glumly, it's now or never!

He bolted from the chair, giving it a wicked yank as he did. The chair hit the floor as his hands collided with the panel by the bed. His fingers flew over the panel, but the lights seemed to dim with the slowness of a sunset at the beach. He heard an unfamiliar curse as the Antarean lumbered after him. Wes was closing his eyes in anticipation of being throttled severely when the lights suddenly went out.

In pitch blackness with fear pounding between his ears, Wes stayed his post and was greeted by what sounded like a wounded elephant trying to run the hurdles. With a howl, Grastow toppled over the chair and crashed to the floor. Immediately, Wes felt a hand on his foot. He jerked away, while his fingers feverishly worked the panel, careful to keep the lights out while opening the door. The door whooshed open, and light from the corridor shafted across the room, revealing the Antarean sprawled across most of the floor. Wes leapt over him and landed between Grastow's legs, which kicked blindly at the teenager, sending him tumbling out of the room.

In the corridor of deck 32, Wes staggered to his feet, realizing he had only a few seconds to guarantee his escape and continue his mission. He rushed to the nearest comm panel and pounded it furiously.

"Ensign Crusher," he gulped, "to O'Brien! Come in, transporter room three!" He heard groaning and glanced behind him to see the Antarean crawling out of the cabin on all fours.

"O'Brien here," came the laconic Irish lilt. "What can I do for you, lad?"

Breathlessly, Wesley ordered, "Beam me directly from these coordinates to the class-one cleanroom of the Mircrocontamination Project on deck 31!"

"Whoa now," replied O'Brien. "You're only one deck away. What's the matter with the turbolift?"

Fire burning in his pink eyes, Grastow caught sight of Wesley and rose up from the floor to his full height.

"Do it now!" barked the ensign. "I'm on special assignment for Worf—it's a matter of life and death!"

"Whose death?" O'Brien asked skeptically.

"Mine!" shrieked Wesley, as Grastow bore down on him. "Energize!"

The Antarean's massive arms wrapped around whirling fragments of light, the phosphorescent residue of the transporter effect. Wesley Crusher himself was gone.

The ensign's eyes were still screwed tightly shut, and he could almost feel Grastow's hot breath on his neck. Nevertheless, the slight tingling in his being told him that he had transported, and he opened his eyes to find himself in the eerie pod room on deck 31. He was alone.

At his transporter controls, O'Brien tried to home in on Wesley's communicator badge. He wanted a fuller explanation, and he wanted it now. But, oddly, Wesley's badge was still on deck 32, while the readouts clearly indicated that the person had transported to deck 31. O'Brien shook his tousled red hair in complete puzzlement. If this was some kind of youthful prank, he would make sure that the young ensign ended up in the old doghouse.

Well, there was no way to contact him now. O'Brien was doubly mad at himself. First, he shouldn't have performed a direct-beam without a full explanation. Direct-beaming was too energy inefficient for normal traffic, and the tactic was usually reserved for medical or security emergencies, such as transporting wounded crew members to sickbay. But worse, he had transported Wesley into a protected environment with no protective clothing! If he ever found out, Karn Milu would raise holy hell over that. The transporter operator was torn whether to tell anyone what he had just done, or to confront Wesley privately about it later. Maybe, just maybe, the lad had a plausible explanation for all this. He had mentioned something about being on assignment for Worf.

O'Brien did a quick scan of all the ship's systems and decks and could find nothing wrong anywhere, despite the presence of the Kreel delegation on board. Finally, his sense of duty overwhelmed his fear of a dressing down, and he resolved to contact Worf. The boy had dropped his name, so let the Klingon deal with him.

Life and death, indeed!

* * *

In the pod room, Wesley borrowed some sterile, dust-free gauze from a dispenser and held it over his mouth and nose. He didn't want to set off alarms merely by breathing. At first, he had been surprised to find himself alone with the pods, knowing that Emil Costa and Karn Milu had arranged to meet there. But he had reached the room by the fastest possible method, he told himself, and they would have to take separate turbolifts to deck 31, walk through the manufacturing and research facilities, change into suits in the transition room, and take the lateral turbolift equipped with air showers and ultraviolet baths to reach this cleanroom. Therefore, he was crouching down behind the farthest pod in the back of the room, safely hidden, when the door opened.

A white-suited, helmeted figure entered. It could have been anybody, but Wesley surmised from the pronounced stoop and nervous shuffling that it was Emil Costa. The teenager gulped, remembering the distraught scientist was carrying a phaser, and he hunkered down even farther behind the last of the eight class-zero pods.

Emil anxiously prowled the room, stopping only to stare at pod number one for several minutes. What must he be thinking? Wesley wondered. His wife had died because of that contraption. The ensign ran his hands along the smooth, cold glass of the pod in front of him—its contents were a milky bluish gas which pulsed with tiny pinpoints of light, like a city in the fog. Wes couldn't see its identifying screen, but he could guess that it was a simulation of some planet's atmosphere. Maybe amino acids were playing in those murky swirls, or enzymes. Who knew? Vacuums, weightless states, anything was possible in the confines of a pod. For several days during his tutoring, he had worked with Emil in pod number six, watching the famous microbiologist induce mitosis in exotic single-celled animals. Emil Costa had seemed to enjoy playing God.

Now the scientist stood bent and forlorn, staring at the object of his lifelong partner's death. How could Worf, or any of them, suspect Emil of killing Lynn? Couldn't they see how broken he was? How fearful? He was giving up everything: career, friends, the project he had created, even the *Enterprise*. It was like he didn't care anymore. Sometimes Lynn may have been a thorn in Emil's side, but Wesley knew that she was the kind of thorn that stuck forever. She had always been a part of him, a part he was lost without.

Wes was almost moved to rise from his hiding place to comfort the old man, when the door opened and a stocky figure in a white suit entered. Immediately, the new arrival removed his helmet and wiped a hand over his bristling eyebrows and thick stand of graying hair. Though Wesley was expecting to see him, it was still a shock to see Dr. Karn Milu at this surreptitious meeting.

"Go ahead and take your helmet off," said Milu to the old man. "There's no one around to see us, and I don't want the ship's intercom to pick us up."

With quivering hands, Emil Costa removed his helmet. "What about the monitors?" he asked.

The Betazoid waved a disdainful hand. "With all those meddling engineers crawling around here, we had to turn them off anyway. This is hardly a class-one cleanroom at the moment."

"Yes," nodded Emil, stealing another look at pod one. "Did you kill her?"

Karn Milu laughed. "Don't be ridiculous," he scoffed. "It *was* an accident. Considering Lynn's mental state—a predictable accident, I'm afraid. We should have done more to prevent it."

"She didn't want me to tell you the origin of the submicrobe," Emil croaked. "She knew it was wrong."

"But she initially agreed!" exclaimed Milu angrily. "You *both* did. You can't keep it a secret—an organism that is so small it is virtually undetectable but an organism that is impervious to all known agents and biofilters? The applications are unlimited, especially for weapons!"

The Betazoid's tone of voice grew kindly, fatherly. "Emil," he sighed, "in all our years of service to the Federation, we have never sought any personal gain. This is our last chance to retire wealthy men, instead of penniless icons."

Looking confused, Emil ran a quivering hand over his close-cropped hair and muttered, "What good is money?"

"Not much good in the Federation," Milu admitted. "But elsewhere, you could live out your final years as a king. Think of it, Emil," he winked, "you could have a harem of Orion slave girls who would make you feel like a young man!"

Emil swallowed hard. "To whom would you sell it?" he croaked.

"The Ferengi have already expressed an interest," answered the Betazoid. "There are factions within the Romulan Empire who would pay dearly. As we have discussed so many times, the Federation—with its open policies—would never be able to keep this discovery secret. It is best to profit now."

Emil Costa wrung his hands indecisively. "I don't know . . ." he rasped.

"Come now," replied Karn Milu with a disarming smile. "I'm not asking you to get your hands dirty— I'll handle all the arrangements. All you have to do is tell me the planet we were orbiting when you discovered the submicrobe. If your wife hadn't been so thorough in her attack on your records, I might have been able to deduce it myself."

Emil's spine suddenly stiffened. "I'm glad she did it!" he declared. "Maybe we haven't always been as honest as we should have been, but selling out the Federation is something we've never done!"

Karn Milu was no longer smiling. "I've risked a lot for this deal," he snapped. "Just tell me the name of the planet, and I will see that you are well taken care of for the rest of your life."

Wesley sat on his haunches, so wracked with anticipation that he didn't realize he was choking himself with the strip of gauze until his sudden intake of breath.

The two scientists whirled in his direction. "Who's there?" growled Karn Milu.

Sheepishly, Wesley rose to his feet. "Uh, hello," he stammered. "Don't tell him, Dr. Costa."

"What are you doing, Wesley?" wailed Emil. "I wouldn't have told him!"

But Karn Milu was taking no chances. He strode purposefully toward the young ensign and gripped him by his neck. Wesley was too stunned and too surprised at the Betazoid's incredible strength to struggle. Before he knew what was happening, Karn Milu was dragging him toward pod number one. Slapping at his chest where his communicator badge should have been, Wes encountered nothing but a hole and his own skin.

"Open the pod!" Milu ordered Emil Costa.

Emil hesitated for a second, then sighed reluctantly and initiated the sequence which opened the double-sealed hatch. Head bowed, the old man turned away.

"No!" Wesley screamed, but the stocky Betazoid

pinned his arms to his sides and stuffed him inside the air-tight container. In the cramped confines, the boy's head struck a solid mass of tubing, and he was dazed while the scientists sealed the pod.

When he came to his senses, both men were gone. Wesley screamed and pounded on the smooth convex walls, but not even a whimper could be heard outside the class-zero unit. With horror, the boy realized they could have killed him easily by programming the pod for a vacuum. But they had let him live . . .

At least until the air ran out.

Had Deanna Troi been in a happier frame of mind, she might have enjoyed watching the farce playing out in front of her. But now it was just a distraction that was keeping both Guinan and Will Riker from talking to her. Commander Riker had shown dubious judgment in bringing six strapping Kreel into the Ten-Forward Room. And once they had found out there was all the free synthehol you could drink, they had refused to leave.

"Admiral Ulree," Riker said forcefully, "unless we leave this place immediately, we will miss our estimated departure time."

"That's why they call it *estimated*," Ulree laughed, downing another synthehol in three gulps. "We've got lots of time." He wiped his crooked mouth, pushed his tumbler toward Guinan, and sneered, "Keep it coming."

The proprietress frowned good-naturedly and shook a finger at the hulking figure. "You're just being a glutton," she accused him. "Why don't you go with Commander Riker, and I'll give you a rain check when you come back to the *Enterprise*."

"Rain check?" asked Ulree.

"I'll owe you one," she explained. "Or as many as you want."

"I'll take them now!" Ulree declared, pounding his glass on the counter. His fellows did the same. "You never know what may happen later, so we had better drink up now."

Guinan appealed to Riker for help, and the first officer scowled and motioned to her to refill their glasses. No matter how much synthehol they drank and how inebriated they felt, they should be able to shake off the effects of the Ferengi product. It had always been proven safe. But for Kreel? Will wondered if they possessed enough self-control.

"Why can't you be hospitable?" asked the female Kreel, Kwalrak, who boldly sidled up to Will and rubbed a hairy shoulder against his.

Will almost recoiled, but he decided to try to make an ally among the unruly band. "You know," he smiled charmingly, "you've just used up the time we had allotted for your visits to Engineering and Weaponry. I thought you wanted to learn about us?"

The leathery female shrugged and wrapped a gangly arm around his. "We *do* want to learn about you," she purred, fixing him with large bloodshot eyes. "We want to learn everything there is to know. But there's so much more than gadgetry to share between our races. Tell me, Riker, what do you think about *joining* with the Kreel?"

Will considered whether to acknowledge this bald double entendre or not, and he decided that, under the circumstances, a little deviousness might be forgiven. "There will be more time for getting to know one another aboard the shuttlecraft," he whispered, cocking a seductive eyebrow toward the door. "Federation shuttlecraft have very *private* accommoda-

133

tions. Can't you get Admiral Ulree and his party to move faster?"

Kwalrak lowered her triangular head as much as her thick neck would allow. "Let me see what I can do," she smiled coyly.

She approached Ulree and his cronies and spoke to them sternly in a low voice. In a matter of moments, the Kreel were yelling at one another, creating a cacophony rarely heard aboard the *Enterprise*. Kwalrak apparently held her own, shouting down their every objection point by point. Still, Riker was almost certain they would come to blows, until Kwalrak nodded decisively and motioned toward the door.

Ulree shrugged, finished his drink, and skulked out, followed by the others. Passing Riker, he could be heard to mutter, "Just because she's beautiful, she thinks she runs things."

Glumly, Deanna Troi watched them leave, certain now that she wouldn't have a chance to discuss the Lynn Costa case with Will Riker for close to an hour. Disappointed, she sought out Guinan, who was collecting the empty glasses left by the Kreel.

"Guinan," she sighed, "Emil Costa is leaving the ship, and we can't prove a thing. Have we been wrong? Have we overlooked something? Or worse, was I right originally to consider suicide? If that's the case, then I should have done much more to save Lynn Costa's life." Deanna snorted derisively, adding, "I thought a sabbatical away from the ship would solve all their problems. I failed her miserably."

"No," said Guinan warmly, taking the Betazoid's youthful hands in her older, darker hands. "Not knowing the full story cannot be called failure. Sometimes the mystery is revealed to us a piece at a time, or never fully revealed to us. You must be patient, Deanna, you and Worf both."

"Yes," Deanna absently agreed. But she didn't really believe it, or feel like being patient. She stared out the window at the stars beyond, now appearing to hold perfectly still as the *Enterprise* kept station behind the slow-moving asteroid called Kayran Rock. She wondered if anything more would ever be revealed to them.

Lieutenant Worf quickened his step as he approached the almost hidden entrance to the cleanrooms on deck 31. He was still shaking his head over the cryptic message from the transporter operator, O'Brien. Why in Khitomer was Wesley Crusher direct-beaming to the pod room? And without his communicator badge? Worf had asked Wesley Crusher to keep an eye on Emil Costa, plain and simple, not presume he had the run of the ship. If Emil Costa had taken one last trip to his workplace before leaving the *Enterprise,* what of it? Maybe he was sentimental.

There was little enough time left, Worf thought disgruntledly, to spend it chasing down teenage ensigns. Then O'Brien's words, "life and death," crossed his mind. To Worf, Ensign Crusher was inexperienced, naive, and sometimes overconfident, but he was never frivolous.

He stopped at the voice-activated door and barked, "Worf requesting entrance."

"Lieutenant Worf not cleared for this facility," the computer replied politely but firmly.

Worf bristled for a moment, then growled, "Security override, level one."

Now the door opened, and Worf shouldered his way through. Maybe Wesley had had the right idea, direct-beaming through this place. He jogged down the empty corridor between the gigantic darkened rooms devoted to research and manufacturing, with their ghostly shapes and robotic arms, through the class-one-thousand corridor and the first air showers, between rows of smaller laboratories, where white-suited denizens plied their alchemic and medicinal crafts. None of them paid him any heed as he jogged past them, his strength and alertness intensifying with each step.

He reached the door marked TRANSITION ROOM 3, CLASS 1000, and skidded to a stop. "Worf," he growled. "Security override. Open immediately."

The door flashed open, and he was in the round transition room, with its racks of white garments, neatly stacked helmets, showers, lockers, and changing stalls. Worf didn't know why, but the hackles on his back were rising in alert. He drew his phaser and made his way quickly toward the turbolift marked MICROCONTAMINATION.

He heard the racks of jumpsuits and coats rustling, but he was a split-second too slow as he whirled on his heel and was struck by the phaser beam. It ripped through his body like an electric charge, deadening nerve endings as it went, and he suppressed a howl. But the wound was low, on his thigh, and the charge didn't reach all the way to his brain. Worf collapsed to his stomach and tried to roll away, but most of his coordination was gone.

He got off one wild shot into the rack of garments when a second beam struck him in the shoulder. His head exploded in a single blast of pain before everything went blank.

Chapter Nine

WITH RELIEF, Captain Picard spied his first officer leading the Kreel contingent into the cavernous shuttlebay. He suppressed a smile to see that Riker had to slow his usual striding charge to a gait more in step with the Kreel, who swayed awkwardly on their bandy legs. The captain couldn't afford a real smile, because Data's presence beside him was a reminder that the shuttlecraft should have left six minutes ago. Data's intricate schedule for the shuttle landings on Kayran Rock was dependent upon *their* shuttle getting a timely start, which it wasn't. Jean-Luc Picard hated to be late.

"Captain!" called Riker with equal relief. Picard and Data strode forward to meet the party. "May I introduce the Kreel delegation," said the first officer. He smiled charmingly as he indicated each muscular humanoid in turn, "Admiral Ulree, First Assistant Kwalrak, Ambassador Mayra, Colonel Efrek, Orderlies Akree and Efrek."

Picard nodded in appreciation at the difficulty of Riker's task in remembering all those names and titles. "Captain Jean-Luc Picard," he replied with an abbreviated bow. "Welcome to the *Enterprise.*" He motioned to the tall sallow-faced android. "This is Commander Data."

Admiral Ulree leaned into Data's face and sniffed him suspiciously a few times. "It's not a joke," he observed. "You really have made a lifeless machine that looks human."

"That's not how we look at it," remarked the captain. "To us, Data is a living being whose physiology and intellect are quite different than ours—but in many ways superior. As far as being a machine, *we* are the ones who are mass-produced, while Data is unique."

Picard smiled warmly at the android; then he motioned toward the gaping entry of the personnel shuttlecraft *Ericksen.* "I am sorry we have to leave so quickly, but the ceremonies await. We can become further acquainted en route."

"Yes, indeed," purred Kwalrak into Riker's ear.

Rolling his eyes slightly to Picard as he passed, Riker led the Kreel into the passenger section of the *Ericksen.* The full-sized shuttlecraft was outfitted with four rows of plush seats, each row accommodating two passengers luxuriously and three comfortably. Kwalrak took Riker's arm and dragged him to the rear of the vessel, while the rest of the Kreel scrambled for window seats.

Outside the shuttle, the captain's cordial smile twisted into a scowl. "Now where is Emil Costa?" he whispered.

"He would seem to be late," the android agreed. "Shall I find him?"

A female voice sounded crisply over Picard's communicator badge, "Ensign Hamer to Captain Picard. All luggage has been stowed, all systems have been checked, and the course has been set for Kayran Rock. We can leave on your order, sir."

"Thank you, Ensign," replied Picard. "I would like to give that order, but we are waiting for a final passenger. In the meantime, Commander Data and I will take our seats." He turned to Data with concern. "Let's sit down, then we'll try one last time to contact Emil Costa."

"No need, Captain," replied the android, blinking his pale golden eyes toward the doorway. "I hear him approaching."

Looking disheveled and dragging a duffel bag that made him walk more lopsidedly than a Kreel, Emil Costa staggered into the holding area. "I-I am sorry, Captain," he panted, his frail chest heaving with exertion and sweat beading his white scalp. "Several last minute arrangements . . ."

"Yes, yes, Doctor," muttered Picard. "Take your seat."

"I will take your bag," offered Data.

"No, no," croaked Emil, "that's quite all right." He hurried into the main cabin and sank into a seat, stowing his bag under his legs. Then the disheveled scientist stared forthrightly at his hands, avoiding eye contact with the others.

Picard afforded Data a puzzled glance as he strode in to take a seat that had obviously been saved for him beside the imposing Admiral Ulree. The two chatted amiably, and Picard answered questions about the shuttlecraft.

"Nice," murmured Ulree, not bothering to hide his envy. "If the Federation won't give us transporter technology, they should at least give us a few of these. If we like them, we'll buy them—if the price is right."

The door clanked shut behind him, and Data still

hadn't spotted an empty seat among all the dangling Kreel arms. He was about to head to the more familiar environs of the cockpit when he heard Commander Riker hailing him.

"Over here, Data!" called Will Riker desperately from the rear of the craft. He pushed Kwalrak off his chest and struggled to sit up. Disgruntledly, the red-skinned female uncurled her long hairy limbs from Commander Riker, and he was able to straighten both his posture and his uniform. Riker was glad they had packed their dress uniforms and were still wearing their heavy-duty reds, which could take more of a beating.

"If you wish to lounge, Commander," said Data, "I will sit elsewhere."

"Yes, we wish to lounge!" exclaimed Kwalrak, hugging Riker possessively.

"Not now," insisted Riker, yanking himself free from her grasp. "We're filled to capacity, and we have to make room for Commander Data."

"I can sit in the cockpit," remarked Data.

"No!" Riker growled. He grabbed Data and force-fully inserted the android between himself and the Kreel first assistant. Kwalrak sneered and slid over to make more room for the android.

"Thank you," Data bowed respectfully to the sinewy female. "I am unaccustomed to being a passenger aboard a shuttlecraft. Usually I serve as pilot."

Riker snuggled his big shoulders into the thick upholstery and sighed, "You're an honored guest today, Data. You don't have to do anything."

"Being an honored guest," observed Data, "does not make me incapable of piloting the shuttlecraft."

"It's a matter of protocol," Will insisted pleasantly. "That's somebody else's job today. Yours is to sit back and act like a dignitary, because that's what you are."

"I am unaccustomed to being a dignitary," said Data. "What does one do?"

Beside him, First Assistant Kwalrak purred, "Just watch Riker. *He* knows what to do."

Data turned to study the bearded first officer, but Riker's eyes were shut and he was smiling contently. Riker considered shepherding the Kreel to be his hardest duty of the day, and he was going to relax now that it was over. As if in consent, the lights in the cabin dimmed to a warm golden hue, forcing everyone to speak in whispers. The shuttlecraft glided off its pad, and there was a moment's weightlessness while the artificial gravity adjusted and the elongated vessel launched into space, filled to capacity.

Trapped inside the class-zero pod, his air thinning to the point where standing in a crouch was making him dizzy, Wesley Crusher worked feverishly. The pod had been idle since Lynn Costa's death, but Wes was throwing together its standard components— specimen receptacles, monitoring equipment, robotic shakers, and sterile tubing—to begin a new experiment.

The computer controls were outside the container, and Wesley couldn't manipulate them by either voice or hand. What a time to be without a communicator! He tried to forget his problems and concentrate on what he knew about these computer subsystems, one of the few subsystems that were so complex they were kept apart from the main computer to avoid taxing it. Nevertheless, Wes knew the pod's computer was never totally "off" and that it was set by default to respond to certain types of experiments at all times. Wesley figured he could rig a small experiment that would trip the monitoring equipment. Maybe, hoped the teenager, if the experiment became contaminated, it would set off an alarm.

If it didn't, *he'd* be the next experiment.

Wesley rigged up the simplest experiment he could think of, an organic/inorganic particle detector set to go berserk at the wrong kind of contamination. He removed a circuit board from a particle counter and set its switches manually to default to inorganic matter. That way, the slightest detection of organic matter would set it off. He hoped. At least he wouldn't have to worry about programming the environment; his own body and what little oxygen was left would furnish that. Unfortunately, there would be no way of judging his success until he—or someone—heard the alarm. Wesley tried not to think of what would happen if no one heard.

He slipped the board back into the particle counter and held his breath waiting for the indicator lights to shine. He was hardly breathing by the time they finally did, and it wasn't due solely to excitement. At the tip of a robotic arm, Wesley found the tiny receptacle he had installed as the collector, and he tapped it with his fingertip to make sure it was awake. There were many ways he could have chosen to contaminate it, but sometimes the simplest is the best. Wesley took dead aim at the funnel and spat.

It took two attempts to really load it with spittle. More than that would be overkill, decided the boy, slumping to the floor. He tried to modulate his breathing, because there wasn't anything else to do but sit and wait—and breathe until he was rescued or the air was all gone.

Wes fought off weariness and tried to stay alert to any movement outside the pod. The gray tint of the glass was light enough to let him see just past the window to the class-one-hundred cleanroom beyond. If the alarm was going off, someone should be appearing out there just about now. . . . Wes clicked his fingers.

And an apparition in white stared down at him through a bubble visor. Wes blinked in amazement as the angelic vision straightened up and moved to the control panel. Its slim fingers played the controls for a moment until the hatch whooshed open, and Wesley was almost sucked out with the foul air.

The savior lifted Wesley out as if he were a baby and held him for an instant. "Are you in need of medical attention?" he asked.

"Not right now," gasped Wesley. "They . . . those two sealed me in there. Emil Costa . . ."

Saduk gently set Wesley down and took off his helmet to reveal his stoic Vulcan face. "Emil Costa is the only reason I am here," he reported. "He asked me to check on an experiment for him, or else I wouldn't have been in this area. Are you sure you are all right?"

"Yes, yes," stammered Wesley, confused. "I don't know why he called you, but we've got to stop them . . ."

The Vulcan interrupted the boy's sputtering. "One thing at a time, Ensign Crusher. There is a man outside this room who is either dead or badly wounded."

Wesley peered at him. "Where?"

Saduk motioned toward the door, and, despite his dizziness, Wesley was the first one out. His eyes saw no dead man among the scattered enclosures in the class-one-hundred cleanroom. Instead, he saw a very live Klingon staring past one of the large white pyramids toward the spotless floor. As he drew closer, Wesley could see a white bootie sticking out from behind the pyramid.

Lieutenant Worf was aiming his tricorder at a

plump white-suited figure sprawled on the floor. Wesley rushed to get a closer look—and wished he hadn't. The boy had to grab his mouth to keep from gagging. Most of the man's chest cavity had been burned to a blackened crater, and chunks of his suit had melted around the jutting ribs.

"No rush to call sickbay," Worf muttered. "This is the work of a phaser set on full. I was far luckier—my attacker had his phaser set to stun."

"You were shot too?" gasped Wesley. "What is going on here!"

Worf knelt down beside the disfigured body and removed his helmet. Wesley gaped and Saduk looked impassively at the familiar bristling eyebrows and shock of graying hair. The determined jaw was frozen in death.

"Karn Milu!" exclaimed Wesley. "Wow!"

Worf glared at the youngster. "Report, Ensign Crusher. What do you know about this?"

Wesley gulped, "He and Emil Costa had an argument over a submicrobe the Costas discovered and kept secret. It's apparently indestructible, and Karn Milu wanted to sell it. I was listening, but they caught me and sealed me in a pod. All the while, Emil Costa had a phaser!"

Worf banged his communicator badge. "Security alert! Capture Dr. Emil Costa immediately. Use all precautions—he is armed with a phaser and should be considered dangerous!"

The alert went to every part of the ship instantaneously, including the shuttlecraft, which was still close enough to the ship to be tied into its communication system. Aboard the *Ericksen,* all small talk abruptly stopped, and Picard sat up in his seat, as did Riker and Data. If they hadn't believed their ears the first time, they did the second.

"Repeat," said the Klingon, "capture Emil Costa and use extreme caution!"

The captain swiveled in his seat to find Emil, but instead he got a good look at the business end of a phaser.

"Don't move!" the scientist shrieked, waving the phaser frantically at the full passenger compartment. He staggered to his feet. "I'm not going back there! I'm not going back to the *Enterprise!*"

Riker started to rise from his seat, but Picard motioned him down. Undoubtedly, Ensign Hamer was already turning the small vessel around.

"What is this!" growled Admiral Ulree.

That exclamation brought the shaky phaser to bear on the Kreel admiral, an action that was too threatening for one of his orderlies. The orderly snarled and leapt to his feet—and got drilled in the chest for his efforts. He collapsed back into his comrade's hands, stunned into unconsciousness.

"Don't move!" Emil screamed insanely. "I-I know how to use this thing! Don't make me shoot you!"

No one was moving now, that was for sure. "Doctor," Picard said evenly, "you are endangering your life as well as all of ours. Please put the phaser down, and let's discuss this."

"No, no!" insisted Emil, backing toward the cockpit. "I'm not going back there—ever! They're after me!" He rushed past the partition into the cockpit, and they heard the muffled voice of Ensign Hamer trying to reason with him.

Clearly, they heard Emil shout, "What are you doing? Don't turn back!"

"Data," snapped Picard, knowing the android was more impervious to phaser fire than the rest of them. Picard motioned him toward the cockpit.

Before Data got halfway there, they heard a shriek

from the cockpit—and it wasn't Emil Costa. The shuttlecraft took a sudden lunge to port, and Data sprawled across Picard's lap as everyone was thrown into a heap. It was Riker, crawling on hands and knees, who reached the cockpit first.

What he saw horrified him. Ensign Hamer was unconscious, and Emil Costa was systematically shooting up the controls with his phaser. Sparks and smoke billowed everywhere, and Riker ignored his own safety to corral Emil in a bear hug. He easily wrestled the frail scientist to the deck and slapped away the phaser.

But that was the least of their problems. The tiny vessel continued to pitch wildly, totally out of control, dumping Kreel and humans first to starboard, then back to port. The cabin filled with noxious smoke, and the Kreel howled like frightened children.

"Data!" cried Picard over the chaos. "Get the helm!"

"Controls are shot to hell!" answered Riker. Underneath him, Emil Costa was sobbing pitifully, and Riker shoved him away with disgust. He grabbed the phaser, pocketed it, then fumbled along the wall for a fire extinguisher.

Data, also more impervious to smoke, found the extinguisher first and began showering the controls with white foam that hit its mark, then evaporated. As soon as he was certain the fire was contained, the android gently moved Ensign Hamer's unconscious body and sat at the helm. A momentary glance showed him everything he needed to know.

Captain Picard reached his side and slid into the co-pilot's seat. "Status?" he breathed.

"Stabilizers are out," answered Data. "Navigational and communication systems are dead, and the conn is inoperative except for basic readouts. The computer is operating at perhaps ten percent efficiency and is trying to compensate for the loss of the stabilizers. Impulse engines are not the least bit damaged. In fact, we are picking up speed."

The captain slapped his communicator badge. "Picard to *Enterprise.*"

"Out of range," said Data noncommittally. "The *Enterprise* is moving in the opposite direction."

The captain repeated his request several times, but there was no answer. Then Commander Riker poked his head into the cockpit. "We have some injured back here," he reported. "How is Ensign Hamer?"

"She has merely been stunned," answered Data. "But she faces the same danger that we all do."

"Danger?" asked Riker.

The android raised his eyebrows and said simply, "We are headed toward the greater Kreel asteroid belt with no way to correct our course or speed."

Picard and Riker took their eyes off the smoldering control panel and peered worriedly out the window. In the distance, they could barely make out a band of brown objects floating lazily in the starscape. From this distance, they looked like dust particles, but they well knew that most of those chunks of space litter were larger than the shuttlecraft. A few were larger than the *Enterprise.*

Shouts and commotion sounded behind them in the passenger compartment. "I'll handle that," said Riker.

He turned to see two of the Kreel pummeling a helpless Emil Costa. "Stop that!" ordered the first officer.

Admiral Ulree turned his wrath on the human. "This man has willfully injured two of my officers!" he snarled. "We will punish him!"

"There'll be time for punishment later," warned

Will Riker. "Now return to your seats." He felt for his phaser and hoped he wouldn't have to use it.

The gangly humanoids paused in their violent activity and looked at one another. Reluctantly, Admiral Ulree waved them away, and they dropped the injured scientist onto the deck and returned to their seats. Seconds later, the shuttlecraft bucked violently, and Riker picked up Emil Costa and found seats for both of them.

"What is happening?" asked Kwalrak nervously.

"Nothing," Riker lied. "Data is making repairs."

He glanced toward the cockpit, hoping his lie had a germ of truth in it.

"Worf to the bridge!" ordered Lieutenant Commander Geordi La Forge.

Worf, who was striding down a barren corridor on deck 31 with Wesley Crusher in tow, slapped his communicator badge and responded, "I have to find Emil Costa."

"No need," answered the engineering officer. "I know exactly where he is—or rather, where he should be."

"Where?" growled the Klingon.

"I don't know where *you've* been," said Geordi with a slight scold in his voice, "but he left with the captain, Commander Riker, and Data in the shuttlecraft over thirty minutes ago."

Worf stopped in his stride and scowled. "I was unconscious. Get them back."

"We're trying," Geordi moaned. "They're not where they should be, and they don't respond to repeated hailing. We've been keeping station with Kayran Rock and lending them logistical support, but now we're breaking off to search the sector."

"I'll be right there," replied Worf. "Out." He turned

to Wesley and said, "Find Counselor Troi and give her a complete report about Karn Milu's death and what you witnessed. Then join me on the bridge."

"I should go to the bridge right now," insisted Wesley.

The Klingon growled softly, "Obey my order, Ensign."

"Yes, sir!" snapped Wesley. "I hope you find them."

"We will," nodded the big Klingon, striding away.

Data inspected the singed circuitry under the shuttlecraft console and made a split-second decision. Normally, he refused to make assumptions without knowing all the facts, but a small ship careening out of control wouldn't last long in an asteroid belt. Something had to be done. Captain Picard sat beside him, saying nothing, but the tense muscles in his neck and jaw revealed his concern. The asteroids were getting closer. They didn't look like dust anymore but more like exactly what they were—jagged carbonaceous rocks hardened into deadly projectiles by the cataclysm which formed them eons ago.

The android sat up and reported, "Captain, I believe I can divert the remaining computer circuits into the navigational system. We may be able to steer, but we'll lose what little stabilization we have, including the artificial gravity."

"Make it so," ordered Picard. "I'll tell the others to buckle themselves in."

Jean-Luc rose from his seat and returned to the passenger compartment. The Kreel looked sullenly at him, and Emil Costa, blood caked on his nose and lips, looked up sheepishly.

"I'm sorry, Captain," rasped Emil.

"A little late for that now," muttered Picard, his lips thinning with anger. "We've lost our stabilizers, and in order to steer, we'll have to forego the artificial gravity. So, everyone, please buckle yourselves in."

"I demand to know what you're doing!" growled Admiral Ulree.

"Admiral," sighed the captain, "what we are doing is trying to save all of our lives. This craft is out of control at the moment, but we are endeavoring to correct that problem."

"What about the asteroid belt?" asked Kwalrak.

"Buckle yourselves in," ordered the captain with finality. "And secure the wounded as well."

When he returned to the cockpit, Picard was gratified to see Ensign Hamer sitting up groggily. "Captain," she murmured, "I'm sorry, but I didn't know how to stop him . . ."

"No apologies necessary," replied Picard, laying a comforting hand on the young woman's shoulder. "Commander Data has the helm, and I suggest you return to the main compartment and strap yourself in."

Whoozily, the ensign rose to her feet. "Yes, Captain," she answered before leaving the cockpit.

Data was still working under the control panel in a convoluted position only a contortionist—or an android—could achieve. "Please seat yourself, Captain," he suggested. "When I connect the harness array, we will lose all stabilization, but the helm may respond."

"*May* respond?" the captain repeated.

"We have not had the benefit of a thorough evaluation," Data reminded him seriously.

"Of course not," said Jean-Luc, adjusting his own seat restraint. "I just wish you had a little more confidence."

Data observed, "This is not a situation that inspires confidence."

"What will happen to you?" asked the captain worriedly. "You're not buckled in."

Data's face was still hidden under the console, so Picard couldn't see if it manifested any sort of concern. "I will be weightless," said the android. "Please restrain me if I appear to be in danger."

The captain reached down and got a firm grip on the android's waistband. "Proceed."

As swiftly as possible, Data unplugged the computer array from the stabilizers and connected it to the helm controls. He was already floating by the time the connector was seated in its slot, and the shuttle went into an immediate spin. Even though Captain Picard gripped him firmly, Data's head banged against the burned-out console several times.

With all the strength he could muster, the captain hauled the android into the pilot's seat and buckled him in. Out the window, the stars and asteroids spiraled like a kaleidoscope, and Picard couldn't stand to look at it for very long. Data ignored the disorientation and weightlessness to concentrate on forcing the helm to respond. After several moments of intense activity, his efforts began to pay off, and they could feel the craft veering slightly from the course set during Emil's rampage. Nevertheless, the looming asteroids looked so immense that avoidance seemed impossible.

"If I can set a course bearing mark-three-four," said Data, "I may be able to skirt the outer edge of the belt and emerge below it."

Already, smaller chunks of debris swirled around the spinning ship. "Use your best judgment," the captain replied.

The android nodded, then applied his slender fingers to the trim-pot controls. The cabin rang with thuds as several small asteroids hit the outer hull. One of the Kreel screamed, and the others began a low chant. Probably a death dirge, thought Picard.

"This is not working," observed Data. "The helm is responding too sluggishly at this speed."

Picard asked, "Can't the thrusters slow us down?"

The android shook his head. "Thrusters would be ineffective with impulse engines on full."

"Wait!" exclaimed the captain. "If we can match the speed and the course of the asteroids, we can drift safely among them."

"Yes," agreed Data, "but once we disengage the impulse engines, it is unlikely we could start them again. We would be trapped."

The ship shook with the impact of another small asteroid, and the wailing grew louder in the back. They were closing fast on a mammoth black asteroid as large as some moons.

"We haven't got much choice," Picard said grimly.

"Yes, sir," answered Data, already making the course adjustments. Then he reached under the console, felt his way for a moment, and yanked out a mass of circuitry. The console protested with more sparks, but the impulse engines died immediately. Inertia kept the craft moving at the same velocity, however, and they drew close enough to count the pocked craters on the gigantic asteroid. Data fired the thrusters manually and kept firing until the little vessel finally began to slow down. The asteroid loomed so large before them that Picard involuntarily closed his eyes and braced himself for impact.

When he opened his eyes, the entire window was filled with the ravaged crags of the black asteroid. But they weren't gaining on it anymore. Picard swallowed and sank back in his seat. "Well done, Data," he sighed.

"Now that we have no need for navigation," said

the android, "I will rewire the computer for gravity and stabilization."

The captain nodded in agreement. "I know subspace communications are out, but see if you can rig up a distress signal."

"Yes, sir," replied Data.

As the android worked on his new assignments, Captain Picard swiveled in his seat. He almost unfastened his restraint, then remembered that he was still weightless. "To all hands!" he called loudly enough to be heard even at the rear of the craft. "We have stabilized our speed and position. We are in no immediate danger."

A few seconds later, the Kreel first assistant, Kwalrak, drifted into view over Picard's head. Oddly, a weightless Kreel possessed none of the awkwardness of a walking Kreel. With her long muscular arms to guide her, Kwalrak maneuvered gracefully around the weightless cabin.

She stared in dismay at the blackened controls, then remembered her purpose. "Captain," she gulped, "Admiral Ulree would like to congratulate you on regaining control of the shuttlecraft, but he warns you not to remain long in the asteroid belt. We have lost many ships here."

"Understood," nodded Picard. "Tell the admiral and the rest of your party that we appreciate their patience. We will leave here as soon as possible."

Kwalrak bowed her triangular head and floated away. Jean-Luc watched her go, then slumped back into his chair, wondering how long "as soon as possible" would be. Data was working diligently with circuits that looked like they belonged in a junk pile. At the moment, thought Picard, the entire shuttlecraft was just another piece of space junk drifting in a lazy solar orbit through the greater Kreel asteroid belt.

Chapter Ten

WORF STOOD BEHIND GEORDI at the mission ops station on the bridge and looked worriedly over the chief engineer's shoulder. Other shuttle traffic was registering in the sector as delegations made their way to Kayran Rock, but there was no sign of the *Ericksen*.

"Damn!" cursed Geordi, punching up an earlier screen. "They got off to a late start, but it was all routine—until you put out that security alert."

"An error on my part," Worf admitted glumly.

"In hindsight, yes," agreed the engineer. "But you couldn't have known that the shuttlecraft had left. How long were you unconscious?"

The Klingon shrugged, "Fifteen, twenty minutes. It seemed like only a moment to me."

"Maybe you should check into sickbay," Geordi suggested. "You must've received quite a jolt."

The scowl on Worf's face told him that such a course was unlikely. "Have you scanned for wreckage?" asked the security officer.

"Yes," answered Geordi, "and we've been scanning repeatedly. It's like they vanished. The only thing that would account for it is a complete change of course and a shut-down of all communications. It's like they were *trying* to hide from us."

"Remember," said Worf grimly, "aboard that shuttlecraft is a man with a phaser who has already killed two people."

"That's a cheery thought," muttered Geordi. "But where would they go? How could Emil Costa even think he could evade a starship in a shuttlecraft that's only capable of impulse power?"

"He's insane," Worf replied.

"Right," frowned Geordi.

Worf leaned forward and pointed to a section of the screen. "There," he said.

"The asteroid belt?" asked the engineer in amazement. "He's insane, but is he *that* insane?"

"It's within range," added the Klingon.

A third voice broke into their conversation. "Commander La Forge," said the communications officer, "we are being hailed by the Kreel vessel *Tolumu.*"

Geordi straightened up and heaved a sigh. "On the screen," he ordered, striding briskly from the aft section of the bridge into the command area. He glanced back at Worf. "And keep the view localized on my face."

"Aye, sir," the young officer answered tensely.

A red triangular head mounted on broad naked shoulders filled the main viewscreen. His fearsome countenance did not look at all happy. "This is Colonel Jarayn," the Kreel announced. "We just tried to contact Admiral Ulree and his party on your starbase, and they say they haven't arrived yet. In fact, they have no idea where they are. They are still aboard the *Enterprise,* I presume."

"No," answered Geordi forthrightly. "The shuttlecraft left the *Enterprise* approximately forty minutes ago with the admiral and his party as well as our three ranking officers, Captain Picard, Commander Riker, and Commander Data. Their whereabouts are unknown, and we are attempting to locate them now."

The ferocious face turned several darker shades of red, and Colonel Jarayn's massive shoulders tensed. "Are you serious?" he snarled. *"Could they be dead?"*

"Missing," corrected Geordi. "We have no reason to believe they are dead. But I won't mislead you, Colonel—we don't know where they are."

The red-skinned humanoid was shaking with rage. He shrieked, "We give you an asteroid, let you build a starbase in our solar system, and entrust our highest-ranking officers to you—*and you lose them!* I should blow you out of the sky!"

"That wouldn't be advisable," Geordi answered calmly. "We know their last position, and we know the capabilities of our shuttlecraft. You certainly are within your rights to lodge whatever kind of complaint you want, but it's in your own best interests to help us locate them."

Geordi looked back at Worf, whose hands were poised over the weapons console. "We have reason to believe, Colonel," he continued, "that they may have flown off course into your asteroid belt."

The translator wouldn't even take a guess at the string of Kreel expletives that greeted that remark. "We should have known," howled the Kreel, "anyone who allies themselves with Klingons . . ."

"Please," said Geordi, holding up his hands. "We've allied ourselves with thousands of races throughout the galaxy, including the noble Kreel. This is an unfortunate accident, but threatening us and cursing us won't help. What would help is if you sent us the best charts you have for the asteroids in this sector. Our computer will compare your charts with our current readings and pick up any irregularities."

The Kreel colonel seemed to calm down minutely. "This wouldn't have happened," he growled, "if you would just give us transporter technology!"

Geordi shook his head. "That's a discussion for later. We will await your transmission. Out."

"They can't be trusted," warned Worf.

"I don't think we have much choice," muttered the VISORed officer. As if he had been doing it all his life, Lieutenant Commander La Forge sat in the captain's chair and motioned to the officers manning the conn and ops stations. "Take us to within fifty thousand kilometers of the asteroid belt and keep station. Divert all scanners to the asteroids and analyze anything that isn't chondrites, achondrites, silicates, or metallic iron."

There came a chorus of "Aye, sir's."

"Kreel data coming in," announced the communications officer.

Data had restored artificial gravity and stabilization to the shuttlecraft, and it no longer pitched and yawed. It just floated behind the immense black asteroid. He could have used the thrusters to put some distance between them and the giant rock, but then they would have gone sailing off in the other direction, unable to stop without impulse engines to compensate. As it was, the android marveled that he had slowed them manually to what seemed to be the correct speed. It wasn't really correct, he knew, and eventually they would collide with one or more asteroids. That could be in a few days or a million years.

The asteroids themselves showed ample signs of having banged into one another fairly often. Although they appeared at casual observation to be orbiting the Kreel sun at the same speed and trajectory, they weren't. Gravity kept the herd together but also kept them off kilter, subtly attracting one to the other. Eons of major and minor collisions had put some space between the bigger bodies, but the debris from those collisions still ricocheted through the belt. The asteroids had no real synchronicity and were like countless small planets all in the same general orbit.

Captain Picard returned to the co-pilot's seat after having tried to reassure the Kreel they would be rescued. "I told them the truth," he muttered. "There was no point in pretending that we're going to fly out of here under our own power. That would be foolhardy, even with full navigation and helm. And they realize that."

"Yes," said Data, never taking his eyes off a circuit board full of isolinear chips. "Our survival thus far is quite remarkable."

Picard ran his hand over his bald pate. "Data," he whispered, "we need that distress signal."

Data peered closely at the miniaturized circuits, remarking, "The distress code generator does not appear damaged, but its support circuitry is badly burned. The tools in the emergency kit are rudimentary, but I think I can effect repairs."

"Make it so," Picard said with more intensity than usual.

A few meters away, Will Riker again found himself in the back of the shuttlecraft. This time, however, Kwalrak wasn't hounding him. In fact, Riker found that he had been ostracized for sitting next to Emil Costa. The old scientist hunched beside him, looking as forlorn and miserable as a person could look. Riker would have felt sorry for the man, if he hadn't behaved like a reckless maniac and endangered all their lives.

"Why did you do it?" he asked tensely.

The old man stared at him with haunted eyes that pleaded for help and understanding. "They would have killed me if I had stayed aboard the *Enterprise*," he whispered earnestly. "I couldn't go back, no matter what!"

Riker frowned, "Who would have killed you?"

Emil hissed, "The same ones who killed Lynn."

"Who exactly is that?"

Emil shook his head as if this question had weighed greatly on him for some time. "I don't know," he sighed. "Karn Milu may have something to do with it, but I don't know for sure."

"Karn Milu," replied Riker thoughtfully. "Why would he mean you harm?"

"That damn submicrobe!" Emil cursed. "I wish I had never found it. It cost Lynn her life!" He covered his face with his hands and sniffled softly.

Will Riker sighed and shook his head. He had never pegged Emil Costa as someone who would go around the bend, but he supposed the trauma of losing one's wife could do it. Emil might persist in saying he had nothing to do with his wife's death, but his actions of today indicated a shocking mental disorder of some sort. If they survived this incident, Emil Costa would be kept busy for the rest of his life with examinations and inquiries. Together with his wife's death, his perverse actions signalled a tragic end to an outstanding career.

Wesley Crusher paced nervously, anxious to get this over with and get back to the bridge. He never for an instant doubted that the shuttlecraft would be recovered with all safe and accounted for—he just wanted to be there when it happened.

"Go on," Deanna Troi said patiently, aware the boy's mind was wandering from his story—and why.

"There isn't much more to say," Wesley shrugged. "After Saduk let me out of the pod, we went out into the class-one-hundred area, and I saw Worf. He was checking the body with a tricorder." The boy shuddered with a mixture of disgust and excitement. "You should have seen Dr. Milu's body—it had a hole in it as big as a dinner plate. Burned to a crisp!"

Deanna nodded, glad it had not been her luck to make the grisly discovery. "Nothing else struck you as important?" she continued.

Wesley shook his head slowly for a moment, then shook his finger, recalling, "There was something Saduk told me—that Emil had alerted him to go to the pod room and check on an experiment. In effect, Emil saved my life. So I really don't think he meant me any harm. Of course," the teenager frowned, "Karn Milu couldn't say that."

"But Worf could," the counselor replied puzzledly. "Emil apparently shot both of them, but one he shot to kill and one to stun. What do you make of that?"

Wesley shrugged, "He likes us better than he does Karn Milu."

Deanna blinked at the unexpected joke, but she felt the frustration in it. Revelations kept piling upon one another, but not solutions. Knowing of the mysterious submicrobe and Karn Milu's pursuit of it brought some clarity to these terrible incidents, but no relief. Now Will, the captain, and Data were caught up in this murderous web. Wesley's account of what he had seen and experienced had been duly recorded by the computer, and there wasn't much else Deanna could do for the moment.

"Let's get to the bridge," she declared.

"All right!" exclaimed Wesley.

The ensign reached the door of the consultation room first and almost walked right into the hulking figure of Grastow. Wes stumbled backward, but recovered quickly and reached for his missing communicator.

Deanna Troi was a few seconds behind him, but she instantly appraised the situation and leveled the Antarean with angry black eyes. "If you move one muscle," she warned, reaching for her badge, "I will have you beamed directly to confinement."

"No, no," said Grastow sheepishly, "I mean no one harm. I helped Emil get off the ship, and that's all I promised him I would do. Here, I came to return this."

Grastow's hand proffered a shiny communications badge, stuck to a few centimeters of red cloth. Cautiously, Wesley snatched it from the mammoth palm.

"I would understand fully if you put me in confinement," the Antarean said with a bow. "I have interfered with the duties of a Starfleet officer, and I freely admit it. In no way is this an excuse, but I owe so much to Emil and Lynn Costa that I would gladly do whatever they requested of me. I am ready to serve my punishment."

"Here's your punishment," said Deanna Troi sternly. "Everyone aboard that shuttlecraft—Captain Picard, Data, and Riker, six Kreel ambassadors, and Emil himself—is lost. We don't know where they are. And Dr. Karn Milu is dead. So restrict yourself to quarters and think about what your reckless activities have done."

Grastow swallowed hard, and Wesley was certain he was going to cry. Deanna pulled at his elbow.

She dragged Wesley away, but he looked back over

his shoulder at the dejected researcher. That would be one more leaving the Microcontamination Project, he thought sadly.

"There is one problem," Data told Captain Picard. The android was again lying on his back under the shuttlecraft control panel, and his voice seemed to float up through the instruments. "The more energy we divert to the distress signal, the less we will have for life support."

Picard's lips tightened. Life support was a problem he had hoped to put off for a little while longer. He knew there was a finite limit to the vessel's power cells and regenerative ability, but he didn't want to be reminded of it. Not so soon. Nevertheless, Data had opened the box.

"How much time do you estimate we have left for life support?" asked Captain Picard in a voice that was barely audible. He knew Data would hear him.

The android answered softly as well. "Theoretically," he began, "a personnel shuttlecraft is equipped to provide for ten passengers for two weeks. However, factoring in the damage we sustained and the metabolism of the eleven individuals on board, I would lower that estimate by fifty percent. Boosting the distress signal to maximum output would further exhaust our energy by fifty percent."

"Three or four days." Picard nodded grimly. "That was my estimate too. We are not to discuss this with anyone but Commander Riker."

"Understood, Captain," replied Data.

Will Riker rounded the partition, managing a weak smile. "Did I hear someone mention my name?"

"Yes, Number One," said Picard softly, "but we'll speak later. What are our guests doing?"

"Mostly glaring at Emil Costa," answered Riker.

"They've grown very quiet. The Kreel who was stunned has recovered fully, but I believe the other orderly dislocated his shoulder when he fell."

"The Kreel are very fatalistic," Data observed. "They probably believe they are already dead."

"We're far from that," vowed the captain.

But they were almost deafened a moment later when the *Ericksen* thundered and shook from a shower of asteroids striking its hull. Riker and Picard instinctively crouched to the deck, and Data sat up. There was no screaming from the back, just accepting moans.

"We are lucky!" shouted Data over the terrible din. "Without that large asteroid to partially shield us, we would have been destroyed by now!"

"I don't feel lucky!" answered Riker.

Picard shouted, "How long before you can start the distress signal?"

"It is on, Captain," replied Data. "Energy consumption is at maximum!"

They crouched down, shielding their ears and their minds from the crashing assault on the ship's hull.

Ensign Wesley Crusher had just taken his customary seat at the conn station when he had something to report. "Distress signal!" he announced. "Bearing five-mark-eight!"

"I read it too," reported Worf. "Standard repeater —it could well be the *Ericksen.*"

A quiet cheer went up in everyone's heart on the bridge, but there was too much work to be done for congratulations.

Wesley shook his head worriedly, "It's getting weaker."

Geordi rose from the captain's chair and leaned over Wesley's shoulder. "How far away is it?"

"It's fluctuating," he said, "but I make it at seventy to eighty thousand kilometers."

"We'll have to get closer to transport them," warned Worf from his station at the rear of the bridge.

Geordi patted Wesley's shoulder. "Do you think you can get us another twenty thousand kilometers closer to the source?"

"To be honest," answered the teenager, "I don't know. According to the Kreel charts, we're fifty-two thousand kilometers from the first big asteroid, which measures two kilometers in diameter. But there are bound to be smaller asteroids that don't show up in the Kreel charts or on our scanners, and we're certain to hit some of them."

"Shields up," ordered Geordi.

"Shields," answered Worf.

The engineering officer peered over Wesley's shoulder at a readout that had a Kreel chart superimposed over it. "It looks like that signal is coming from an asteroid," he said puzzledly.

"It's very near to one," Wesley agreed, "and it may interfere with transporter operations. To be certain we're in transporter range, we should draw to within forty-five thousand kilometers. I'll have to do a manual override, because computer navigation would never allow us to get that close."

"Do whatever it takes," ordered Geordi. "We need to get a good read on them before we can start transporting." He called out, "La Forge to O'Brien!"

"O'Brien here," answered the transporter operator.

"Lock on to the distress signal," said the acting captain. "I want to beam the entire shuttlecraft to the main shuttlebay."

"I wouldn't suggest that," countered the Irishman. "With this interference, it would be safer to lock on to biological readings only. We don't know what we'll bring over if we don't."

"Okay," muttered Geordi, "but be quick about it. When we lower the shields to transport, we could get clobbered."

"Aye, sir," answered O'Brien. "Transporter Room Two is standing by to assist."

"Await my order," said Geordi tensely. "Out."

The engineer left the young helmsman to do his job as he returned to the captain's chair. With mounting concern, he watched an endless array of dark shapes slowly drawing closer on the main viewscreen.

He heard Deanna Troi shift nervously in her seat beside him. "I sense they are alive," she offered. "But unsafe."

"We've got to get them out of there and fast," vowed La Forge. "Asteroids are so unstable—one little collision can start a pool table effect."

"Pool table?" asked Deanna.

"An Earth game," scowled Geordi. "You don't want to know."

A low rumble echoed throughout the saucer section. "Shields holding," announced Worf.

"Sorry," said Wesley nervously, "I couldn't avoid it. That one was almost a kilometer in diameter."

"You're doing fine," said Geordi.

A succession of thuds sounded just over their heads. "Shields holding," said Worf.

"The Kreel commander is hailing us," said the communications officer. "He says what we're doing is extremely unsafe."

"Thank him," answered Geordi. "Tell him we are attempting rescue."

"Forty-eight . . . forty-seven . . . forty-six . . ." Wesley counted down, "forty-five thousand kilometers!"

He spread his fingers across his control panel. "Slowing down to tracking speed."

"Well done, Wesley," Geordi gulped, rising to his feet. "Open all channels. Captain Picard, anyone aboard the shuttlecraft *Ericksen*—do you read me?"

On the shuttlecraft, eleven pairs of eyes and ears widened at once. Geordi's voice sounded loudly over all four Starfleet combadges, including Ensign Hamer's in the passenger compartment. The startled exclamations were almost louder than the continuing asteroid bombardment.

"Picard here," responded the captain. "Good to hear your voice, Geordi! We are adrift behind a large asteroid and are passing through a shower of smaller ones."

As if for emphasis, the shuttlecraft was bashed so soundly that Picard, Data, and Riker were all knocked off their feet. Wails came from the back, and Data was the first to straggle to his knees and gaze out the window.

He slapped his badge. "Data to La Forge!" he called. "Beam us up immediately. We are on a collision course."

Picard and Riker struggled to their knees and saw that Data was not exaggerating. The last impact had sent them careening at a new angle toward the outer edge of the giant asteroid. Data grabbed the thruster controllers and laid into them with all his might. The effect was minimal as they sailed closer and closer to the curved wall of pitted rock.

Aboard the *Enterprise,* Worf announced, "Shields down!"

"Transporter Room One," snapped Geordi, "beam up eight. Transporter Room Two, wait two seconds, then pick up stragglers."

"Acknowledged," said O'Brien in Transporter Room One. "Energizing."

O'Brien couldn't be blamed for locking on to his commanding officers first, and Picard, Data, and Riker dematerialized from the cockpit of the *Ericksen*. They were quickly followed by Admiral Ulree, Kwalrak, and three other startled Kreel. Only Ensign Hamer, the wounded Kreel orderly, and Emil Costa remained aboard the out-of-control vessel. Ensign Hamer smiled reassuringly at Emil and the orderly, as if to say they were more expendable but would probably be rescued anyway.

They were, seconds later, just before the small craft tore into the asteroid and exploded into millions of glistening bits. Each fragment spun off in its own trajectory to add a bit of sparkle to the ageless boulders of the Kreel asteroid belt.

Chapter Eleven

HIS HEART STILL PALPITATING, Will Riker stepped off the transporter platform and sucked in a breath of air.

"This has been an outrage!" shrieked Admiral Ulree to Captain Picard. He waved an extremely long arm around the room but couldn't find Emil Costa. "I don't know what you've done with him, but I demand custody of that maniac who tried to kill us!"

"One moment," Picard answered. "Let's make sure we got everyone off safely."

"Captain," interjected Engineer O'Brien from behind his transporter controls, "everyone is off the shuttlecraft, and the other three persons are in Transporter Room Two."

"Worf to Captain Picard," called a deep voice.

Picard tapped his insignia. "Picard here."

"Captain," said the Klingon, "I thought it best not to join you."

"Understood," said Picard. "Where are you?"

"In Transporter Room Two. We have taken the wounded Kreel and Ensign Hamer to sickbay, and Emil Costa has been placed under arrest."

"Is that your security chief?" asked Admiral Ulree.

"Yes, it is," answered the captain.

"May I speak with him?"

Picard nodded, "Mister Worf, can you hear Admiral Ulree?"

"Quite clearly," answered the Klingon, his voice betraying none of the irony of dealing with an ancestral enemy who had no idea he was Klingon.

"You place that man under high security!" the admiral ordered. "Because we intend to bear him over for trial!"

"On what charge?" asked Worf.

The grizzled Kreel admiral blinked and scratched his hairy chest. "I'm no lawyer," he grumbled, "but attempted murder comes to mind. What about hijacking, assault, and endangerment? I don't think we have any shortage of charges, and the attack took place in *our* solar system!"

"We will maintain custody," answered Worf, "because we intend to try him for a more serious crime—murder."

"If this is a trick . . ." growled the Kreel, pumping himself up to a threatening size. He glared at Picard who returned his gaze noncommittally.

"No trick," Worf's deep voice assured him. "Captain, I regret to inform you that Karn Milu is dead; he was killed by a phaser."

Now Picard looked as angry as his Kreel counterpart. "Are you saying that Emil Costa murdered him?"

"Just before he got on the shuttle," answered Worf. "Or someone did. Unlike Lynn Costa's death, this cannot possibly be construed as an accident."

O'Brien interrupted, "Captain, the Kreel vessel *Tolumu* requests an immediate audience with their personnel. I could beam them directly there."

"That is up to the admiral," said Picard, nodding to the Kreel officer. "This entire unforgivable incident was caused by the fact that we didn't want to embarrass our guests by using transporter technology. But they have already been transported once, and I have no wish to delay them further. Admiral, do you wish to return to your ship?"

"Let them wait," scoffed the Kreel. "Just get us to the party—we're late enough as it is!"

"Beam us down," purred Kwalrak, eyeing Riker lasciviously.

"We intend to fight for custody of that criminal!" bristled Colonel Efrek. "But later."

Jean-Luc smiled wearily and tapped his badge. "Captain Picard to bridge. I commend all of you for your quick work in rescuing us. Set course for Kayran Rock and maintain station as planned. After our unexpected detour, we owe our Kreel guests some prompt service. Please inform the *Tolumu* that all their personnel are safe and accounted for and will contact them from the starbase. Out."

Data overheard Admiral Ulree confiding to Kwalrak, "They may be good at transporters, but they're terrible with shuttlecraft."

Lieutenant Worf dragged Emil Costa by the arm down the high security walkway toward the containment cells. The scientist was beginning to struggle, and Worf tightened his grip and walked faster.

"I am innocent!" yelled Emil. "I didn't kill anyone! Listen to me!"

Eyes straight ahead, Worf growled, "Interrogation will begin immediately after you have been safely confined."

"All right, all right," said Emil, slouching into step. "I admit, what I did aboard that shuttlecraft was insane, but I was desperate to get off the *Enterprise*. With two deaths now, you can see why!"

The ridges furrowed skeptically on Worf's brow. "Dr. Costa," he said testily, "I'm not interested in hearing excuses."

They rounded the corner, and Worf ushered the wizened scientist into one of the comfortably appointed cells. The Klingon stepped out and pressed a button. Realizing he had just been imprisoned, Emil sprang toward the open doorway but bounced harmlessly off the invisible forcefield.

Worf saw him gingerly touch his nose, which was still caked with blood. "I will get you some medical attention," he offered.

"No, that's all right," muttered Emil, slumping toward the bed. "I've got a sink here—I can clean myself up. I don't really want to see anybody else at the moment, anyway."

"I have many questions to ask you," said Worf, "the most important of which is: Did you kill Karn Milu?"

"No," muttered the old man. "When I left him, he was alive."

"Did you kill your wife?"

"No!" Emil shrieked. "Get out of here! *Go away!*" He sprawled across the bed and sobbed pitifully.

Worf remained, impassively studying the famous scientist. The frustration at not having prevented Karn Milu's death grated upon the Klingon, but they couldn't have acted any differently. The captain had been correct to let Emil Costa go when Lynn's death looked so much like an accident, but in so doing, they had lost another life.

However, Worf was not forgetting that his own death could have been the third murder. But Emil had spared him, which was very puzzling considering his probable mental state at the time. In fact, there were many inconsistencies in this chain of events—one carefully planned and executed murder, one brutal mindless killing, a timely phaser stun, and the willful sabotage of an entire shuttlecraft filled with people. At the rate he was going, Emil Costa would have to be considered the most dangerous man in the galaxy.

But he didn't look dangerous, the frail white-haired old man curled up in bed sobbing pathetically. He didn't seem at all like the kind of desperate lunatic who would willfully murder two people and endanger the lives of a dozen more. At least, thought Worf gratefully, they only had two cases of murder to prosecute. They had come uncomfortably close to having a dozen murders, complicated by the murderer's suicide.

In reality, the Klingon would have preferred to try Emil for his rampage aboard the shuttlecraft, because there had been so many witnesses. But he had committed himself to prosecuting the scientist for the murder of Karn Milu, and he was damned if he was going to back down on his word to a Kreel. They would prosecute the most serious crime first.

Thankfully, they had a strong witness in Ensign Crusher, as well as an obvious motive. Karn Milu had been hounding Lynn and Emil for details of a discovery they were keeping secret, contrary to Starfleet regulations. Emil could hardly deny complicity in that coverup. Lynn's destruction of the computer records now made perfect sense in this twisted scheme of things, and he couldn't forget Shana Russel's testimony that she had heard Karn Milu threaten Lynn's life. All this over one exceptionally sturdy submicrobe, thought Worf with amazement.

"What drove you to do it?" he asked the researcher. "Did Karn Milu tell you that *he* killed your wife?"

"He probably *did* kill her!" Emil moaned in a distraught German accent. "But he never told me about it, and I swear he was alive when I left him.

172

You've got to believe me, Lieutenant, I didn't kill anyone!"

Deanna Troi and Wesley Crusher quietly entered the security chamber and stood behind Worf.

"Wesley!" shrieked Emil, charging toward the force-field and being repelled. "Tell the lieutenant that I didn't kill anyone! Tell them that you only saw us arguing! *I swear I didn't kill anyone!*"

Wesley started to speak but Worf glared at him. "Ensign," he warned, "you are a material witness in this case. You cannot converse with the suspect. In fact, it would be a good idea if you didn't converse with *anyone* regarding this case, except the captain, Counselor Troi, and myself.

"I don't mean this to sound like punishment," the Klingon continued, softening his tone. "I am extremely grateful for your help, even if you didn't entirely heed my warning not to endanger yourself. But, Ensign Crusher, you are restricted to quarters until summoned to testify. Go over your own memories of what you witnessed, and don't let other people make suggestions to you. The less you know about subsequent events in the shuttlecraft, the better. I haven't seen your account to Counselor Troi, but that deposition immediately after the fact will be our most important piece of evidence."

"Yes, sir," replied Wesley. He glanced at Emil, shrugged helplessly, and started for the doorway.

"Wesley!" shouted the scientist, "I need a lawyer. If you could pick anybody on board to represent you, who would it be?"

Wesley stopped and looked toward the security chief, who nodded his approval for the boy to answer that question.

Wesley answered without hesitation, "Data."

"Get me Data," the old man told Worf, shuffling

toward the sink at the rear of his cell. "I won't answer any more questions without him."

"Data was with you on the shuttlecraft," Worf protested. "He could be a witness against you."

"Not in a trial concerning the death of Karn Milu," countered the old man, wetting a cloth and washing the blood off his face. "If that's the crime you are charging me with, Data can be my attorney."

"He is correct," added Deanna Troi. "Data had no involvement with this case until the shuttlecraft incident."

With a scowl, Worf heaved his chest and banged his communicator badge. "Security team to containment unit one," he ordered. "Emil Costa will be guarded by security teams rotating in two-hour shifts. Maintain this schedule until further ordered. Worf out."

"A whole security team?" scoffed Emil. "Four men to guard *me?*"

Worf fixed him with a baleful glare. "We haven't had anyone shoot up a shuttlecraft in some time. We consider you extremely dangerous and irrational."

The Klingon tapped his badge again. "Worf to Captain Picard."

"Picard here," answered the captain crisply. "We are just about to embark for Kayran Rock, but I will not be gone long. I just want to make sure that our guests are well treated."

"Understood," answered Worf, "but there is a condition you should be aware of. Dr. Costa refuses to answer questions without legal representation, and he has requested Data for that purpose."

"Data as defense counsel?" asked Picard slowly, mulling over the concept. "We'll decide this when I return, but I suppose we should ask Data himself. He knows more about the regulations and legal requirements than I do."

"Captain," said Worf, "with so many crew members as witnesses, we may spend considerable time resolving this case."

"Undoubtedly," grumped the captain. "I will do what I can to see that Dr. Costa is afforded a speedy trial, but we might as well accept the fact that we will be stationed at Kayran Rock for an indefinite period."

The Klingon knew that Admiral Ulree was probably within earshot, and the captain was making this last statement as much for his benefit as Worf's.

"We are in transporter range," added the captain. "I will make the necessary inquiries regarding the trial. Out."

Forcing himself to be cordial, Worf turned to Emil Costa and pointed to the food slot in his cell. "Have yourself something to eat, Doctor," he suggested. "Your screen is not connected to the main computer, but you can read periodicals and fiction on it. For a measure of privacy, you can lower the blinds. As I previously stated, I can arrange medical attention for you."

"Thank you for your concern," said Emil sarcastically. The old man sat on the bed and crossed his arms, suddenly feisty and rejuvenated. "I am guilty of crimes, yes, but not the murder of either Karn Milu or my wife. I refuse to speak to anyone until you get me my counsel. Get me Data!"

"As you wish," snarled Worf. "You will remain in solitary confinement until Commander Data returns to the ship." He waved everyone out, and the solid double hatches closed on the block of containment cells.

Alone and wishing to remain so for the present, Captain Picard strolled down a deserted corridor in the first starbase built inside an asteroid. Kayran Rock was almost three thousand kilometers in diameter, and only a small pocket had been carved out for Starfleet's use. The natural walls of the corridor were blacker than the blackest ebony, and they glistened with a coat of resin that had been applied to strengthen the carbonized stone. Picard ran his hand over the dark surface, feeling its coldness. The asteroid was really a small planet that had failed to attract an atmosphere, so it had no soft blanket of gases to protect it against the coldness of space.

Spying a lounge area ahead, the captain quickened his step. The chatter and clatter of the reception taking place behind him in the dining hall was barely audible, and it faded completely before he reached the observation lounge. His attention was instantly drawn toward a circular viewport, which exhibited an immense array of stars, framed by a tunnel that had been bored through two meters of asteroid.

The view from inside an asteroid wasn't all that different than from inside a starship, except that these stars held steady—no gentle pulsing or blurring at warp speed. This celestial body was on a leisurely tour of its own solar system.

The captain found a seat strategically located for contemplation of the starscape and sat down. It was extremely quiet, even with a party going on less than a hundred meters away. Picard so seldom had time alone with himself that at first he was stunned to realize that no one knew where he was at that moment. Of course, they could contact him via communicator, but he wasn't aware of the usual bustle of his crew. Even when he was alone in his ready room or his quarters, he was aware of them and they of him. Here, for the moment, he was truly alone.

If only he had something pleasant to think about,

instead of ugly murders, sabotage, and insanity. The events of the last few hours had left him numb and unusually weary. The harrowing escapade in the shuttlecraft was not so troubling—he was accustomed to danger and tense situations. But cold-blooded murder? Insane behavior from an enormously respected scientist? Careers ruined, files destroyed, violence, and extortion over secret discoveries? It was staggering to think that such problems could have remained hidden—and then gotten so totally out of hand—in such a small community as the *Enterprise.*

Of course, Picard realized sadly, they were a small community but not really a close-knit one. The bridge crew was one separate entity; the science branch consisted of dozens of self-sufficient disciplines; and then came all the departments like sickbay and Engineering. Each was part of the whole but each was self-absorbed in its own work and circle of workers. In the few places where everyone on the ship brushed against one another, like the Ten-Forward Room or the theater, the crew members connected only briefly before returning to their primary pursuits. What connected them most, he guessed, was their desire to serve aboard the *Enterprise* and make the most of that opportunity.

They were so wrapped up in their duties, though, that they often failed to see what was going on around them. For example, he had doubted Worf when the Klingon had insisted Emil Costa was dangerous. If he had listened to his security chief, the episode in the shuttlecraft wouldn't have happened and maybe Karn Milu would still be alive. Picard hardly ever second-guessed his decisions, but this was one that bore reflection.

"Jean-Luc Picard!" called a cheery female voice

behind him. He stood and turned to see Ambassador Gretchen Gaelen striding toward him, her arms outstretched.

He hugged the diminutive gray-haired ambassador and she beamed back at him with a grandmotherly smile. "You're looking a bit thin, Jean-Luc," she observed. "Get in there and eat some of my goulash. It doesn't come from a food slot, but from my great-great-grandmother's cookbook!"

"I'm sure it's delicious, Gretchen," Picard winced, rubbing his stomach. "But I've had plenty to eat."

"You've had *nothing* to eat," she corrected him. "I may be pretty busy at these affairs—but I started out as a caterer, and I notice who's eating."

Now Picard was forced to laugh. Gretchen Gaelen was the Federation's master organizer of official ceremonies. He couldn't imagine her as anything but a galaxy-class traveler and ambassador of good will. He didn't even know how many starbases she had opened up, but between the two of them, they had probably been to more starbases than any other two people in the Federation. She was way ahead of him, however, on planetary galas celebrating new treaties and such.

"So what's the matter with you, Jean-Luc?" she persisted. "You're not even wearing the right uniform. Where's your dress uniform?"

"Uh," he hesitated, "I had a change of clothes, but they . . . It's a long story."

"Yes, I know," Gretchen grimaced, "and that long-winded Kreel is in there telling it to everybody. He keeps making himself the hero, although I'm sure that isn't true." She lowered her voice and asked in disbelief, "Is it true Emil Costa tried to kill himself and everyone on board a shuttlecraft?"

Jean-Luc nodded grimly, "It's considerably worse than that."

"The murder charge," Ambassador Gaelen acknowledged. "The Kreel have been talking about that too, but no one seems to know very much. Actually, I've been grateful for these fascinating rumors. Everyone has been so interested in finding out the real story that the Kreel and the Klingons have forgotten to argue! I heard that Emil Costa was trying to escape on the shuttlecraft when the murder was discovered?"

"Those are essentially the facts, as I know them," answered Picard. "Our security chief believes he has sufficient evidence to press a murder charge, and several of my officers will be witnesses."

"You can't be too pleased about this," Gretchen observed sympathetically.

"Not very," the captain admitted. "We could be tied up here for longer than expected."

A sly look crept over the ambassador's kindly face. "The Kreel may try to use this for leverage," she whispered. "What would they want from us?"

Picard shrugged, "They say they want Emil Costa bound over for trial for endangering them."

"Once they find out who he is," warned the elder stateswoman, "they will want him for his knowledge about biofilters and transporters. We must make sure our trial is thorough, so there will be no need to hand him over to them."

"Who would serve as judge?" asked Picard.

Gretchen frowned, "They're not fully staffed here yet, but we have one thing in our favor. Do you know who acting commander of this starbase is?"

"No," answered Picard.

Gretchen beamed, "I am! My replacement is Captain Nadel, but she doesn't take over until after the dishes are cleaned up. I may be able to get the wheels turning on this before I quit tonight. Leave it to me."

"Thank you, Gretchen," said Picard gratefully,

clasping the lady's hand. "Maybe I could go for some of that goulash."

Will Riker gritted his teeth. The inevitable had happened and the sound system was playing dance music. Dinner was long over, and the dignitaries remaining had turned to hot beverages, dessert, and mingling. In the corner of his eye, he had seen two of the Kreel dancing, if it could be called that. He had also seen Kwalrak hovering near the computer to request a song, and she had winked at him.

All in all, thought Riker, the affair had been very dignified. They had missed the opening ceremony but had arrived in time for the grand tour and the sumptuous meal. Admiral Ulree had dominated the dinner conversation with his enhanced version of the shuttlecraft incident; even the Klingon representatives had listened intently. In fact, the Kreel were having such a good time that they had outlasted all but the Federation personnel, most of whom lived on the base. The crowd had dwindled from a high of about two hundred to little more than fifty.

Data had attracted a crowd from the start, and everyone in attendance had shaken his hand at some point in the festivities. With his marvelous memory, Data could be utterly charming, remembering names and histories of people he hadn't even met yet. Once Admiral Ulree had spread the word about the ill-fated shuttlecraft trip, Data had been besieged for his version of the incident. He patiently told the same story to at least a dozen different individuals, his unemotional but fact-filled style making each telling equally compelling.

Will had tried to blend into the black walls, hardly typical behavior for him at parties. But he was content to drink synthehol champagne and listen to tales of drilling through iron silicate. This gathering wasn't really for the diplomats, he decided, but for the brave men and women who had carved a starbase out of cold rock. Riker wanted to hear *their* war stories, not a rehash of the shuttle incident. His quiet observation was ending, however, with Kwalrak loping toward him with a big grin on her crooked face. All around him, the computer took up the strains of the "Blue Danube Waltz."

"Earth dancing music," she beamed proudly. "You see, I know all about you humans. Shall we dance?"

Before he had a chance to reply, Kwalrak wrapped her tenacious limbs around him and moved him along the dance floor. Riker decided there was no point in trying to lead, so he concentrated on where exactly to touch the hairy half-naked humanoid.

"I like this music," she cooed, hugging him closely but exhibiting a certain amount of decorum. This was a distinct improvement over her behavior in the shuttlecraft, thought Riker. He relaxed, certain that if he could survive hurtling through an asteroid belt in a crippled shuttlecraft, he could probably survive a dance. One thing was certain: The Kreel had plenty of intestinal fortitude. They may have moaned, but they didn't blink in the face of death. To Will, their collective wails showed more a recognition of death than a fear of it.

He injected an actual waltz two-step into his aimless lurchings with Kwalrak, but she ignored it. Nonchalantly, she remarked, "They say that man is very famous."

"Who?" asked Riker innocently.

"You know, Riker," she scolded him, "that crazy human who tried to kill us."

"Yes, him," sighed the first officer. "I hope you won't judge all of us by the actions of one disturbed individual."

"Spoken like a true diplomat," smiled the first assistant. "But it's nice to know your species isn't perfect."

"We never claim to be," Riker replied. "But we do the best we can, even if we don't always succeed. Our species has tried to live by one simple rule: Do unto others as you would have them do unto you."

"A nice sentiment," Kwalrak shrugged, "but quite impractical. For example, if you really believed that, why don't you give us transporter technology? You've seen how dangerous shuttle transportation is in this solar system."

"We live by another creed," Riker explained, "and it took us several millennia of trying to conquer each other before we learned the value of it. We don't interfere in the development of other cultures and species. This Prime Directive is the main tenet of our exploration; it keeps us from being exploited or exploiting others."

"We could buy transporter technology from the Ferengi!" Kwalrak threatened. "We already know most of it—only a few pieces are missing."

Riker shook his head doubtfully, "Let me tell you what would happen. If you didn't understand the technology, not having developed it yourself, you would always be at the mercy of the Ferengi. They would sell you the first units cheaply enough, get you dependent upon them, then quickly escalate the prices for everything, including repairs and maintenance. They'd end up owning your planet."

Kwalrak moaned, "If the prices they're offering us now are the cheap ones, I wouldn't want to see the expensive ones."

Riker smiled at her, noting that her large brown eyes were really quite pretty and expressive. "You've achieved space travel," he observed, "and have developed weapon systems that are quite impressive. Why can't your scientists apply themselves to this task?"

Kwalrak shrugged disgruntledly, "Those weapon systems you mentioned . . . they take priority over all other research. We still think we're at war with the Klingons, or somebody."

"Old habits," remarked Riker, shaking his head. "Believe me, we know how easy it is to be at war with the Klingons."

"But you're not exactly at peace," Kwalrak scoffed. "You carry massive firepower aboard that *Enterprise*. I notice you didn't *show* us any of it, but we've heard reports."

"I would've showed it to you," laughed Will, "if you hadn't found the Ten-Forward Room so interesting."

"I found *you* interesting, Riker," she purred, melting into him.

In his younger days, thought Riker, he might have found this interesting, but not now. He enjoyed Kwalrak's company, but her intentions were a bit too bald for his taste.

"Relax," she hissed, as if reading his mind and body language. "This is my way of flirting with you. Ulree would have us both killed if we actually did anything. Though if I really *wanted* you," she warned, squeezing him tighter, "you'd have been mine by now."

Somehow, Riker didn't doubt her, and he was relieved when the waltz ended a moment later. He politely disentangled himself and stepped back, saying, "I wish I had time to get to know you better, but not on this trip."

She stroked his hairy cheek and purred, "You are

cute, Riker. But you aren't going anywhere soon, and neither are we."

While he was mulling that over, the Kreel raked a long fingernail through his beard, turned, and sashayed away. She glanced over her brawny shoulder once before joining the rest of her party.

Riker wandered for a moment among mostly empty tables and tasteful decorations. The floral arrangements were quite striking in their variety, suggesting the wealth of places the Federation called home, and each table had a hologram at its center depicting a phase in the building of the starbase. He marveled again at the extraordinary achievement and wished he could enjoy being here more.

Had it only been three days ago that he and Deanna Troi had been planning a sabbatical for Lynn and Emil Costa? Would that have helped? He felt he should have taken Deanna's request more seriously and done something sooner. More than ever, Riker had meant what he had said at Lynn Costa's funeral: His biggest regret was not having enough time. Not enough time to get to know Lynn Costa, not enough time for himself, for Deanna. . . .

An automated wagon with a tray of desserts scooted past, and Riker followed it apathetically to its next stop. The large hall was gradually shrinking in size as the lights in its farthest corners dimmed. In one corner, the shadows caught Captain Picard and Lieutenant Commander Data engaged in conversation, but they ignored the darkness—or perhaps welcomed it.

The captain repeated the information as simply as he could, "Emil Costa has asked for you to be his defense counsel. What is your reaction?"

The android cocked his head puzzledly, "My initial

reaction is surprise. Emil Costa and I do not know each other very well. Today was the first opportunity I had to spend any amount of time in his presence, and I would not call it a pleasant experience."

"I see," nodded the captain. "Then you would remove yourself from consideration for personal reasons?"

"No," answered Data. "I would be able to ignore that incident in order to act as his counsel. I have not had any conversations with Lieutenant Worf or Counselor Troi regarding the murder investigation, and I consider myself impartial. I assume we will be based here for the duration of the trial?"

"I don't see how we can avoid it," Jean-Luc admitted. "You won't be missing anything exciting on the bridge. But how do you feel about being a trial lawyer, after your own trial experience?"

Captain Picard didn't talk to Data often about the trial on Starbase 173 in which the one-of-a-kind machine had been granted the legal status of a sentient being. Despite his artificiality, the ruling had determined that Data was nobody's property and could not be disassembled like a food slot. It had been an inevitable confrontation and a maturing process for all of them. Still, Picard couldn't help but wonder if courtrooms made Data uncomfortable. They made *him* uncomfortable, and he had only acted as Data's defender.

Data considered the question seriously. "It is true, Captain, I have been on trial for my own life, and I might have an understanding of that position. But isn't that an attorney's job, to articulate his client's side of the dispute?"

"Yes," smiled Picard. "There isn't any doubt in my mind that you would make a marvelous advocate for

Emil Costa. However, when *I* defended *you*, it was an emergency situation, and this isn't. This is a serious obligation, and you don't have to accept it."

"I understand," answered Data. "But nothing in Starfleet regulations would preclude me from acting as counsel for Emil Costa."

"Then you want to do it?" asked Picard.

"I would like to talk with him first."

Picard tapped his combadge. "Number One," he asked, "are you ready to leave?"

"Absolutely."

"Let's say our good-byes," suggested the captain, "and go home."

186

Chapter Twelve

Dr. Beverly Crusher winced slightly as she uncovered Karn Milu's body, but she was beginning to get used to the burned-out crater that had once been the Betazoid's chest. She pointed out its dimensions to Worf.

"Close range," she said, "and brief. A prolonged blast from a phaser set to full would have vaporized the body. Notice the lack of bleeding."

Worf straightened up, having seen enough of this particular corpse. "So," he concluded, "Dr. Milu was not walking or running away from his slayer but was facing him at close range."

"Undoubtedly," Beverly agreed. "I'll put that in my autopsy report, because I don't have much else to put in. There can be no doubt about this one." She covered the body, not wishing to look at the Betazoid's frozen features any longer.

"Yet he shot *me* to stun," Worf muttered puzzledly, his thick brow hooding his eyes. "At least the sequence of events is clear: Emil Costa quarreled with Karn Milu, put your son in the class-zero pod, then killed Dr. Milu. He had to take a special turbolift back to the transition room, but from there he could have escaped down any number of corridors. He must've entered the transition room shortly before I did, heard my voice when I demanded entrance, and hid among the garment racks."

"Whoa," interjected Beverly Crusher. "Back up a moment, Worf. What did you say about putting my son in a class-zero pod?"

The Klingon cleared his throat before stating, "I ordered Ensign Crusher not to mention it to you, but he was observing Emil Costa for me."

Beverly drew in a sharp breath and stared at him. "You had my son tailing a murder suspect?" she asked incredulously. "A man you knew was dangerous? Lieutenant, Wes is not a part of your security detail."

"He had a previous relationship with Emil Costa," Worf explained. "I wished to exploit it, but I also told him not to engage in any activity that could result in his peril. None of us knew the extent of Dr. Costa's derangement, or the involvement of Dr. Milu. They acted together to confine your son in a class-zero pod. Like myself, Wesley was lucky." He glanced down at the blasted body of Karn Milu.

Beverly's anger faded into incomprehension. "None of this makes any sense," she moaned. "Look what that madman tried to do with the shuttlecraft! I just sent the Kreel orderly we had in sickbay back to his ship. He was still shaking."

"We were very fortunate," agreed Worf, "considering the alternative."

The doctor snorted a derisive laugh. "And I always thought Emil Costa was one of the nicest men on the ship. He treated Wesley like his favorite student, a teacher's pet. To think, he could have done this . . . and murdered his wife too. It's astonishing."

Worf stroked his goatee thoughtfully before replying, "I'm not so sure Emil killed Lynn Costa. Without a confession, a trial on that charge could take months and might still prove inconclusive."

"I know," sighed Beverly. "I would have liked to be more specific in my autopsy, but I could only say she died from inhaling toxic gas."

"No matter," replied Worf, straightening the sheet on Karn Milu's body. "Doctor, can you keep this body preserved for a few days?"

"I suppose so," she nodded. "Why?"

"I intend to show it to the court."

"You talk like the prosecutor," Beverly observed.

"Whatever I must do, I will do," Worf promised. "I am determined to achieve justice."

He turned and marched out of sickbay. Beverly Crusher couldn't remember when she had seen a more determined look on his rough-hewn face.

The containment doors opened, and Data strode into the chamber alone. Emil Costa instantly bounded to his feet and pressed up against the invisible force-field of his cell.

"Commander Data!" he called with relief, trying to compose himself. "They were true to their words, I'll give them that—they sent you to help me!"

Data strode to the edge of the cell and peered quizzically at the scientist. "I have not agreed to accept this assignment," he replied, "which is fully voluntary. Why do you wish me for your defense counsel?"

"On Wesley Crusher's recommendation," said Emil, starting to pace. "But more importantly, I'm in a lot of trouble. I know that now. I am willing to admit to every crime I ever committed, going back to the biofilter days, but I am not guilty of *murdering* anyone!"

"For my clarification," replied Data, "you will insist you are innocent of murdering Karn Milu, no matter what evidence is presented?"

"Yes!" barked the old man forcefully. "I am innocent. They can shoot me out of a torpedo tube, and I'll still say I am innocent!"

"Curious metaphor," observed the android. "You realize, Dr. Costa, this stance will preclude any mutual agreement on lesser charges, such as self-defense or accidental manslaughter."

"I am innocent," maintained the frail researcher. "I will never plead guilty to killing Lynn or Dr. Milu, because I didn't do it!" He hung his head. "I don't know why they're dead and I am still alive."

"If you did not kill them," asked Data, "who did?"

"I don't know!" shrieked Emil, banging his fists on the forcefield. "I thought Karn Milu killed my wife . . . when I wasn't deluding myself into thinking that it could be an accident, or suicide. But now that *he* is dead . . ."

Emil Costa gripped his temples and howled, "I don't know who it is, but I know they've been after me!"

"Calm yourself, Doctor," said Data with alarm. "I will plead your case, but I cannot guarantee you will be acquitted. Many people are already convinced of your guilt."

"What have I got to lose?" muttered Emil, slumping onto his bed. "I've already lost everything."

Data nodded slowly, knowing Emil Costa's life would not improve soon. Even if they managed to get him acquitted of Karn Milu's murder, he faced a myriad of charges over his other actions. With or without an acquittal, he would probably face Kreel justice. Data was concerned about Emil Costa's plight, but he was not looking for a new career.

"It is understood," explained the android, "I will represent you only at the trial for the murder of Karn Milu. If you need legal counsel after that, you will have to look elsewhere."

"Understood," nodded Emil gratefully. "By the way, Commander, thank you for saving us on that shuttlecraft. I truly regret what I did. For that momentary lapse of sanity, I will accept the harshest punishment—but not for crimes I didn't commit."

"Good-bye, Doctor," said Data, starting for the door. "I will return when my appointment as your defender becomes official."

"Thank you," the old man smiled wearily.

Deanna Troi lay shivering in her bed, unable to sleep. She pulled a thick afghan over her shoulders, but it didn't help to quell the fear. For hours now, she had felt a nameless dread. It had started when she had first heard the shuttlecraft was missing—no, it had started before then. Really, Deanna admitted to herself, it had started from her dream of Lynn Costa's death. With each new episode of violence, the apprehension grew.

It should be over. The death of Karn Milu, the rescue from the asteroid belt, and now the imprisonment of Emil Costa—it all sounded like the climax of a Victorian play. The villain was safely behind bars, and now everyone could put on their coats and go home. But something was missing, namely the fact that the tension hadn't eased. The dread Deanna had felt all along was not going away; it was intruding deeper into every moment, waking or not.

Was Emil Costa such a vile man that he could be sitting in his cell even now, plotting more murders? Deanna didn't think so. In Emil, she sensed defeat, acknowledgment of mistakes, and extreme regret.

She didn't sense the cold-blooded craving for more revenge and murder she was sensing at this moment.

Deanna shuddered, jumped out of bed, and went to her wardrobe. There was no point in lying around scaring herself. Anyone who had heard what happened to Karn Milu was naturally going to be thinking about violence and death. Plus, she could be wrong about Emil Costa; she had been wrong about his wife. Maybe Emil *was* the source of the danger she still felt so strongly.

What I need is some diversion, Deanna decided. She put on her blue dress with the sparkle in the fabric and checked out her face in the mirror. Hair was okay, and what was troubling the face could only be cured by thinking of something else. Besides, with Guinan as her own personal informant, a trip to the Ten-Forward Room was business.

Deanna Troi hesitated before stepping into the corridor, but the apprehension wouldn't go away. There was no pretending that she would be able to think about anything else, so Deanna touched her communicator badge.

"Counselor Troi to Dr. Saduk," she requested.

"Saduk here," came the crisp Vulcan tones.

"Sorry to bother you," she stammered, "but I was just thinking about Dr. Milu and everything that's happened. Would you like to have a drink with me in the Ten-Forward Room?"

"I would welcome it," he replied. "I will meet you there in approximately twelve minutes."

"Fine," she answered. "Out."

The Ten-Forward Room had never seemed more crowded yet more subdued than in the last few days, thought Deanna. People had wanted to congregate somewhere, anywhere—first to bemoan Lynn Costa's death, then to discuss the rumors, and now to see if it was true that Karn Milu was also dead. No shipwide announcement had yet been made, but enough low voices made it clear that the ship's grapevine was efficiently on-line.

The counselor smiled politely and greeted a few people she knew, but she steered a direct course for the counter where Guinan usually held court. On this busy evening, the hostess was all over the room, but upon seeing Deanna, she gravitated back tō the bar.

"Hello, Counselor," said Guinan glumly, matching Deanna's glum expression. "It's times like this I wish I had something stronger to offer than synthehol."

"It wouldn't help," Deanna frowned. "It's just so distressing, I can't take my mind off these murders."

"And that shuttlecraft business," clucked the Listener. "Crazy. Nobody can believe it."

"I've studied psychology my whole life," Deanna said numbly, "and I still don't understand deadly violence. Does a person wake up one morning to discover that killing is the only solution to his problems, his torment? Is it something that strikes at the moment?"

The Betazoid shook her head and answered her own rhetorical question, "No, it doesn't strike suddenly. Whoever planned Lynn Costa's death had plenty of time to think about it. This is all a piece from the same rotten cloth."

Guinan observed with a wry smile, "You can't prevent madness. The more intelligent we get, the more prone we are to it. We have to consider ourselves lucky that it doesn't affect more of us."

The Betazoid sighed, "I came down here to think about something else, if that's possible. What's the ice cream special tonight?"

"Banana split!" enthused Guinan. "Today only, we include alterations on your waistband."

Deanna grinned, but before she could decide, a voice broke in on the ship's intercom. "This is Captain Picard," came the familiar clipped tones, sounding more solemn than usual. "As many of you have already heard, Dr. Karn Milu, head of our science branch, was brutally murdered with a phaser about six hours ago.

"By Dr. Milu's express order," continued the captain, "there will be no memorial service. His body will be stored at Kayran Rock until suitable transportation is arranged to his home planet. So let this quote from Goethe suffice: 'Death is a commingling of eternity with time; in the death of a good man, eternity is seen looking through time.'"

A moment later, the captain's voice sounded brighter as he told the crew, "Our stationing near Kayran Rock for the inquiry will allow shore leave for all who request it. Sleeping arrangements on Kayran Rock are limited, but some guest quarters are available. Please make your requests as soon as possible, so the computer can draw up the schedule. This is Captain Picard, out."

Several of the people in the room politely excused themselves and bolted for the door.

"Going to make their reservations," mused Guinan. "I've got a screen in my office, if you'd like to use it."

"No thanks," replied Deanna. "I assume the trial will guarantee me passage down to the asteroid."

"Then how about the banana split?"

"Yes," Deanna smiled. "Maybe I can find someone to share it with me."

While waiting for her treat, the counselor studied the people in the lounge area. The combination of expected bad news and unexpected good news had altered their mood for the better. People's voices were louder, and topics other than murder wafted to her ears. Deanna had always marveled at the resiliency of people, especially those aboard the *Enterprise*. Despite the horror of losing two top scientists—three, counting Emil—they were eager to get on with the business of life.

"Hello," said a voice that startled her.

She swiveled on her stool to see Saduk. As before, the lithe Vulcan had sneaked up on her without even trying.

"Hello," she replied, "I'm glad you came."

He took a seat beside her. "We always seem to be meeting following a death."

"In your department," Deanna added. With a shock, she realized that Saduk had a good reason to hate Karn Milu. Milu had passed him up to head the Microcontamination Project in favor of Grastow, merely because the Vulcan had insisted that Lynn Costa was murdered. But Vulcans didn't hate, unless . . .

Unless they were insane.

"Thank you for joining me," she stammered. "I wish it wasn't so soon after another death."

"Another murder," he corrected her.

Guinan arrived with the banana split. "I brought two spoons," she said to Deanna, "because I knew you'd find somebody to help you."

Saduk regarded the heaping concoction with a raised eyebrow. "What is it?" he asked. "It looks unnatural."

"Supernatural," the proprietress grinned. "Enjoy." She bustled off elsewhere.

The Vulcan took a spoon and prodded the confection. "Anything that color, in that amount," he declared, "cannot be healthy."

"It's an Earth dessert," explained Deanna, dipping

into strawberry syrup over a scoop of green pistachio ice cream. "I needed something to cheer me up."

Saduk tried a bite, and not even his most stoic expression could withstand the sugar assault—he grimaced and set down his spoon.

"They use too much of that dreadful spice," he remarked.

"That's why you're so thin," Deanna observed, taking another bite.

"If you are seeking recreation," said Saduk, "I have decided to no longer remain unbonded."

Deanna coughed and spit up a bit of strawberry. She grabbed her napkin, wiped her face, and stared at the Vulcan. "What is that supposed to mean?"

"A change of attitude," answered Saduk, oblivious to any embarrassment he might have caused. "When we talked before, I said I was remaining unattached in order to devote as much time as possible to the Microcontamination Project. The events since then have convinced me that so much self-sacrifice is unhealthy and counterproductive."

Deanna smiled with realization, "Life does seem too short, doesn't it?"

"Another factor in my decision," said Saduk, "is that rewards are not always commensurate with the amount of energy expended."

He wasn't complaining, Deanna felt, just stating a fact. She had certainly felt that way about everything she had done since her initial session with Lynn Costa. Energy and worry she had expended in metric tons to very little effect—she had done nothing to prevent two murders.

"Excuse me," said another male voice, and Deanna looked up from her thoughts to see the warm smile and bearded face of Will Riker. "I'm not interrupting anything, am I?"

"No," answered Saduk, "I was simply explaining my decision to—"

"Nothing urgent," Deanna interjected. "Please sit down, Will."

She ushered him to an empty stool, and he gazed around the somber room. "All of us are feeling our mortality today," Deanna remarked.

"You're right about that," sighed the commander. He turned sympathetically to Saduk. "I'm sorry about Dr. Milu and everything that's happened to your project. If there's anything I can do—maybe assign some extra people—please let me know."

"I suspect the project will be disbanded," replied Saduk.

"No!" cried Deanna with alarm. "That would be terrible."

"When I resign," said the Vulcan, "only Grastow and Shana will remain, and they do not have the experience to manage the project."

"Why are you resigning?" asked Riker with his usual bluntness.

"Personal reasons," answered the Vulcan.

A moment's uneasy silence followed—at least it was uneasy for Riker, who shifted nervously on his stool. "Deanna," he said softly, "I would really like to talk to you privately."

"I can go," replied Saduk. "I am only here because Deanna requested my company."

Riker blinked with surprise at Deanna, who sat up stiffly. "That's right, Will," she admitted. "Dr. Saduk has been helping us with our investigation."

"Then I *am* interrupting you," declared Will, standing and bowing his head to the Vulcan. "Dr. Saduk, if you ever want to discuss reassignment to another branch, please contact me. We don't want *you* to leave the ship too."

"Thank you," nodded the Vulcan. "My plans are as yet unformed."

"Will," Deanna protested, "stay a little bit longer, please. We really weren't discussing anything important."

Riker's embarrassed expression turned to a surprised smile, and he was about to reclaim his seat when his combadge relayed a message: "Data to Commander Riker."

"Riker here," he answered.

"Captain Picard is meeting Ambassador Gretchen Gaelen and the Judge Advocate General in Transporter Room Three. He requests that you meet them in the conference room."

"Acknowledged," said the first officer. "Counselor Troi is with me—is her attendance required?"

"No," the android answered. "The sole purpose of this meeting is to outline the parameters of the trial."

"On my way," Riker replied. He shrugged and smiled apologetically at Deanna. "Now I really do have to leave. One of these days, though, I want to have a long conversation with you."

"One of these days," she nodded ruefully.

"Good-bye," he said to Saduk, then shouldered his way out of the room. While she was watching him leave, Deanna failed to see Saduk rise from his chair.

"Good-bye, Deanna," he said politely. "I must leave as well."

She blinked at him from her reverie. "Thank you for meeting me. I'm sorry you didn't like the sundae."

"I enjoy your company," answered the Vulcan, "but these are not times for conviviality. We shall talk later."

"Good-bye," said Deanna, suddenly feeling very lonely in the room full of people.

* * *

Two older women of diminutive height materialized on the transporter pod. Jean-Luc Picard stepped forward to greet them, hailing the woman he knew first, "Ambassador Gaelen! Judge Advocate General! Welcome aboard the *Enterprise.*"

Gretchen Gaelen stepped down and indicated the unimposing Oriental woman beside her. "Judge Ishe Watanabe, this is Captain Picard."

"An honor," he said, taking her hand.

"A mutual honor," answered the judge with a slight bow. "Our time is very limited."

Jean-Luc motioned to the door. "Come this way."

As they rode the turbolift to the bridge, Ambassador Gaelen tugged on Picard's sleeve and made him bend down to hear her whisper, "I had to pull quite a few strings to get Judge Watanabe on such short notice. Luckily, she was returning from a conference and was in the area." The ambassador winked, "She has a reputation for being efficient."

They emerged onto the bridge and were ushered straight through to the conference room, where Commander Riker, Lieutenant Commander Data, and Lieutenant Worf instantly shot to their feet. Picard performed introductions and offered refreshments, but there was no chit-chat. Everyone took a seat around the conference table, and a businesslike hush fell over the room.

"Thank you for receiving us so promptly," said Judge Watanabe, taking control of the meeting from the start. "We could have conducted our business by communicator, but I felt we needed more confidentiality. Let me tell you my feelings on this matter first, and then we can hear from each of you."

She adjusted her antiquated spectacles and continued, "If I am to try this case, Emil Costa will have a fair trial. Make no mistake about that. I am well aware of Starfleet's desire—and probably your own—to make these proceedings as brief as possible. But they will be as brief, or as long, as they need to be.

"Ambassador Gaelen is concerned about the Kreel's perception of this trial. And so am I."

Worf bristled in his seat and clenched his jaw, but said nothing.

Judge Watanabe went on without taking notice, "However, when I try a case, *I* am in charge. A Kreel official may observe as a friend of the court and may even be able to ask a question, if I deem it appropriate, but I will be the sole magistrate. We can save ourselves a preliminary hearing if both sides agree to the basic facts of the case—that is, time of the murder, murder weapon, site of the crime, etcetera. If all parties agree to these facts at the arraignment, we can go straight to trial."

The woman raised a delicate finger and warned them, "This brings up our biggest problem. If either the prosecution or the defense has a desire to draw out this trial, they can do so easily. We need prosecution and defense attorneys who can grasp the facts quickly and present their cases without engaging in delaying tactics. Can we find two advocates who would be amenable to these conditions?"

Picard sat forward, saying, "Emil Costa has already requested Commander Data to be his counsel. I think I can truthfully say Commander Data will not delay the trial."

Judge Watanabe looked squarely at the android. "Commander Data," she asked, "would you let your desire for a speedy trial compromise your client's case?"

"Never," answered the android. "I am prepared to do a thorough job in whatever time frame is required."

"Very good," nodded the judge.

Worf was fidgeting in his seat, and Picard turned to him, asking, "Lieutenant Worf, do you wish to add something?"

The Klingon sat stiffly in his chair. "I volunteer to be the prosecuting attorney," he said.

Now the security chief had everyone's attention, as he continued with his justification, "I know the facts of the case already, and I would not have to spend time educating an outside prosecutor. My testimony as security chief would be part of the prosecution's case, and I am quite aware of what I want to say. I believe this case is sufficiently simple that I could present it without difficulty."

"Already spoken like a prosecuting attorney," frowned the judge. "No murder case is simple, believe me, Lieutenant. Actually, I have no objections to your serving as prosecutor. I always believe it's best to have attorneys who are familiar with the territory. This is your community," she said, motioning around the room and taking in the whole ship. "It should be settled within it."

The diminutive judge slapped her palms on the table and stood up. "At ten o'clock tomorrow morning," she declared, "report to starbase Meeting Room B for arraignment. The accused must be present."

"We'll arrange sleeping quarters for the participants," Gretchen Gaelen assured them.

"For Emil Costa," added Worf, "make them high security quarters. We will only beam him cell-to-cell."

Riker smiled slyly at Worf, "You're not taking any chances, are you?"

"No, sir," the Klingon said determinedly.

The two women bid the officers of the *Enterprise* good day, and Captain Picard and Commander Riker offered to escort them back to the transporter room.

Whether by accident or design, Worf and Data were left alone with one another.

"Lieutenant," said Data, "I want you to know there is no element of competition in my decision to represent Emil Costa. I simply have an understanding of his predicament."

Worf grumbled, "If you're willing to admit to his guilt, we should have a very agreeable trial."

"I did not say that," Data cautioned. "Emil Costa insists upon his innocence, and so I will present his version of the story as ably as I can. I will also attempt to cast a reasonable doubt upon your version of the story."

Worf's eyes narrowed and his lips pulled back slightly, but he managed to smile. "I intend to see this murderer put away for a long time," he promised. "Are you forgetting what he did to you in the shuttlecraft?"

"Yes," answered Data. "I am forgetting that."

"On the other hand," grinned Worf, "maybe I should let you acquit him. I know what the Kreel do to their prisoners." He marched toward the doorway. "I'll see you in court."

Chapter Thirteen

WESLEY CRUSHER GROANED, rose from his desk, and stretched his arms over his head. He was weary from spending the last several hours recording every detail of his surveillance of Emil Costa. Mainly, he was bored from having no one to talk to except the computer. What had started out to be so exciting had turned into danger, drudge work, and forced confinement. It might be a while before he accepted another undercover job again.

A chime sounded, and Wesley turned eagerly to the door. "Who's there?"

"Wesley, it's me, Deanna," came the reply from the other side of the hatch.

"I'm not supposed to talk to anyone," the teenager sighed. Then he brightened, "But that doesn't include you."

"I just came by to see if you're all right," she replied. "We can talk about that, can't we?"

"Sure," Wesley agreed eagerly. "Come in, Deanna."

Deanna Troi entered the young man's room and caught him tossing an errant sock behind his bed. He pointed excitedly to his computer screen. "I'm trying to get it all down, everything that happened up to the murder. At least, everything *I* saw or heard."

"That's wise," Deanna replied with a comforting smile. "Have you talked to your mother yet?"

"Just briefly," frowned the teenager. "She's annoyed at me for keeping this assignment a secret from her. But that's what Worf told me to do."

"You did the correct thing," Deanna replied. "You're a full ensign now, and your mother will have to accept the fact that you may have assignments that are . . . unpleasant. Worf and I appreciate what you've done, even if we were too late to help Dr. Milu."

"Yeah," agreed Wes glumly. "It still doesn't seem like it really happened. At the time I saw them arguing, Dr. Milu acted like he was in charge. Emil was the one who was scared." The boy shook his head and added, "Of course, Emil was the one with the phaser."

"Do you feel comfortable now?" asked the Betazoid, choosing her words carefully. "Now that Emil Costa is incarcerated and awaiting trial, does everything seem as it should to you?"

"No," answered Wesley, blurting out the truth. "I'm still scared and still don't know what's going on."

"Me too," said Deanna sympathetically. "I think it's residual anxiety. All of us have been slightly traumatized by these events."

The teenager nodded, admitting, "It'll be a long time before I go near one of those pods."

The door chimed again, startling them both. A voice boomed, "This is Lieutenant Worf. May I enter?"

"Come in," called Wesley.

The security officer entered and appeared mildly

surprised to see Counselor Troi. But his face soon returned to a portrait of grim determination, as he tugged on his sash and announced, "The arraignment is set for ten o'clock tomorrow morning at the starbase. Ensign Crusher, your presence may or may not be required, but I would prefer that you beam over there with me tonight. Emil Costa is also beaming directly to a cell on the asteroid."

Worf added solemnly, "I am acting as prosecuting attorney in this matter."

"Excellent!" exclaimed Wesley. "That should expedite matters."

"Yes," Worf replied, "except that Data is acting as defense attorney."

"Wow," said Wesley with somber realization. "He's going to cross-examine me."

The Klingon grumbled, "It was your suggestion, Ensign." His anger softened, and he granted himself a smile. "I've just reviewed the deposition you gave to Counselor Troi a few minutes after the murder. Our case is stronger than I thought. We'll play your deposition for the court, then you will have to answer a few questions. I wouldn't be too nervous. Pack enough uniforms for a few days. I'll return in an hour."

"I should be leaving too," announced Deanna. She gave Wesley an encouraging smile and followed the lieutenant out.

"I'm confident," said Worf, striding briskly down the corridor, while Deanna hurried to keep up. "Crusher's testimony clearly establishes that Emil Costa had a phaser weapon when he went to meet Karn Milu. He had both motive and opportunity. In fact, we have our choice of motives: greed, extortion, and revenge. This is more than a disagreement between two conspirators—Emil Costa also believed that Karn Milu had killed his wife! I have another witness who will testify that Karn Milu *threatened* to kill Lynn Costa."

Deanna blinked in surprise. "Is there anything else I can do to help?"

Worf stopped and bowed his head gratefully to the Betazoid. "Counselor Troi," he intoned, "you've been a valuable asset to this investigation and I hesitate to burden you, but somebody needs to go through Karn Milu's personal files and records. If I have any time to spare, I will assist you."

"Think nothing of it," smiled Deanna. "Betazoids sometimes use arcane methods to keep notes. Let me check out his files and papers."

"Dr. Baylak is now acting head of the science branch," said Worf. "If you need help, see him. In all likelihood, I will be occupied in court, and you may not be able to communicate with me. But Captain Picard will remain on the *Enterprise,* should you discover anything noteworthy."

The Klingon's confidence gave way to puzzlement. "I cannot understand why Emil Costa won't confess and save himself needless anguish? He would certainly qualify for psychiatric care instead of punishment. The only thing our case lacks is an eyewitness."

Deanna's brow looked as troubled as Worf's, and she asked hesitantly, "Is there any way it could be somebody else?"

Worf stared at her as if she had said the unthinkable. "Counselor," he warned, "what we need is support for the case we have, not new theories."

"Understood," said the Betazoid, feeling foolish, "I'll report later."

Worf nodded curtly and marched off to the turbolift. The new prosecutor felt almost light-headed from all the details swirling around in his massive cranium. Legal procedures in the Federation were still modeled after ancient Earth standards, but they had been vastly simplified since the time when arcane language confused normal people and made lawyers rich. In the Federation, law was more in the common sense vein of Solomon, so that people from radically different cultures could grasp it. Yet, there were still many decisions and considerations, and they kept tumbling through Worf's mind, fighting for his attention.

The case against Emil Costa was self-evident, he told himself. All he had to do was present it coherently. True, Data was formidable, but the android was also scrupulously honest and would never resort to tactics that weren't fair. He would do exactly what he promised—argue his case and cast doubt on the prosecution's. So at least Worf didn't have to worry about being tricked by a smooth-tongued orator. Justice would be served, and Emil Costa would be punished.

Thinking about the once-revered scientist brought a surprising twinge of pity, which the Klingon fought down. He was a murderer, plain and simple, and there could be no mitigating factors.

"O'Brien to Worf," came the transporter chief's voice.

The Klingon tapped his combadge and answered, "Worf here."

"We've received the coordinates for the containment cell on Kayran Rock," explained O'Brien, "and starbase security says they're ready. We can beam Dr. Costa over whenever you say."

"Stand by for my command," said Worf. "I'm going to his cell now. Out."

He swiveled abruptly on his heel and marched back toward the turbolift. When he arrived at the containment unit, he saw Data seated by the old man's door, talking to him through the invisible forcefield. Emil was a pathetic sight, and once again Worf suppressed a feeling of sympathy.

Upon seeing the security chief, they stopped their discussion and rose uncomfortably from their chairs.

"Hello, Lieutenant," said Data.

"Hello, Commander Data," the Klingon replied. He turned to Emil. "Dr. Costa, we are ready to transport you to a cell on the starbase. I have requested some clothes for you as well as a medical examination."

"Oh," groaned the scientist warily, "I hate transporting. Isn't there some other way?"

Worf scowled, "You had your chance to go by shuttle. Prepare to beam." He tapped his badge. "Worf to O'Brien. Prepare to beam Dr. Costa to the starbase."

"Acknowledged," said O'Brien.

"Wait!" Emil shrieked. He turned plaintively to Data. "Please, I'm scared . . . Data, will you come with me?"

The idea of an old man begging the android to keep him company in a transporter beam was absurd yet oddly touching, thought Worf in spite of himself. Data turned to him and asked, "May I?"

The Klingon shrugged, "Go ahead." Had it been anyone else, he probably would have refused, but no one was likely to overpower Data, especially a crushed old man.

"O'Brien," said Worf, "lock on to Commander Data as well and beam them both to the containment cell. They can continue their conversation there."

"Locking on to Commander Data," the technician replied.

"Thank you," Emil said sincerely.

"Thank you," added Data.

Worf growled, "Energize."

The accused and his lawyer dematerialized, and all the cells in the containment unit were again empty—that was how Worf liked it. He stepped out into the corridor, and the doors jarred shut behind him.

After wondering whether she should give sleep another chance, Deanna Troi decided that relaxation wasn't in the immediate offing. Better start on Karn Milu's records, she told herself. She took the turbolift to deck 5 and emerged on the main science deck where most of the labs and offices were located. Normally, deck 5 was bustling with activity, but this shift seemed deserted. Of course, the counselor told herself, when the head of the entire branch is murdered and the most famous scientist on board is held for that murder, the rank and file may not feel much like working.

She remembered quite well having been to Karn Milu's office just before Saduk showed them where Lynn Costa had died. That seemed so long ago, but it had only been a few dozen hours. That first death—then so shocking and unexpected—had now paled beside the brutal murder of Karn Milu and the fateful shuttlecraft trip. Events had compounded upon events, offering clarification and a firm suspect—but no satisfaction. Deanna Troi did not feel relief.

She rounded the corridor leading to Karn Milu's office and bumped headlong into a figure hurrying in the opposite direction. Shana Russel recoiled from her in shock.

"I just heard!" the young woman gasped. "I was working in the cleanrooms, and the intercom in my helmet must not have been working. This is horrible! How can he be dead?"

"Calm yourself," Deanna suggested. "This has been

a shock to all of us. Did you think by going to Karn Milu's office you would find him?"

"I don't know what I thought!" Shana wailed with confusion. "This makes it all worse. *What is happening to us?*"

Deanna put her arm around the girl's shoulder and comforted her. "You must be brave," she advised. "Emil Costa is standing trial for Dr. Milu's murder, and you will probably be called to testify, as will I."

"But I don't know anything," protested Shana. "What will I tell them?"

"You must speak to Lieutenant Worf about that."

The young blond woman slumped against the wall. "This is not quite how I imagined it would be," she muttered. "The Costas, the *Enterprise*—I thought I was the luckiest kid in my class. And I learned so much in this last six months, I hoped it could go on forever. But now it's over before it began."

Deanna smiled sympathetically, "You're still aboard the *Enterprise,* and you obviously have work to do. Don't be discouraged. These incidents are an aberration, believe me."

"I do," the girl smiled bravely. "Counselor Troi, would you like to go to Ten-Forward with me?"

"No," answered Deanna. "I've just come from there, and it's quite lively—I'm sure you will find people to talk with. If you missed Captain Picard's announcement, he also informed us that we'll be taking shore leave on Kayran Rock. You may want to get to a computer screen and put in a request."

"I will!" exclaimed Shana, brightening considerably. "Thank you for being so understanding."

"It's my job," Deanna smiled.

The young woman started down the corridor but stopped and turned. "Tell Lieutenant Worf I would be happy to discuss my testimony with him any time."

"I will," Deanna promised.

Now the Betazoid wound her way down a corridor that was totally deserted. She wondered if Karn Milu's door would be locked. If it was, she had only to contact Worf, and he could issue a security override. That wasn't her problem; the problem was the volume of data he would have. Betazoids were inveterate record keepers, and they enjoyed the more arcane aspects of the practice. They seldom kept records only one way.

As chief administrator of the science branch, Dr. Milu's daily proclamations were a matter of record. But how did he arrive at his decisions? When he chose Grastow over Saduk to head the depleted Microcontamination Project, for example, did he keep any log of his thought process? She doubted if he had told anyone the real reason for overlooking Saduk. Personnel assignments were a large part of Karn Milu's job, and Deanna wondered if he operated by intuition, documented reasoning, or a patronage system.

She had admired the man inordinately, and she hoped she wouldn't find more evidence of wrongdoing to tarnish his reputation. She was afraid she would, though. Whatever she rooted out, Deanna told herself, would help Worf find the truth—and that's all that mattered. Karn Milu's privacy couldn't concern him now.

His door whooshed open at her approach, meaning it had been left unlocked, or set to open automatically for anyone who approached. Deanna entered the office and again marveled at the cases of exotic insects, all pinned, labeled, and preserved. Her eyes were drawn to the massive amber desk where a multitude of grubs twisted in eternal suspension. She stopped abruptly.

His computer screen was on.

Of course, thought Deanna, he may have gone off and left it that way. But Karn Milu didn't seem to be the careless type. Would he go off to a secretive meeting and leave his screen on and his door unlocked? Had somebody else been in here in the last six or seven hours?

That was ridiculous, Deanna scolded herself. She should do exactly as Worf had admonished her: Forget half-baked suspicions and get on with the business at hand.

The computer was already opened to Karn Milu's file area, and Deanna worked long into the night. She read as many representative files as she could and listened to his official logs. Still, she didn't find the morass of material she expected. The administrator's private files on the people under his direction were relatively complete but oddly dry and impersonal. His records for the entomology section he also headed were just as maddeningly succinct. Nowhere was the opinionated flair of the man himself.

Even his collection of memos and reports was mostly restricted to official business. Where was a happy birthday message? The odd copy of a favorite poem? A quick to-do list? Where was the person behind these sterile computer records?

This data was strictly for public consumption, the Betazoid decided, pushing herself away from the immense desk. She stood and glanced about the room. Not that she expected to find a sheaf of yellowing papers lying on the floor, but she knew her countrymen could be very surreptitious about their private affairs. Perhaps the ability to communicate telepathically made them somewhat paranoid about keeping information confidential. At any rate, it was not uncommon for a Betazoid to keep a secret diary or notebook.

Unfortunately, it wasn't an easy office in which to search for something odd or out of place, because the walls were literally crawling with bugs. Deanna found herself distracted at every instant by a Regulan mantis or an Andorian silkworm. She was startled when the door suddenly opened automatically.

Deanna caught her breath and turned to greet the new visitor, but no one came in. No one was standing in the doorway. Hesitantly, she moved toward the open door and called, "Is somebody there?"

In response came rapid footsteps. By the time she reached the corridor, whoever had tripped the automatic door was gone. She could run after him, but the corridor broke into a maze of offices beyond the next bulkhead, and she hadn't gotten even a glimpse of the caller. How could she identify him?

The only plausible explanation, thought Deanna, was that he had come expecting Karn Milu's office to be empty and was surprised to find her inside. This did not bode well. Counting herself and Shana Russel, the unseen caller was the third visitor to Karn Milu's office that night.

She touched her insignia. "Counselor Troi to Lieutenant Worf."

"Worf here," answered the Klingon, trying to keep the sleep out of his voice.

"Sorry to interrupt you," she said, "but I'm in Karn Milu's office, and I feel we ought to seal it off. I think people have been coming in and out of here."

"Right away," responded Worf. "I'm on the asteroid, so would you remain there until the security team arrives?"

"Yes," breathed Deanna, feeling uncomfortable for the first time since entering Milu's chamber. "Out."

Now the room and the corridor were both exceptionally quiet. Deanna crossed her arms and began to pace. She didn't know why, but she felt safer leaving the door to the office open and pacing outside in the corridor. That way, she could see who was coming and wouldn't be taken by surprise again.

She was acting like *she* was on guard duty, Deanna thought angrily. What was she so scared about? If she had any sense, she would be using this time to read more files or look for Karn Milu's hidden notes. If the only records he had were the ones she had seen, he wasn't going to be much help in convicting his own murderer. Worf hadn't said it, but she knew he was concerned about having his whole case dependent upon one witness. Wesley Crusher was a credible young man, but if Data placed one single aspect of his story in doubt, his entire testimony might be discounted. She had to keep looking for corroboration and forget her groundless anxieties.

Yet there it was again. The feeling that somebody was waiting out there, just out of sight, waiting to get into Karn Milu's office. Deanna Troi was accustomed to being the observer, and it was very unsettling to know somebody was observing *her*. She heard a noise and stopped her nervous pacing. Listening carefully, she thought she heard footsteps coming toward her, and instinctively she retreated into the office.

The footsteps continued coming, and she knew she wouldn't see their owner until he rounded the corner and was almost upon her. One thing was certain, thought Deanna with alarm, it was only one person— not the security team promised by Worf. She backed away from the door as the footsteps sounded loudly and then seemed to stop—just before the bulkhead. What was he waiting for? she wanted to scream. Was he planning his next move?

A hulking figure rounded the corner, and Deanna gasped. Then the relief poured out of her as she rushed to meet the bearded first officer.

Riker gasped at the hug she gave him. "Well, hello," he grinned, not anxious to let her go. "To what do I owe this warm welcome?"

"Childish fear," she replied, squirming out of his grip. "I've been here by myself, going through Karn Milu's computer records, and I think I must be getting jumpy."

"Worf told me you had some intruders," said Riker, casting a concerned glance around the area. "The security team will be here any second, but I was close by."

"Thank you, Will," she smiled warmly, glad she had his protection and knowing she usually took it for granted.

"While we're alone," whispered Riker, "I've put in for shore leave and I wanted to coordinate it with you. I've been thinking about what you said before this whole thing started, about two people needing to spend time alone together. Why don't we try it?"

"That's sweet of you," she smiled, touching his arm. "I don't know how long I'll be tied up here, or when they'll need me to testify. But if any opportunity . . ."

A contingent of four security men noisily rounded the corner. They snapped to attention upon seeing Commander Riker. "Security team reporting for duty," said their leader.

"Right on time," Will replied curtly. He bowed to Deanna. "About that other matter, please keep it under consideration."

"I will, Commander," she promised.

Chapter Fourteen

FOR ITS FIRST OFFICIAL USE, a meeting room on Kayran Rock had been hastily converted into a courtroom. They must have had the replicators working overtime, thought Worf, to come up with the handsome wooden bench and old-fashioned high-backed chairs. The witness stand even had a waist-high enclosure around it, complete with gate. The only hint of modernity in the room were the forcefield rods surrounding the chair where the accused would be sitting. Once activated, Emil Costa would be securely confined, yet able to converse with his counsel and see and hear everything that transpired. He would also be protected in the unlikely event of attack from someone in the courtroom.

No one was in the room at the moment but Worf, who was always early and earlier than usual this morning. He had only himself to look after, starbase security now being responsible for Emil Costa. The novice prosecutor sat at the table opposite the one with the forcefield and turned on his tricorder. There were more efficient instruments for storing notes than a tricorder, but Worf felt comfortable with the familiar hand-held device. Earlier this morning, he had uploaded Dr. Crusher's autopsy report, a transcript of Ensign Crusher's deposition, and other pertinent information into both the tricorder and the starbase computer. Then he had made sure Karn Milu's corpse and Emil Costa's phaser had been beamed to base security. With all this, Worf wasn't entirely pleased with his preparations, although he couldn't think of anything he had failed to do.

One by one, others entered the courtroom as the hour approached ten. First there were clerks, who busied themselves making sure the recording system was working and that all the participants had water to drink. One of them placed a gavel on the bench. Then security officers entered the room and checked the forcefield. These workers acknowledged Worf's presence but were careful not to interrupt his somber contemplation. He felt oddly removed, like the star of a play whom the stagehands had been ordered not to disturb. He almost wished he could change places with them.

Then Data arrived. The android, of course, needed no tricorder, carrying the equivalent of several hundred of them in his head. "Good day, Counselor," he said to Worf.

The Klingon smiled in spite of himself. "We really could make this a lot shorter," he suggested, "if Dr. Costa would confess."

"That is true," acknowledged Data. "However, Dr. Costa maintains his innocence."

"Unfortunately," shrugged Worf.

The accused himself arrived next, accompanied by security officers on each arm. Emil Costa's appearance was considerably improved over the last time Worf had seen him, thanks to a new suit of civilian clothes and attention to his cuts and bruises. He sat erect in his chair, his close-cropped white hair bristling as he smiled confidently. Quite insane, Worf thought to himself; he definitely needed the care he was going to get when this was all over.

Then two Kreel spectators swaggered into the room. Immediately, Worf looked away from them—not simply because they were repulsive but because he assumed they would be staring at him. They were certainly not accustomed to seeing a Klingon wielding authority.

"All rise," intoned one of the clerks, "for Judge Advocate General Watanabe and friend of the court, Admiral Ulree."

They rose to watch a diminutive Oriental woman enter the courtroom, followed shortly by a grizzled hairy Kreel. Worf would have liked to avoid looking at Admiral Ulree, but he had no choice because the Kreel was staring directly at him.

"What is *this* doing here?" he bellowed, pointing toward the Klingon. "I was told these were to be *civilized* proceedings!"

Judge Watanabe was small, but she looked as if she was going to throttle the gangly humanoid. "That will be quite enough of that," she countered. "Lieutenant Worf is the security chief of the *Enterprise* and a logical choice to prosecute this case."

Ulree puffed his chest out and rocked on his spindly legs. "This trial will be a mockery with *him* trying it!"

Worf was grinding his teeth furiously, but he said nothing. Any outburst, he knew, would jeopardize his standing with the court. He did, however, glare at the rude admiral.

"I will not take part in this sham!" Ulree declared.

"You certainly will not!" agreed Judge Watanabe. "You are banned from this trial."

The Kreel blinked at her in utter surprise. "You can't do that," he mumbled.

"I most certainly can," she insisted. "We agreed to a Kreel observer, but not to you exclusively. You will be replaced by a Kreel who has some inkling of propriety and decorum."

Ulree snarled, "Someone who can stomach Klingons?"

"At the very least," answered Judge Watanabe with finality. "You are dismissed. In fact, you are banned from the starbase until these proceedings are over." For emphasis, she motioned to the security guards to take action.

Now Worf didn't want to look away—he was enjoying it too much. The admiral huffed and puffed a bit more, then he swaggered toward the door, announcing, "I appoint my assistant, Kwalrak, to take my place."

Looking confused, one of the Kreel spectators rose to her spindly legs. "Me?" she asked.

Judge Watanabe looked toward Data and Worf. "Does either of you have any objection?"

"No," they answered in unison. As soon as Admiral Ulree had made his exit, Judge Watanabe seated herself behind the impressive bench, and Kwalrak was directed toward a chair at the side of the bench. Worf almost felt sorry for the female Kreel, because she looked as if she had just been stunned by a phaser.

"I will do the best I can," Kwalrak promised Judge Watanabe.

"As a friend of the court," said the magistrate, "you may observe and offer suggestions on Kreel opinion in this case, but I am the sole judge. You may also ask a question of a witness, if I deem it appropriate."

Watanabe settled into her seat and banged her gavel once. "This court is now in session. Today we are hearing the arraignment of Dr. Emil Costa on the charge of murdering Dr. Karn Milu. Both the accused and the deceased are Federation subjects, and the alleged crime took place on the starship *Enterprise,* a Federation vessel. Therefore, our judgment will be binding in all Federation territories and in all worlds where the Federation has treaty obligations, including this one."

The judge centered her spectacles on the bridge of her nose. "Murder is a very serious crime," she said. "In some societies, it is a capital crime, punishable by death. In our society, however, the emphasis is on rehabilitation and understanding. I say this at the outset, because I wish everyone present to know that the primary purpose of this court is to determine guilt or innocence, not punishment. Should the accused be found guilty, he will be remanded to Starfleet for psychological and physical evaluation. Sentencing will be determined by a separate panel."

"Excuse me," said Kwalrak hesitantly, "what if we, the Kreel, wish to try the accused on separate charges?"

"You will petition Starfleet for extradition," the judge answered. "The terms are covered in our treaty."

Kwalrak nodded, looking momentarily satisfied.

"As to the charges at hand," continued Judge Watanabe, "I have reviewed the material furnished by Lieutenant Worf, and there seems little doubt that Karn Milu was killed by a phaser discharged at close range. Commander Data, do you wish to refute that finding?"

"No, Your Honor," answered the android. "We do not refute that finding."

"Stardate 44263.9 is given as the approximate time of death. Do you refute that finding?"

"No, Your Honor."

"Do you refute the place of death as the starship *Enterprise,* deck 31, in the class-one-hundred cleanroom operated by the Microcontamination Project?"

"No, Your Honor."

Judge Watanabe nodded and turned to Worf. "Lieutenant Worf, do you wish to make a formal charge?"

"I do, Your Honor," answered the somber Klingon. "I charge Emil Costa with the murder of Karn Milu."

"Are you prepared to try him now?"

"I am."

Judge Watanabe nodded and turned to Data, but her eyes drifted to the drawn face of Emil Costa. "How do you plead?"

"Innocent," replied Data. He glanced at his client and gave him a slight but comforting smile.

"Are you prepared for trial?"

"Yes, Your Honor."

The judge banged her gavel with authority. "Let the record show," she announced, "that Emil Costa has pleaded innocent to the murder of Karn Milu and will be bound over for immediate trial. The court will reconvene in one hour to hear opening arguments."

The diminutive jurist stood, and all eyes followed her out of the courtroom.

Deanna Troi rubbed her throbbing temples, almost wishing the computer had never been invented. She focused momentarily on the grubs frozen in Karn Milu's desk—at least they weren't crawling across the screen like the army of information she was trying to absorb. Between the Costas' records, Karn Milu's records, and all the interrelated cross-collaterized reports from all the scientific departments that came in contact with them, she had probably read more files in the last three days than in the last three years. Nevertheless, she had seen nothing to corroborate Wesley Crusher's story.

Deanna was well aware that Betazoids could be secretive, but she had never known one to be so obtuse. These seemed to be the files of an unimaginative second-class clerk, not the Federation's most esteemed entomologist. She was about to concede the fact that Worf and Wesley were on their own in attempting to convict Emil Costa, when a security officer poked his head in the door of Karn Milu's office.

"Commander La Forge wishes to enter," he announced.

"Please," she responded, "let him enter."

Deanna rose from the amber desk to meet the chief engineer. "Geordi," she sighed, "thank you for coming."

"Think nothing of it, Counselor," he grinned with his usual good cheer. "To tell you the truth, I don't have much to do at the moment. I've been working on an experiment to speed up the turbolifts during an alert, but following an asteroid around doesn't keep Engineering very busy."

"I imagine not," she smiled. "Still, I won't keep you long, and your help will be greatly appreciated."

"What can I do?" asked Geordi.

The Betazoid motioned around the elegant office with its horde of motionless insects. "I have reason to believe," she explained, "that something is hidden in this office, some storage medium. I've looked everywhere—and so have those security officers outside—but we can't find anything. I thought, with your special kind of vision . . ."

"Say no more," said Geordi, taking a leisurely stroll around the colorful but cluttered office. With his

VISOR apparatus functioning as his eyes, La Forge scrutinized a case of orange and blue beetles. "Sorry about what happened to Dr. Milu," he said softly. "You must feel his loss more deeply than the rest of us."

"We weren't that close," Deanna admitted, remembering how inferior she always felt in the presence of the full-blooded Betazoid.

Geordi moved to another case, shaking his head. "Talk about sensory overload," he winced. "Do these things look as frightening to you as they do to me?"

"Yes," she admitted.

He turned and walked slowly toward the opposite wall. "Dead bugs don't give off electromagnetic impulses, do they?"

"Not that I know of."

He stopped before a dark wooden case that contained a dozen phosphorescent centipedes and carefully pried it open. As Deanna moved closer, Geordi's fingers reached hesitantly toward one particularly large and ugly specimen. "If you'd rather do this," he gulped, "just let me know."

"You're doing fine," Deanna replied evenly.

Geordi wasn't careful enough, and the exotic insect crumbled to dust beneath his fingers. But underneath it, mounted to the board, was an isolinear optical chip.

"Bingo!" he crowed, plucking the chip from its mounting.

The counselor finally let out a breath. "Thank you, Geordi!" she enthused. "Let's see what's on it."

Within seconds, Geordi had plugged the chip into a slot on Karn Milu's console, and Deanna was trying to access it from his keyboard. Their excited expressions turned to alarm as gibberish scrolled across the screen.

"I'm sorry," said the chief engineer glumly. "Something must have damaged the contents."

"No," murmured the Betazoid with dawning realization. She slumped back in her chair, looking even more crestfallen than Geordi. "I've heard of this, but I've never seen it. It's a subliminal code."

"Code?" shrugged Geordi. "Let's have the computer analyze it."

"You don't understand," muttered the Betazoid. "This isn't just code based on some mathematical or relational equation. It's distinctly Betazoid, and it depends upon subliminal thought patterns. Karn Milu himself did not know the code when he wrote it."

"Come again?" asked Geordi.

Deanna shook her head forlornly. "I don't know exactly how it works," she sighed, "but it's like making a coded imprint of the contents of your subconscious. He wrote it while in a trance, knowing, though it looked like gibberish to him as well, he could read it in the future if he concentrated."

"Hmmm," said the human, "I think I know what you mean. On ancient Earth, people from certain religions used to speak in tongues and write in unknown languages. But they had no way to interpret what they had done."

"They weren't Betazoids," replied Deanna. "They only had half the key."

Head bowed, the chief engineer paced. He stopped and snapped his fingers. "I bet Data could . . ." He caught himself. "Data is occupied at the moment, isn't he?"

"It doesn't matter," muttered Deanna, turning off the computer screen. "Only the person who writes it can read it. There is no code more effective."

"Can you go into that kind of trance?" asked Geordi.

She shook her head again and managed a tight-lipped smile. "I'm not even full Betazoid."

Geordi put a comforting hand on Deanna's shoulder. "Give it a try," he suggested. "You don't know what you can do until you try."

"Of course, I'll try," the counselor promised with a determined jut of her chin. She pulled the isolinear chip from its slot and gripped it in her delicate fist. "Something has been hidden from us all the time—I feel it. Perhaps this is it."

"Call me if you need any help," offered Geordi.

The Betazoid yawned so quickly she could barely cover her mouth in time. "Unless I get some sleep," she blinked, "I won't be able to decipher my own name. Thank you, Geordi. I will probably call you again in a few hours."

Worf saw no reason to be verbose in his opening statement to the court. He rose to his considerable height and looked Judge Watanabe in the eyes; she stared back intently.

"No one disputes the fact," he began, "that Karn Milu was brutally murdered aboard the *Enterprise* by a phaser weapon set to full. As our witnesses will testify, the slaying occurred seconds after a severe altercation between Karn Milu and the accused, Emil Costa. A witness will testify that Emil Costa went to see Karn Milu *armed with a phaser,* which he used later to try to hijack a shuttlecraft. Plus, Emil Costa had ample motive: Not only did he think Karn Milu had killed his wife, he was under severe pressure to reveal a secret discovery to him. Against Starfleet regulations, the Costas together with Karn Milu were plotting to sell a discovery made aboard the *Enterprise* to non-Federation parties."

Worf flexed his big shoulders and folded his arms, making it perfectly clear what he thought about such activities. "After reviewing the evidence and testimony," he rumbled, "I believe you will find Emil Costa guilty of the murder of Karn Milu."

Worf sat down, and Judge Watanabe thanked him. All eyes in the courtroom turned to Commander Data, sitting erectly in his chair with his typical alertness. The android nodded and rose fluidly to his feet.

"Your Honor," he said with a slight bow, "Emil Costa professes his innocence to the charge of murder. Yes, he did have reason to argue with Karn Milu, but an argument does not make a murder. The truth is that anyone on the *Enterprise* in possession of a phaser could have killed Karn Milu. I am not saying that Emil Costa should be exempt from suspicion, but there is not a preponderance of evidence. The prosecution's entire case consists of one overheard conversation. There is no witness to the murder of Karn Milu, and no one saw Emil Costa threaten his superior with the phaser he was carrying.

"My client admits to lapses of judgment," Data told the hushed courtroom, "for which he has suffered . . . greatly. But you will have to decide whether one overheard conversation warrants a murder conviction."

Wesley Crusher paced what must have been the most elegant guest quarters within the starbase, a suite suitable for visiting dignitaries. He cared little about the sumptuous furnishings but was thankful for the tunnel-like port which gave him at least a partial view of the stars. At one point, he thought he had glimpsed the *Enterprise*. Then again, maybe the blip in the black sky had been a Kreel vessel. It didn't matter, because nothing in the sky or the starbase's library could divert his attention from the testimony he was about to deliver.

Worf had told him to be ready any time today, and he was. In fact, he was weary of recounting the events to himself in a sort of demented rehearsal. But he couldn't help himself—he was nervous! When he accepted this assignment, it hadn't dawned on him that he might become the star witness in a major trial. He was proud of his stint as an investigator, but he wondered if maybe he hadn't done his job a little too well.

Then he thought about Dr. Milu and wondered if he should have done better. But given Emil's apparent mental condition, how could Wes have prevented Dr. Milu's death? At least, because of his alert work, they knew the reasons for both of the killings, and the events leading up to them. Dammit, Wes cursed under his breath, it would all be so much easier if only Emil Costa acted like a murderer.

The chime of the door made him jump. "Enter," said Wes, knowing it had to be security.

It was a new one, a young woman who was sort of cute. But she was all business as she motioned him out. "Step lively, Ensign," she ordered. "Your testimony is required."

Wesley stepped bravely into the corridor and received a jolt of déjà vu—Grastow was looming in the hallway only a meter away. Involuntarily, Wesley started. But a moment later, he saw the security officers on either side of the big Antarean.

"I'm just a witness," Grastow shrugged. "I mean

you no harm, Ensign Crusher, please believe that. Although I'm not ashamed of my actions, your anger with me is quite justified."

"Anger?" spat Wesley. "I think you're crazy!"

The hulking baby-faced humanoid nodded sadly, "Perhaps I am."

"Move on," said the female officer, steering Wesley away. Her fellow officers flattened Grastow against the wall as they passed.

Getting more confident every moment, Worf watched the complete video playback of Wesley Crusher's account of his eventful visit to deck 31, as related to Deanna Troi. He had thought about calling Deanna too, but the young ensign's testimony stood on its own. Counselor Troi skillfully kept him talking, asking only for clarifying statements. She never led him to conclusions, which he had plenty to make on his own. It was a terrible indictment, rife with violence and treachery. Murder seemed an almost logical conclusion, thought the Klingon.

When the deposition was over, Worf turned to the young ensign in the witness chair. "Now that you and the court have seen this statement, do you wish to change anything?" he asked.

"No, sir," answered Wes. "I might add a few things."

"Such as?"

"Well," said the teenager, "I haven't really expressed how scared Emil Costa was—both before his wife's funeral and after, when he was hiding in Dr. Grastow's quarters. When he grabbed that phaser out of his drawer, I really had the feeling it was for protection."

Worf stared at the boy for a moment, then turned

away. "Are you telling the court," he asked thoughtfully, "that Emil Costa was expecting violence?"

Data interjected, "Objection. That is asking the witness to conclude what another person was thinking."

"Objection sustained," Judge Watanabe nodded. She turned to Wesley. "Please don't answer that question."

"Yes, Your Honor," gulped the youth.

Worf strode back to his table and leaned on the heavy piece of furniture. "Would you describe Emil Costa's behavior as agitated during his meeting with Karn Milu?"

"Yes."

"And you are certain you heard Emil Costa accuse Karn Milu of killing his wife?"

The teenager nodded emphatically, "He said that, yes. But Dr. Milu insisted her death was an accident. All he wanted to talk about was the submicrobe they had found."

Worf rose to his full height again. "Would you say the men were threatening one another?"

"Yes," answered Wesley. "It wasn't a pleasant conversation."

Worf nodded sagely, asking, "Later, when you were rescued from the pod and saw Karn Milu's body in the outer laboratory, what were your initial thoughts?"

Wesley tried not to look at Emil Costa. "I thought Dr. Costa had killed him," he whispered.

"Could you please repeat that answer a little louder?" asked Worf.

"I thought Dr. Costa had killed him!" Wes said too loudly, shrinking into the big wooden chair.

Worf nodded triumphantly and turned to the judge. "I have no more questions at this time," he declared. "May I reserve the right to recall this witness later?"

"You may," Judge Watanabe nodded, glancing at First Assistant Kwalrak. The Kreel apparently didn't wish to interject. "The bench may have some questions at a later time. Commander Data, you may cross-examine the witness."

Data stood and walked swiftly to the witness stand. "Good day, Ensign Crusher," he said simply enough. Wesley relaxed slightly and gave Data a smile, which he ignored. "For clarification, when you last saw Karn Milu and Emil Costa together, they were working cooperatively to confine you in a pod? Is that correct?"

Wesley shifted nervously. "That's correct," he said.

"They were not arguing?" Data continued.

"No," answered Wes.

"In fact," concluded Data, "they were acting together against a common threat—you. Wasn't the argument over by this time?"

"Yes," admitted Wesley, "but they could have started back up again."

"Why would they?" asked Data. "According to your testimony, Emil Costa was about to get his fondest desire—he was about to leave the ship. In a few minutes, he would be rid of Karn Milu forever. His wife's destruction of the computer records made their secret absolutely safe. Why would he jeopardize all this to kill Karn Milu?"

Wesley's mouth hung open, but he couldn't talk. He just shook his head and slumped back in his chair.

Worf bolted to his feet. "I object," he growled. "That is asking the witness to conclude what another person was thinking!"

"Overruled," said the judge. "Ensign Crusher's interpretation of these events is all we have." She turned to the nervous young man. "Have you an answer to the question?"

"I think I do," Wesley answered. "Emil also had the idea it was Karn Milu who killed his wife."

"However," countered Data, "isn't it true that Karn Milu insisted to Emil Costa, as he had insisted to everyone, that Lynn Costa's death was an accident?"

"Yes."

"Can you say Emil Costa was positively convinced his wife was murdered?"

"No," muttered the teenager. "Like all of us, he wasn't sure what exactly happened to her."

Data stood rooted to his spot in front of the witness stand, his golden eyes never leaving the young ensign. "Ensign Crusher," he said softly, "Emil Costa has been your tutor and friend, and a friend to your mother, for almost three years. Is that not true?"

"It's true," Wes answered with pride.

"Do you think he is capable of murdering someone?"

Again, Wesley's mouth opened but no words came out. He looked with embarrassment at the judge, then Worf, before shaking his head. "No," he rasped, "I can't believe he did it."

Worf's erect posture buckled just a little.

In the sanctity of her darkened room, Deanna Troi drifted in and out of sleep. Her dreams were filled with the spirit of Karn Milu. His image, his face, his voice, his thoughts, and his coded writings fought for her subconscious. The code appeared to her like love letters, heartfelt attempts to communicate his secrets. Of course, they were love letters to himself, and she told herself she shouldn't read them. But she knew he wanted her to read them.

She pulled herself awake from the troubling dream, realizing there was no escape in that direction. There was nothing to do but get over the weariness and the fear of failure and decipher those letters. She slid out of bed and splashed some water on her face.

It wasn't very often that Deanna Troi thought about drinking a beverage containing a stimulant, but her mind was thinking about some stiff English tea at that moment. She picked up the isolinear optical chip— just because it was comforting to hold it—and padded over to the food slot.

She punched the machine's wake-up button. "Small pot of English tea," she requested.

After several seconds, there was no synthesized voice response, and nothing happened at the delivery tray. Deanna hit the button again. "Computer," she ordered, "may I please have a glass of water?"

The complex mechanism hung in the wall like a shiny crater, and nothing happened.

"Computer?" Deanna Troi said evenly, "is this food slot working correctly?"

No answer—it was dead. Deanna didn't have time to worry about the inert machine, because she was already plotting an alternate course. If she wanted something to drink, she would have to go out, she reasoned. If she was going out, she might as well corral Geordi into helping her analyze the code with the computer. That would be a better starting place than staring at it, hoping for inspiration.

She yanked on her tight-fitting jumpsuit and touched her insignia badge. "Troi to La Forge," she announced. "What are you doing, Geordi?"

"Counting asteroids," he answered. "Do you know there are over four million asteroids in this one belt? I don't know how many, because I stopped counting at four million."

"Trying to read this code may prove less productive than counting asteroids," Deanna cautioned, "but I'd like to try. Can you help me run it through the computer?"

"Absolutely," Geordi enthused. "I'll meet you in Engineering—half my staff is on shore leave."

"On my way. Out."

Deanna only needed to take one thing with her, Karn Milu's secret isolinear chip. She gripped it in her hand and hurried out of the cabin, forgetting the broken food slot.

Chapter Fifteen

"VAGRA II," croaked Emil Costa to the rapt observers in the courtroom. "That's the planet where I found the submicrobe. I trapped it myself while we were in orbit and did all the preliminary tests myself."

Data was surprised when Judge Watanabe put Emil Costa on the stand before the defense had presented its case, but he didn't object. He understood her desire to comprehend the secret dealings between the deceased and the accused. She was looking for the truth, he sensed, not flexing her authority.

The judge increased her intense stare as she leaned forward to ask the defendant, "When did you decide to keep this discovery hidden from your colleagues and superiors?"

The frail scientist squirmed in his seat but managed to put a measure of professional pride into his voice. "I knew it was special right away," he said. "I tested it on Lynn's newest filters and found it was invincible— this little submicrobe throws all our previous work out the window. Lynn and I immediately transferred the test data to our private file and started making only oblique references to it. All we knew was that we wanted to control the discovery until we had a clear goal for it. The applications for weaponry or sabotage are frightening."

Emil took a drink of water and leaned forward in his chair, keeping his voice low. No one had trouble hearing him in the hushed courtroom. "To avoid discovery," he swallowed, "I ejected the only sample we had into space. No one but Lynn and I knew where to get more. We went to Karn Milu for advice, and that was our first mistake. He said we should sell the information to the highest bidder, in secret. The secrecy made sense to us, because if word ever got out, everyone would flock to Vagra II to trap their own specimens. With the open policies and reviews of the Federation, they would never be able to keep it a secret. Karn Milu offered to arrange all the details of the sale for a twenty-five percent cut. We agreed, without giving him any hard information.

"But Lynn got cold feet," he rasped, his eyes tearing slightly. "The implications worried her. Without even telling me, she erased every record that might remotely reveal the existence of the submicrobe. I was aghast at what she did, although it did serve to safeguard the secret even more. Milu got desperate and started to threaten Lynn. By this time, I was in complete agreement with my wife and wanted nothing more than to forget about the whole thing.

"That was not to be," he said hoarsely. "Lynn had felt we were in danger for some time, but I never took her seriously . . . until her death. Now I know how right she was. It was a terrible thing we did, and we've paid for it . . ." Emil's voice cracked into a sob, and he struggled to compose himself.

Judge Watanabe leaned toward him and asked, "Would you like a recess, Dr. Costa?"

He sat hunched and motionless, like a cheap hologram devoid of life. The judge cleared her throat and announced, "I believe we can excuse this witness until he is called by the defense. Lieutenant Worf, you may continue with your case."

"Yes, Your Honor," said Worf, standing slowly. He waited until the old man shuffled down from the witness stand. By his own testimony, Emil Costa had just opened himself to even more charges. He would not be a free man in his lifetime, Worf realized, no matter what happened here.

"At this time," intoned the Klingon, "I wish to present physical evidence." He nodded to a security officer, who placed a small palm-sized device on the bench. First Assistant Kwalrak eagerly poked at it. "This is the type I phaser weapon confiscated from Emil Costa less than half-an-hour after Karn Milu's murder. This is the weapon he used to hijack and disable the *Ericksen.*"

"Objection," protested Data. "That is a separate matter."

"Yes," admitted Worf, "except that it proves without a doubt that Emil Costa was armed with a phaser of the same type used to kill Karn Milu. He had the opportunity, the motive, and the weapon."

"One moment, Lieutenant Worf," said Judge Watanabe with a hint of confusion on her ageless face. "Excuse my ignorance, but weaponry is not my strong suit. Is there any way to determine positively whether *this* is the murder weapon?"

"No," answered the security chief. "Small phaser weapons, such as this, are made in the replicator. All are identical and have an identical firing pattern, with a slight variance when the power is running low. This phaser weapon was fired repeatedly aboard the shuttlecraft before it was forcibly removed from Emil Costa. His fingerprints and blood are all over it."

Kwalrak slammed the weapon down and hissed at Emil, "Why did you shoot Kreel? They had done you no harm!"

Judge Watanabe banged her gavel and leveled the Kreel female with a critical gaze. "Please," she cautioned, "let's confine our inquiry to the single charge of murder. Without a doubt, other charges are warranted, but we are trying the most serious charge first."

Disgruntledly, Kwalrak sat back in her seat and folded her huge arms. "We will wait," she grumbled, "as long as this is not a subterfuge to deprive the Kreel of justice. But I think we should recall this witness and find out more about the weapon."

The judge nodded in agreement and turned to Data. "If your client is recovered and you have no objection, the bench would like to ask a few more questions."

Data glanced at his client, who had apparently recovered from the emotional reliving of the events leading up to his wife's death. The aged scientist nodded gamely, so the android said, "I have no objection."

While Emil was taking his seat, Kwalrak turned to Worf, an action which seemed to dismiss any lingering tensions. "Is it normal in the Federation for civilians to carry phasers?"

"Not at all," he replied sternly. "This is a severe breach of security."

Judge Watanabe turned to the defendant. "Then the first question is, where did you get this weapon?"

The scientist hung his head, looking guilty enough to bring a slight smile to Worf's face. "I replicated it—while I was consulting with a group who were doing a study on replicator maintenance," he said sheepishly. "Yes, I know it's another crime I have committed. But Lynn was so scared that she insisted upon having some sort of protection. I replicated two of them."

Several pairs of eyebrows rose at once. "Where is the other one?" asked Worf.

"I don't know," Emil shrugged with confusion. "Lynn left it somewhere, or it was stolen . . . I don't remember."

Worf charged toward the witness and bellowed, "You replicated phaser weapons without authorization, then left them lying around where anybody could take them?"

"Calm yourself, Lieutenant Worf," cautioned Judge Watanabe. "Granted, this is a serious matter, but it's not our immediate concern. Dr. Costa, let me clarify this: You positively admit to having carried a concealed phaser weapon from the time you left Dr. Grastow's cabin, throughout your meeting with Karn Milu, then on to the shuttlecraft bound for this starbase?"

Head bent, the old man croaked, "I do. But I never fired it until I got on the shuttlecraft and they started to turn back. I swear! I was out of my mind, but I couldn't stand to go back there!"

Worf relaxed even more. If Wesley Crusher's testimony had been less than impressive for its total honesty, then Emil Costa's honesty was even more damning. The court was getting the picture of a deeply disturbed individual who would not hesitate to fire a phaser weapon indiscriminately.

"Dr. Costa," snarled the Kreel observer, "the boy said in his videotape that you were 'settling matters once and for all' when you went to see Karn Milu. If not to use it, why were you carrying that phaser?"

All eyes turned again to the wizened old man with the close-cropped hair. His hands shook feebly, but he returned the lopsided gaze of the triangular Kreel face. "I was afraid," he confessed. "I was more afraid than any time in my life. My wife was dead, my career was over, and I didn't know what would happen next. I didn't know who had killed Lynn—or even if she killed herself—but I knew it was because of my discovery."

He laughed derisively, *"My* discovery! This little submicrobe made a mockery out of all our work, our plotting and scheming, *our whole lives!* It was too late to save Lynn, but maybe, I thought, I could salvage our reputations by taking the secret to my grave. You think people like us, at the end of a famous career, have nothing to protect? You would be wrong—we have *everything* to protect. We fear being replaced, we fear being made useless, and we fear being discovered."

With bleary eyes and clenched fists, Emil grunted, "Most of all, we fear being discovered for grabbing the credit while letting others do the work."

Leering lopsidedly, the Kreel leaned forward. "Then you were prepared to kill him to keep your secret?"

"I don't know what I was thinking," he muttered. "I knew Karn Milu would be angry when I said the deal was finished, but what could he do to me? Take away my beloved wife? My career? My self-respect? They were all gone before I went to the pod room.

"I've done some terrible things," brooded the scientist, "but not murder. I never killed anyone."

"Who did?" asked the Kreel.

Emil folded his hands and shook his head emphatically. "I don't know," he swallowed, "but they must still be aboard the *Enterprise.*"

* * *

239

Engineering was running with a skeleton crew, all nonessential personnel having beamed down to the asteroid for a day's outing. The computer was being very logical in scheduling shore leave, thought Geordi La Forge, letting as many people as possible from the same department go together. It was too seldom, he decided, that the Engineering staff got to fraternize and meet one other's family and friends. He wondered how many of them were attending the murder trial?

That was something he wouldn't mind seeing, with Worf and Data pitted against one another. But Geordi got enough away assignments—he didn't mind holding down the fort while others had fun. Still, it was a little disconcerting to look around the cavernous engine room and see so few warm bodies pulsing red in his VISOR.

"Geordi," said Deanna impatiently, "how long is this going to take?"

The chief engineer peered down at the computer screen. Now that Deanna had snapped him out of his reverie, he had to admit the computer was taking too many seconds over this one problem. "Computer?" he asked, "what's happening with the code?"

"The data in question has insufficient recurrence factor to be code," replied the cordial female voice. "It does not match any recognized or hypothesized system of symbols, numerals, letters, words, phrases, or signals. It appears to be random."

Geordi looked at the counselor and smiled. "Computers always were lousy mind readers."

Deanna patted the chief engineer on the back and assured him, "It was a good try, Geordi. I can't say I'm surprised—I didn't think it would be that easy."

"That code of yours is the real thing," he allowed,

shaking his head, "pure stream of consciousness. Like beatnik poetry."

"Beatnik poetry?" asked Deanna.

"Beatniks were a substrata of Earth society from the mid-twentieth century," the human replied. "They recited surreal poetry that was rhythmic and often accompanied by bongo drums or a saxophone. Didn't mean a thing, except to the poet."

"I see," Deanna nodded, the idea of poetry suddenly intriguing her. She didn't know if it would work, but she had a burning impulse to walk in a holodeck setting and try to remember some Betazoid poetry from her youth. "Thank you, Geordi," she said, squeezing his hand and rushing toward the door.

"You're welcome!" he called after her puzzledly.

Upon reaching the turbolift, her combadge sounded with a polite male voice, saying, "Security officer Queryl to Counselor Troi."

She tapped her badge. "Troi here."

"An environmental technician is requesting entrance to your quarters to fix your food slot."

"My food slot?" she recalled with surprise. "Please, let him in. And thank him for his prompt attention."

"The appointment can wait until you're present."

"No need for that," answered Deanna. "I may not return to my quarters for some hours. Out." Thinking of the peculiar meters of Betazoid poetry, she gave the turbolift deck 11 as her destination.

Dr. Grastow shifted his massive bulk but still didn't fit comfortably into the wooden witness chair. Lieutenant Worf was not about to give him much chance to get comfortable. Prowling in front of the witness stand, he snapped, "How would you define your relationship with Dr. Costa?"

Grastow gazed warmly at the old man seated between the forcefield rods. "I idolize him," he admitted in his distinctive high-pitched voice. "I exist only to serve him."

"Were you serving Dr. Costa after his wife's funeral," asked Worf, "when you lied to his friends, saying he was unwell, while he hid in your quarters?"

"Yes," answered Grastow, "it was his wish."

"What about later?" replied Worf. "When you forcibly restrained Ensign Crusher and prevented him from leaving your quarters?"

The Antarean nodded gravely. "I knew it was wrong," he said, "but Emil wanted to be alone. I was the only person he fully trusted."

"Why was that?" growled Worf. "What power does he hold over you?"

"He and Lynn saved my planet," Grastow answered simply. "I would be dead, my parents dead, my world dead—were it not for the Costas. I exist only to serve him."

Worf shook his head impatiently and growled, "The character of the accused is not the issue."

"I believe it is," proclaimed Grastow. "Emil couldn't hurt anybody."

The Klingon paced, then stopped and leveled Emil with a pointed finger. "In preparation for his meeting with Karn Milu, did you see the accused arm himself with a phaser weapon?"

The humanoid squirmed and looked down at his beefy fists. "Yes, I did," he muttered.

"Why did he think he needed it?"

Grastow snipped, "He didn't say."

"You didn't think it was odd he was carrying a phaser weapon to meet his superior, a man with whom he had been a close associate for a number of years?"

"Uh, yes," gulped Grastow, "but I knew he was in a distraught frame of mind."

"Yet," growled Worf, "you kept doing his bidding, which included assaulting a Starfleet officer and aiding in the possession of a concealed weapon, even though you knew he was mentally disturbed?"

"Objection," interjected Data. "The witness is not a trained psychologist."

"I withdraw that question," muttered Worf. "Let's just say, Dr. Grastow, you were willing to break Starfleet regulations on behalf of Emil Costa. Is that correct?"

The Antarean nodded sheepishly, "Yes."

"How much did you know about the secret dealings between Karn Milu and Emil Costa?"

"Nothing!" claimed the big man emphatically. "I knew nothing."

Worf shook his head grimly and observed, "Then you sabotaged your career for nothing."

Somehow, the big Antarean managed to slump a bit farther down in his chair.

"This is a chance to resurrect your career for *something*," insisted Worf. "Won't you please tell us whatever you know about the secret dealings between the Costas and Karn Milu?"

The witness shook his massive head.

"Did you ever hear them discuss a secret discovery, a submicrobe that was indestructible?"

Grastow gave the Klingon a quizzical stare. "No," he said with finality.

"No further questions," murmured Worf, returning to his seat.

Judge Watanabe turned her attention to Data. "You may cross-examine."

The android stood and nodded politely to the witness, "Good day, Dr. Grastow."

"Good day," he chirped, brightening a little.

"How long," asked Data, "have you been working with the Costas in the Microcontamination Project?"

"I came to the *Enterprise* with them," the witness proclaimed proudly. "That was approximately three years ago. Only Dr. Saduk has been with them longer."

"Then you, Saduk, Lynn and Emil Costa joined the crew of the *Enterprise* at the same time?"

"Yes, we did," answered the Antarean, becoming talkative as he became more cheerful. "We've always been a very close-knit group, that's why I can't believe the terrible things that have happened to us."

"You testified," said Data, "that you are so loyal to Dr. Costa that you would break Starfleet regulations for him."

Warily, Grastow answered, "Yes."

"Does that include committing murder?"

"Objection!" barked Worf. "This witness isn't on trial."

Data countered, "I only wish to demonstrate to the court that others on the *Enterprise* may have had the motivation and opportunity to kill Karn Milu."

"Objection overruled," Judge Watanabe answered thoughtfully. "Let the witness answer."

Grastow squirmed in the tight-fitting chair. "I don't know about murder," he said squeamishly. "It never came up."

"Let us pose a theory," offered Data. "Dr. Grastow, if you possessed the missing phaser weapon, you could have followed the others to the cleanroom on deck 31 of the *Enterprise* and seen Emil Costa and Karn Milu arguing *after* they had disposed of Ensign Crusher. Perhaps you waited until Dr. Costa left, then confronted Karn Milu yourself. Would you commit murder to save Emil Costa's reputation?"

Abruptly, the defendant leapt to his feet and shook an aged fist at his own attorney. "Don't incriminate yourself, Grastow!" he crowed. "You weren't there— you didn't do it." In his agitation, the old man moved too far and hit the forcefield. He was knocked back onto his chair and nearly impaled on the backrest.

The security officers instantly shut off the barrier, and Worf was the first one to reach the fallen man. He caught him and gently steered him to his seat.

"I request a recess," said the Klingon.

Judge Watanabe sat forward intently, asking, "Are you all right, Dr. Costa?"

"Just bruised," he wheezed, clutching his chest. Then he looked gratefully at Worf. "Thank you."

Judge Watanabe removed her spectacles and rubbed her suddenly small eyes. "Due to the lateness of the hour," she announced, "we shall adjourn this court until ten o'clock tomorrow, when we will resume with Dr. Grastow's testimony."

While the others were rising from their chairs, Emil gripped Worf's brown hand with his withered pale one. "I didn't kill him," he breathed. "My life is over—I have nothing to gain by lying. To find his murderer, you must keep looking."

Worf stepped back and let the security officers remove the frail scientist. He stood motionless, watching the room gradually empty, thinking about the tangled web of interpersonal relationships that had constituted the Microcontamination Project. On one hand were the opportunistic Costas and Karn Milu; on the other were the loyal assistants, Grastow, Saduk, and Shana. She was the newest member of the group, yet she had been the first to point a finger at Karn Milu's involvement in Lynn Costa's murder. What might the others know that they hadn't said?

The Klingon shook his head, thinking this would be

another night without sleep. He didn't know exactly why, but he was going to heed the old man's admonition and keep looking.

It was one of those overcast days ruled by a good stiff breeze—the kind of day Deanna remembered so well from her youth. The meadow was alight with orange col blossoms, no more than a few centimeters tall. The giant mela reeds whipped in the breeze, their blue tassels hurling winged seeds into the wind, and the moss squished pleasantly under her boots. A drizzle struck her in the face, and she thankfully turned her face skyward to lick the rain with her tongue.

She hugged her old shawl tighter around her shoulders and recalled how it had been knitted by a friend of her mother. She wanted to feel like a child again, to rediscover the primitive emotions of childhood: poetry, frivolity, the joy in taking a walk, and the hurt of an unkind word. These were the triggers that allowed a Betazoid to access parts of the mind shut off to most species. A spirit of playfulness was the essence of discovery.

She walked along, marveling at the authenticity of the holodeck setting and wondering what was over the next hill. Why had she never tried this before? Because, she sighed to herself, she had never had to reach back quite so far to her roots. Betazoids could not only read emotions, she knew, they felt a compulsion to be completely honest about them, seeing them not as weaknesses to be hidden or exploited but as common bonds of experience and empathy. How could one sense emotions without experiencing them first? Deanna had kept hers in check—for the most part— during her tenure aboard the *Enterprise,* but now she had to forget that and open up every part of her mind and senses.

If she knew how Karn Milu was feeling, she told herself, she could decipher the meaning behind his subconscious ramblings. She didn't have to decipher every letter, just the portions dealing with the Costas and the Microcontamination Project. She was certain he had recorded some word, some note about his dealings with them. He would not have gone to all the trouble to make the isolinear chip if he hadn't wanted to leave some record.

One word, she told herself as she ran down a flowered incline, the wind slicking back her hair. One word, one name, might lead to others. Lynn, she thought, the one who had started it all. She would look for Lynn Costa's name, and she would know it when she saw it, somehow.

Deanna twirled for a moment, her scarf billowing behind her, as she chanted the nonsense words of a nursery song remembered from long ago. Aglow with exertion and the warmth of fond memories, she stopped spinning and shouted to the wind, "End program!" The room returned to a black segmented enclosure.

She toweled off on her way back to her quarters, feeling refreshed and renewed. Before entering, she paused at the doorway and sent a thought message to Karn Milu, asking him to help her. It was silly, she knew, but emotions and thoughts could linger. Deanna entered her quarters and sat down at her computer screen. She plugged in the optical chip and went right to work.

An odd melange of characters and symbols, apparently typed at random, crawled across the screen. She lightly perused the strange formations, waiting for something—anything—to jump out at her. The image of Lynn Costa was firmly fixed in her mind, and she knew Lynn's name would appear somewhere in the coded manuscript. She just knew it.

For two more hours, the Betazoid plied the apparent gibberish, never wavering from her belief in her powers. With a sense of playfulness, she tried to chant the nonsense, sing it, and babble it like a happy baby. All the while, the only likeness in her mind was Lynn Costa. How did Karn Milu feel about her?

"A hag," he called her. She blinked again, having read it right in front of her on the screen.

Suddenly, small clumps of the alphabet soup made sense. Names and simple words leapt out at her. Excitedly, she paged through more screens, looking for another appearance of Lynn Costa's name. She found it again, this time surrounded by other names she recognized. All the names were from the Microcontamination Project.

"Queen hag," it said here. She opened another document window to record the raw translations of Karn Milu's subconscious ramblings.

"Lynn," she repeated aloud, "is the queen hag. Emil is a naughty jester. Saduk is the heir-apparent. Grastow is a footman. Shana is jasmine."

She stopped abruptly and peered again at the jumbled letters on the screen and the words she had typed beside them. What did terms like footman, jasmine, and jester mean?

The counselor sat back and scratched her head. Now that she had deciphered the precognition code, she had found another code underneath. It reminded her of the word association tests employed by some psychologists. At this point, Deanna needed a second opinion, another mind off which to bounce all the theories and possibilities. Worf was the logical choice, but she wondered whether the trial on the asteroid was over for the day? It wouldn't hurt to try to contact him, she finally decided, because his communicator would be disabled if he was still in court.

Worf was in his quarters on the asteroid, quarters that were entirely too plush for his liking, with lots of blond wood and cheerful colors. He was studying another piece of evidence, wondering if it warranted being introduced. He held the blue vial carefully between his fingers, although it was hardly breakable. Even if they were trying Emil for his wife's murder, he thought glumly, the vial and Guinan's related testimony only proved that he drank alcohol and went to the pod room.

He remembered how, early on, the blue vial had been the first incriminating link between Emil and the slaying of his wife. It was as if finding the vial had been planned, to point them in Emil's direction. Worf bolted upright in his chair, his nostrils flaring at a maddening notion. What if Karn Milu's murder had been purposely planned to further condemn Emil Costa? He slammed his fist on the table, sending a crack down the center of its exotic blond veneer.

A sound on his combadge interrupted his anger. "Troi to Worf," came an excited voice.

"Worf here," he snarled. "I must talk with you."

"Then we're on the same wavelength," Deanna replied. "We've found an isolinear optical chip hidden in Karn Milu's office, and it contains coded notes, some of which I've been able to read."

"I'm returning to the ship," concluded Worf, jumping to his feet. "Where are you?"

"In my quarters," said the Betazoid. "I'll see you there. Out."

As Lieutenant Worf charged toward his doorway, Deanna Troi stood slowly, stretching her back muscles and neck. Despite the mental rigors of the last few hours, finding the key to the code hadn't seemed like work. Instead, she felt relaxed and invigorated, and she remembered the many times Karn Milu had urged her to practice her telepathy and develop her powers further. He would be proud of her, she felt.

Tea, thought the Betazoid, turning toward the food slot a few meters away. Had she not imagined a brimming cup of tea at that moment, she never would have seen the slight trail of steam spewing from the slot. Damn, she muttered to herself, I thought they fixed that thing.

Deanna took a single step, and her mind lost control of her legs. She pitched forward, gasping. Luckily she fell on an expanse of carpet, and her mind stayed alert the seconds she needed to grip her insignia badge and shout, "Troi to sickbay! Emergency! Emerguh . . ."

Her voice trailed off, and the Betazoid lapsed into an unconsciousness so profound that her lungs stopped breathing and her heart stopped beating.

Chapter Sixteen

WHEN WORF REACHED the nearest transporter room on the starbase, he was surprised to find Data waiting in line with about a dozen others to return to the *Enterprise.* From the laughing, carefree mood of the crew members, it was evident they were returning from shore leave. Four individuals were being transported at a clip, so the line to the platform was moving briskly. Worf fell into step behind Data.

"We could pull rank," he suggested to the android, "and go ahead of them."

"Yes, we could," Data agreed with a cock of his head. "But it would not be fair. These people are returning to their posts, whereas I am going to the *Enterprise* for recreation."

Worf smiled, "You aren't pleased with the way the trial is going?"

"Not particularly," answered the android. "I do not believe you are proving Emil Costa's guilt beyond a reasonable doubt, but it troubles me to think that the real murderer may be at large."

Worf clenched his fists and brooded, "You aren't the only one. I wonder if we'll ever know the whole truth?"

"Lieutenant Worf," came the familiar voice of Beverly Crusher, "report to sickbay immediately."

He tapped his badge and answered, "On my way, Doctor. What happened?"

"Deanna Troi," she began, choosing her words carefully, "has had a close brush with death. I don't want her speaking to anyone at the moment, but she insists on speaking to you."

"Acknowledged," growled Worf, charging onto the platform and motioning dazed travelers out of the way. Data was not far behind him.

Upon reaching the doors of sickbay, they found the entrance guarded by a stalwart Dr. Crusher, who stood barring their way with her arms crossed. "I want Deanna to sleep," she proclaimed, "but she insists she has to talk to Worf. Not anyone else, Data."

"But, Doctor," he protested, "is Counselor Troi all right?"

"She's had a very narrow escape," said the doctor grimly. "But she's stable and will recover completely . . . *with rest*. Data, will you please go to the bridge and alert Captain Picard and Commander Riker as to what happened? Tell them Deanna is all right, and we'll have the details later. In the meantime, no visitors until I give the order."

She snorted impatiently at the Klingon. "I wouldn't allow Worf, except my patient won't go to sleep without talking to him."

"Yes, Doctor," the android nodded obediently. He hurried off.

Beverly stepped aside and let the Klingon bull his way past. Then she led him the length of the examination room. "She's in the intensive care unit," explained the doctor, "but the danger has passed."

"What happened to her?" asked Worf with alarm.

Beverly glowered with frustration, "I'm not really sure. When she came in here, she wasn't breathing. Something caused all the functions of the brain to stop, all the voluntary and involuntary reflexes. We shocked her back to life. When she's stronger, we'll run some tests, but I would expect to see traces of poison."

"Who brought her in?"

"She called sickbay herself," the doctor shrugged. "The computer analyzed her voice patterns and deemed them sufficiently traumatized to initiate a direct-beaming. Or else," said Beverly, stopping and gazing at Worf, "Deanna would not be with us anymore."

The Klingon snarled low in his throat, and the hair on the back of his neck tingled with anger. He followed Dr. Crusher into the intensive care unit.

Deanna lay propped up in bed, her complexion pale. As Worf entered, she mustered a wan smile. He noticed she was lying perfectly still, as if the slightest motion was too much of an ordeal at the moment.

"Two minutes," cautioned Beverly Crusher, shutting the door behind her.

Worf knelt beside the bed. "I'm sorry I put you in danger," he muttered.

"Nonsense," she whispered. "We're getting close now, Worf, and the guilty one is getting desperate. In my quarters," she breathed, "get the isolinear chip. But be careful—the gas may linger. See what Karn Milu meant by the 'queen's hag' entry."

"What?" Worf asked with a startled blink.

"It may be nothing," sighed the Betazoid, sinking wearily into her pillow. After a few seconds, she lifted her head and summoned enough strength to clearly tell him: "In his secret records, Karn Milu wrote: Lynn is the queen hag, Emil is a naughty jester, Saduk is the heir-apparent, Grastow is a footman, and Shana is jasmine. That's just one entry in his notes, and we must have the chip to see them all."

"Rest," he cautioned her. "You have done enough." Worf rose to his feet and tapped his insignia. "Worf to La Forge."

"La Forge here," said the chief engineer. "It's good to talk to you."

"Meet me at Deanna Troi's cabin," he answered. "And bring two tricorders."

"Right away," Geordi responded puzzledly.

"Out," said Worf. He tapped his combadge again. "This is Lieutenant Worf. I want a security team in sickbay on around-the-clock status. No one is to see Counselor Troi without the permission of Dr. Crusher. Worf out."

He turned back to tell Deanna good-bye, but she was already asleep.

In the command area of the bridge, Captain Picard stood stiffly, his jaw clenched, and Commander Riker prowled anxiously beside him. He stopped pacing long enough to ask, "How did it happen?"

Data shook his head, "I do not know, and neither, I believe, does Dr. Crusher. The only thing the doctor seemed sure of was that Counselor Troi would recover."

Riker stroked his beard, then his hand curled into a fist. He turned impatiently toward Picard. "Permission to leave the bridge, sir?"

"No, Number One," replied the captain sympathetically. "We have to respect Dr. Crusher's orders. But," he said curtly, "we should find out what exactly is going on here."

"There exists the unproven possibility," said Data,

"that Counselor Troi's sudden illness may be related to the murder investigation."

The first officer shook his head with frustration and disbelief. "Captain," he barked, "would you like to contact Worf, or shall I?"

"You can," Picard answered, "but please remember, so far the Lieutenant has been right about many aspects of this bizarre situation with the Costas. If I hadn't doubted him, we might have avoided that business on the shuttlecraft."

Riker took a deep breath, realizing he didn't often hear his superior question his decisions. He also realized he knew less than any of them about the events leading up to the shuttlecraft incident. Calmly, he requested, "Riker to Worf."

The deep-voiced response came instantly, "Worf here."

"Lieutenant, we've just heard about Deanna Troi. Is everything under control?"

"Yes, sir," answered the Klingon. "When I left her, she was asleep and recovering. We talked, and Dr. Crusher assured me she will recover. I am on my way to her quarters now to determine what caused her collapse."

"What do you think it could be?" asked Will.

"She seems to think it was some sort of gas," Worf replied. "Geordi and I will investigate until we're sure there's no danger, then we'll call in an engineering team."

"Be careful," added Picard. "Let me know if there's anything we can do."

"Thank you, Captain," Worf said crisply. "We may need to ask the court for a delay. Tomorrow, following Grastow, I was going to call Counselor Troi as a witness."

"I'll get the delay," promised Picard. "You get to the bottom of it. Out."

"Out," answered Worf, stepping off the turbolift onto the familiar residential deck where most of the bridge officers lived. From a turbolift on the other side of the corridor stepped Geordi La Forge, carrying two tricorders. He tossed one to Worf, and the Klingon immediately set off down the walkway.

"What's going on?" asked Geordi, falling into step behind the big humanoid. "I thought you had this thing all sewed up?"

"I was deceiving myself," snarled Worf as he increased his stride.

They rounded a bulkhead, and Worf halted when he saw the open doorway of Deanna Troi's cabin. He continued cautiously a few more meters before stopping to consult his tricorder.

Geordi stopped and flipped open his tricorder. "What are we looking for?" he asked.

The Klingon's hooded eyes never wavered from his readouts. "A gas that can kill someone in seconds."

"I'm picking up some strange residual trace elements," said the chief engineer, "but not in a quantity to be dangerous. It looks like somebody was nice enough to air out the room for us."

"Niceness had nothing to do with it," snarled Worf, cautiously moving into the doorway. When none of the indicators on his tricorder shot up, he stepped into the room.

Geordi followed him, but they went to different parts of the cabin: Worf to the computer screen and Geordi to the food slot—which had been blasted with a phaser.

"Look at this!" marveled Geordi, kneeling beside the blackened crater and jagged metal that had once been a food slot. Black streaks stretched like the points of a star from the gaping hole. Inside, charred wires were covered with steaming green goop. "Direct shot," he observed.

Worf rifled through Deanna's desk and computer console but could find no isolinear optical chip. The screen was off, and both the primary and secondary chip slots were empty. *"Do'Ha'!"* he cursed.

"What's the matter?" asked Geordi.

"It's gone," growled Worf, "the isolinear chip!" He whirled around the room, as if the perpetrator might still be present. "After Deanna collapsed, somebody came in here to steal the chip. When they didn't find her body, they made a quick decision to destroy the evidence of their murder attempt." He glared at the scorched food slot.

"I'll bring in some people from Environmental to go over this food slot," said Geordi, standing and wiping the smudges off his hands.

"We're too late," grumbled Worf. Head uncharacteristically bowed, the Klingon headed toward the door. "I'm going back down to Karn Milu's office. Maybe he left another chip, or other records."

"One moment," called Geordi, halting Worf briefly in the doorway. "I know you've got a lot on your mind, but I completed that speed-up of the turbolifts you asked for. If you ever want to test what it's like to go fifteen percent faster, just give your destination as speed test and you'll take the express trip to Engineering."

"Thank you," nodded Worf, striding away.

Geordi called after him, "Do it when you first get on. Don't do it when the turbolift is in motion, or you'll get the ride of your life!"

Worf barely heard the engineer's last words as he strode angrily down the corridor, away from Deanna Troi's cabin. Again, the murderer had anticipated their actions and beaten them! For all his cleverness and certainty, Worf had been wrong about Emil Costa, unless Costa was working in league with somebody else on the ship. But who else felt threatened enough to commit two murders? Nearly three murders!

Deanna Troi had found something, the first piece of evidence that hadn't been obvious. That was what irked Worf the most—he had dutifully followed the trail of bread crumbs laid out for him while missing the feast. While he had played courtroom on Kayran Rock, Deanna Troi had been doing his job, ferreting out the murderer. At the one instance when he had truly been needed—to protect his crew mate and the evidence—he had been off strutting and making speeches.

Worf grunted angrily as he rounded a bulkhead and headed for the turbolift. Where was he going? He didn't even know. He had told Geordi he was going to Karn Milu's office, but he was certain the office had been picked clean of clues. They had had their opportunity and failed.

The turbolift doors shut, and he had to declare a destination. "Deck five," spit the Klingon.

"Acknowledged," said the friendly computer voice.

It was a jaunt of only one deck, and Worf stepped out a moment later into a corridor lined with darkened offices and meeting rooms. The science branch was either too shaken to do much work, thought Worf, or too busy enjoying shore leave.

The Klingon walked slowly down the corridor, thinking the worst was yet to come. He would have to go on trying a case in which he had no confidence, or turn his prisoner over to the Kreel. Neither decision was remotely palatable. He knew the Kreel cared more about Emil Costa's knowledge than his guilt or innocence, but the man, if truly innocent of murder, had suffered enough. He didn't deserve to become a Kreel prisoner . . . indefinitely.

Worf expected to find his security team waiting outside Karn Milu's office, but he did not expect to find Dr. Saduk conversing cordially with them. The two officers promptly sprang to attention upon seeing the security chief.

"At ease," he said. "Hello, Dr. Saduk."

"Lieutenant Worf," nodded the Vulcan. "I am glad you arrived. I was just requesting entrance to Dr. Milu's office."

"May I ask why?" queried the lieutenant.

"I thought," said the Vulcan, "that Dr. Milu may have left instructions in his log concerning the future of the Microcontamination Project. As you might surmise, we have been in limbo for several days. We don't know whether we are to continue operation, under whose direction, or with what staff. If we are to continue, we must restaff immediately."

The lieutenant pointed to the door, and one of his officers pressed a button to open it. The Klingon stepped slowly into the ornate office, trailed by the graceful Vulcan. "Whose responsibility was it," asked Worf, pondering the bug-infested walls, "to staff the Microcontamination Project?"

Saduk crossed immediately to the massive amber desk. "With the exception of Shana Russel," he replied, "the Costas had staffed the project before coming here. Shana's been with us for six months, and now she could become the senior member of the team."

"Are you thinking of leaving too?" asked Worf.

"I am," the Vulcan replied, flicking on Karn Milu's computer screen. "Both Emil and Grastow may be sentenced for crimes and be unavailable. If Grastow is not convicted of any crime and Dr. Milu appointed him before his death, Grastow will take charge of the project. That would hasten my departure."

"At least you're honest," observed Worf. "You want that job, and you won't stand for anybody else getting it."

"I am the best qualified," replied Saduk factually, slipping into the dead Betazoid's chair. He peered at the data popping onto the screen. "Do I have your permission to look at his log?"

"Go ahead," muttered Worf, sinking into one of the guest chairs. "I could suggest to the captain that you be given the post. With Karn Milu dead, the captain could make the determination."

"I would be grateful to you and the captain if that was the final outcome," Saduk replied, never taking his eyes or hands from the computer console. "If Grastow has already been appointed, however, that obstacle would be harder to overcome. Plus, the captain would be within reason to simply cancel the project. It has proven rather ill-fated."

Worf wasn't going to argue with that statement. He almost envied the way the Vulcan was going to walk away from it all. His mind was jumping from one troubling aspect to another, wondering how he could ever get this investigation back on course. Snippets of words, conversations, actions, and images were flitting through his brain, not giving him a single thing to grasp. What had Deanna Troi said to him in sickbay, words that were all that remained of the stolen optical chip? Worf prided himself on his memory, and trying to recall the cryptic phrases gave him something concrete to think about while the Vulcan probed the computer.

"Nothing pertinent in his log," the Vulcan declared,

pushing his chair back. "I believe it will be up to the captain to make a determination."

"Lynn is the queen hag," Worf repeated aloud, "Emil is a naughty jester, Saduk is the heir-apparent, Grastow is a footman, and Shana is jasmine."

Saduk blinked and furrowed his eyebrows slightly. "That is interesting," he remarked. "Are those your impressions of us?"

"No," the lieutenant shrugged. "Karn Milu's. Do they mean anything to you?"

"Individually," answered Saduk, "they have a degree of meaning. Lynn would certainly be considered the queen, although I never considered her difficult. Emil was more capable of laughter and the human trait of joking than the rest of us, and one could say he had been naughty. I *am* the heir-apparent, although apparent is not positive. As I understand the term 'footman' it could mean a servant—I leave it to you to say whether Grastow qualifies. As for Shana being Jasmine, I did hear Dr. Milu call her that once."

Worf bolted upright in his chair. "Wait," he said, "you say Jasmine is a *name?*"

"He used it as such," replied Saduk. "I only heard him call her that once. Perhaps she reminded him of somebody he used to know named Jasmine."

"Perhaps," frowned Worf, rising gradually to his feet. "When we first met in this office, he seemed not to remember her name."

"I thought that was odd at the time," remarked the Vulcan, "since *he* brought her aboard the *Enterprise* and assigned her to our project."

The Klingon moved behind the Vulcan and hovered over his shoulder. "Look up Shana Russel's personnel file," he ordered. "See what data Karn Milu kept on her."

Saduk keyed in the appropriate commands, and they both stared in amazement at the results. Records on Shana Russel were almost nonexistent, dating only from her arrival aboard the *Enterprise*.

"Computer," Worf intoned, "what is Shana Russel's background?"

"Data incomplete," said the computer after a moment. "Removed at request of Dr. Karn Milu."

"What?" snarled Worf with surprise.

"Data incomplete," repeated the computer. "Shall I request an update from the starbase?"

"How long will that take?"

"Approximately six-point-seven minutes."

"Patch it to my command post," barked Worf. He headed for the door, stopped, and looked back at Saduk. "Thank you. As far as I'm concerned, you deserve that job, and I will tell the captain as much."

The Vulcan nodded agreeably, his saturnine face and expression never changing.

Worf walked down the corridor to his command post, noting how deserted deck 1 had become. He hoped the others were enjoying Kayran Rock more than he was. The Klingon thought briefly about poking his head into the bridge, but he didn't want to face a blizzard of questions concerning Deanna Troi's status. She was recovering and resting, and Dr. Crusher could tell them that. He wasn't anxious to discuss the trial, either. Data could give them an account and do it more objectively than he would. Worf knew he had to forget the trial, reverse course, and start over. He had no idea whether Shana Russel's missing personnel files meant anything or not—missing, secret, and erased computer files were common practice with this lot—but it was a place to start.

He stepped into his command room without passing a single crew member, which was a welcome respite in his present frame of mind. Worf went to his food slot to get a glass of water, and, thinking of Deanna Troi, he hesitated before activating the device. He held his breath until the glass of water innocuously appeared.

Worf sank into the chair behind his command console and punched up the data he and Deanna Troi had been studying only a few days ago. At that time, the Costas had been the primary focus of the investigation, with not much thought paid to the others who orbited around them. They were the shining stars—and now they had gone nova and were about to disappear altogether.

As he reviewed their careers—the early battles, followed by remarkable achievements and altruistic endeavors, culminating in assignment to the *Enterprise*—he realized how far they had risen. In the annals of Federation science, they were legend. But at what cost? Their ambitions had degenerated into greed and treachery.

The computer voice broke into his thoughts. "Received data from starbase," she announced. *"Enterprise* computer updated. Do you wish the data by screen or audio?"

Worf already had screenfuls of data, so he replied, "Audio."

"Shana Russel," said the computer, "born Jasmine Terry on Earth, city of Calcutta. Age, twenty-five standard years. Received bachelor of science degree—"

"Wait," said Worf, leaning forward curiously. "When did she change her name?"

"Eight-point-five months ago."

"Jasmine Terry," he repeated aloud, tasting each syllable. He knew where he had heard the first name, but where had he heard that surname before? "Correlate the name Terry," he told the computer, "with similar names in the records on Lynn and Emil Costa."

"Searching," replied the computer. "One match found. Megan Terry was a co-worker with the Costas approximately twenty-six years ago in the Dayton biofilter experiments. She sued them for scientific plagiarism over biofilter version 8975-G, which was eventually accepted as the Federation standard, but her case was dismissed due to lack of evidence."

"Correlate Megan Terry and Jasmine Terry," demanded Worf.

"Mother and daughter," answered the computer.

"That's enough of that," said a voice behind him. "Elevate your hands."

Worf did as he was told, knowing the intruder was in possession of a phaser and was not adverse to using it. He twisted his head enough to see Shana Russel emerging from the lavatory. She was dressed in dark nondescript clothes with a backpack strapped to her shapely torso. She was also carrying a phaser aimed at his head.

"I should have set the phaser on full," she muttered, "when I shot you before."

"Why didn't you?" he asked.

The young blond woman smiled innocently, "I liked you. Even *I* make mistakes. Now stand slowly, keeping your hands up, and back away from that console. I've got this phaser set to full now."

Worf did exactly as he was told. He had dealt with dangerous and unpredictable creatures from all over the galaxy, but few of them seemed as cold-heartedly ruthless as Shana Russel/Jasmine Terry.

"Your mother," he said, backing toward the wall, "was the one who really perfected the biofilter?"

Shana's pretty face clouded with anger so ugly it bordered on dementia. "It was worse than that!" she hissed. "All three of them were equals in the project, but Emil was having an affair with my mother. He promised to leave his wife if she would turn over the results of her work to him—*she* was the one who was really making progress. Like a fool, she believed him. They stole her work and got her reassigned, while they soared to acclaim. Emil wouldn't acknowledge *me* at all."

"He knew you?" asked Worf.

"Not really," she grimaced with pure hatred. "He never admitted to being my father, but he is."

The Klingon stood perfectly still, realizing the petite blonde was pathologically insane. She must have suffered daily harangues from her mother, proclaiming how the Costas had ruined both their lives. As a Klingon orphaned by the ravages of war, he understood the powerful force of revenge, and he also knew the toll it could claim.

"You succeeded in destroying them," he complimented her.

Shana smiled broadly, "I know. Killing Lynn was satisfying because of the complexity involved. But watching Emil suffer was so . . . fulfilling. He had no idea who I was, or what was happening to him."

"But Karn Milu knew who you were."

"Of course," she answered, "he knew my mother and her whole history with the Costas. When he wanted someone to spy on them over this business with the submicrobe, he came to my school to find me. We decided to change my name to hide my identity, and he spent his sabbatical teaching me Betazoid mind techniques to fool Deanna Troi." The former Jasmine Terry smiled, "I've always been a good student."

"Why did you kill him?" Worf asked calmly.

The woman shrugged, "He was the only one who knew who I was. Plus, killing him resulted in even more suffering for Emil. How could I resist?"

"And Deanna Troi?"

"If anyone could uncover me," answered the murderess, "I knew it would be Counselor Troi. When I planted that device in her food slot, I also planted a transmitter to keep track of her discoveries." Shana shook her head regretfully. "It's a pity. If she had only died as planned, you wouldn't have known about the isolinear chip and we wouldn't be having this conversation."

The woman pressed a panel on Worf's desk, and the door opened, revealing a corridor that had been emptied by shore leave. She motioned with the weapon, "I'll follow you to the turbolift. If you make the slightest wrong move, I'll slice you in two."

"Understood," said Worf, stepping briskly into the corridor. "Where are we going?"

"To get a shuttlecraft," answered the young blonde. "I'm afraid my tour aboard the *Enterprise* is over, and so is yours."

Worf didn't argue. With very deliberate motions, he walked toward the turbolift, feeling the phaser perhaps a meter from his back. He entered first and moved to the rear of the shining enclosure, leaving plenty of room for the woman wielding the weapon.

"I'm glad you're cooperating," she smiled. "Perhaps, with a little luck, we can reach one of the Kreel planets. With what I know, they might be willing to shelter me. Of course, you can drop me off and leave."

"Whatever you say," Worf replied congenially, ignoring the obvious lie. "Deck four, please."

As they began to move, Shana leaned confidently against the side of the lift. "I'm glad you're taking this so well," she cooed. "You might think about staying with me."

"New destination," said Worf suddenly, "speed test."

He had a chance to brace himself, but Shana was still reclining against the wall when the floor dropped out from under them. The artificial gravity was slow to adjust, and she crashed into the roof, shrieking, then bounced along the far wall. Worf rolled into a curl and did the same thing with less damage. They whizzed through the center of the ship as the gravity struggled to catch up, and it finally dumped them in a heap on the floor of the flying turbolift.

Even with her injuries, Shana fought the Klingon for control of the phaser. He made the fight brief, punching her in the face and knocking her unconscious. Worf was struggling to his feet when the doors opened and deposited them in Engineering.

A startled Geordi La Forge gaped at them. "Worf!" he wailed. "What happened?"

The Klingon muttered woozily, "Belay that request for the speed increase." Then he collapsed.

Geordi pressed his insignia badge. "La Forge to sickbay. I need Dr. Crusher in Engineering."

Chapter Seventeen

"Now SIT DOWN THERE," Beverly Crusher told Worf, pushing him back onto the examination table. Worf wasn't so weak that he couldn't out-muscle the good doctor, but her tone of voice told him he shouldn't try.

He twisted his head from side to side. "What happened to Shana Russel?" he asked.

"Still unconscious," she sighed, checking his readings on the luminous panel behind him. "We could bring her to, but she has some minor internal injuries, so it's better to let her rest."

"I'm not injured," muttered Worf, sitting up before she could stop him. "I just bumped my head."

"Apparently, her head isn't as thick as yours," the doctor snapped, pushing him back down. "But at least she's lying quietly."

He saw a member of the security contingent hovering in the doorway and called him with a booming, "Ensign Cavay!"

The fresh-faced ensign hurried toward him and skidded to attention. "Yes, sir," he replied.

"Until further orders," said the Klingon, "you are

to personally guard Shana Russel and see she doesn't go anywhere."

Dr. Crusher scoffed, "She's not going anywhere."

"Yes, she is," countered Worf. "As soon as she's able, she's going to confinement."

Beverly Crusher waved a hypo at her agitated patient. "Are you going to relax long enough to let me examine you, or do I have to use this?"

Worf tried to release the tenseness from his shoulders and accept the bed underneath him. He had won, he told himself, he had caught her. She wouldn't murder again; the contamination was ended. He pressed his insignia and said hoarsely, "Worf to Captain Picard."

"Picard here," answered the captain with obvious concern. "Geordi told us what happened. Are you and the young lady all right?"

"She's the murderer, Captain," rasped Worf. "Shana Russel killed Lynn Costa and Karn Milu in order to ruin Emil. Her mother was Megan Terry— check the computer playback . . ."

"You relax, Lieutenant," ordered the captain. "I'll arrange her transfer to the starbase. Make your report as soon as you're able."

"Yes, sir," replied Worf, trying to relax. He bared his teeth in triumph as he whispered, "This time, it's certain."

Emil Costa paced in his small but comfortably appointed cell on Kayran Rock, wondering what was happening. For sixteen hours, he had not been summoned to the courtroom and had not received any word from Commander Data, or anyone else for that matter. Meals and library materials had become his entire existence, and he finally began to realize what long-term imprisonment would be like. He had been so intent on defending his innocence on those ridiculous murder charges, he hadn't realized what kind of life he would have after the other trials were over. Now he knew, and it caused him to pace all the more worriedly.

He was surprised a moment later when the outer door opened, and Captain Picard, Commander Data, and the female Kreel walked toward him.

"Captain!" he swallowed, moving to the edge of the forcefield. "What a surprise. Hello, Commander Data, First Assistant Kwalrak."

He was relieved by the captain's smile. Even the normally reserved android looked pleased. "Dr. Costa," began Picard, "you will be happy to know that the murder charges against you have been dropped. Shana Russel has confessed to both murders."

"Shana Russel!" he gasped, sitting on the foot of his narrow bunk.

"Her name is actually Jasmine Terry," explained Data. "She is Megan Terry's daughter, and she claims you are her father."

"Megan . . ." rasped the white-haired scientist, his eyes glazing over with a deluge of memories and regrets.

"We will arrange for you to view her confession," said Picard sympathetically. "At the moment, we have a matter that is more pressing—what to do about the charges stemming from the shuttlecraft incident. First Assistant Kwalrak has talked to her superiors, and we believe we can reach an agreement. If you will plead guilty to charges of assault and endangerment, the Kreel will agree to allow you to serve a term of five years under house arrest, here on this starbase. In exchange, you will agree to teach classes in biofilter development to young Kreel."

"You see," interjected Kwalrak with a lopsided grin, "we have realized that just buying transporter technology, without having the knowledge to support it, would enslave us to the vendors. We want to learn how to develop it ourselves. And Doctor Costa has an excellent broad-based understanding of the principles behind transporters."

Picard looked at the doctor and added, "You won't be doing the work for them—you'll just be teaching. Staying here on the starbase will ensure that. And it will ensure that the Federation will drop any additional charges related to your handling of the new submicrobe."

The old scientist looked at Data and smiled quizzically, "You're my lawyer, shall I take this deal?"

"The alternative," answered the android, "is to be bound over to the Kreel for trial on their home planet. The Federation would not be able to assist you. If you feel you can live inside this asteroid for five years, you should take the deal."

"I've lived in far worse places," said Emil, rising to his feet. "Consider it done."

Captain Picard nodded to the attending security officer, "Release him."

A small chime sounded, and the old man reached out to make sure the forcefield was gone. He gratefully stepped out of the cell and shook Data's hand. "Thank you," he gushed, "you're a wonderful lawyer."

"Do not thank me," said the android, "thank Lieutenant Worf and Counselor Troi."

Deanna Troi was strolling down a corridor, feeling vigorously healthy for the first time since the attempt on her life. She also felt a bit at loose ends, knowing the investigation had finally been concluded. Sweet little Shana Russel, she mused, a cold-blooded murderess. It was somewhat flattering, she decided, to know that Karn Milu had spent several weeks training the girl in order to circumvent Deanna's insight.

Suddenly, a strong hand gripped her arm, and she turned to see the beaming face of Commander Riker. "Good to see you up and about," he grinned. "Where are you going?"

"To the bridge," she answered hesitantly, having no real reason to go there.

"No, you're not," he said, steering her toward a turbolift. "You're going to Kayran Rock with me on shore leave."

"I am?" She frowned puzzledly. "I didn't put in for shore leave."

"I requested it for you," he winked, "for the same time as mine."

A surprised smile graced the Betazoid's face, and she bounded into step beside him. She whispered conspiratorily, "How long can we be gone?"

"We're not due to leave for ten whole hours!" he beamed. "I figure we'll stay until they come after us."

Deanna gripped Will's arm and suppressed a giggle as the turbolift doors closed around them.

On the bridge, Lieutenant Worf straightened to attention when Captain Picard and Commander Data entered. Data took his position at the ops console, beside a smiling Wesley Crusher at the conn. Except for the absence of Commander Riker, the bridge crew was at full complement for the first time in several days.

"Status, Lieutenant?" Picard asked Worf.

"Maintaining station with Kayran Rock," answered the Klingon. "The last scheduled shore leave will end in ten hours. We are cleared to leave at that time."

"Lieutenant," said Jean-Luc Picard, "it's good to see you on the bridge again."

"Thank you, Captain," he nodded. "It's good to be back."

"As for the job you did while you were away," the captain went on, "I have something to say."

"Yes, sir?" asked Worf.

"Well done."

THE EXPLOSIVE NEW

STAR TREK: ®

HARDCOVER

PROBE

by
Margaret Wander Bonanno

Pocket Books Hardcovers is proud to present PROBE, an epic length novel that continues the story of the movie STAR TREK IV.

PROBE reveals the secrets behind the mysterious probe that almost destroyed Earth—and whose reappearance now sends Captain Kirk, Mr. Spock, and their shipmates hurtling into unparalleled danger...and unsurpassed discovery.

The Romulan Praetor is dead, and with his passing, the Empire he ruled is in chaos. Now on a small planet in the heart of the Neutral Zone, representatives of the United Federation of Planets and the Empire have gathered to discuss initiating an era of true peace. But the talks are disrupted by a sudden defection—and as accusations of betrayal and treachery swirl around the conference table, news of the probe's reappearance in Romulan space arrives. And the *Enterprise* crew find themselves headed for a final confrontation with not only the probe—but the Romulan Empire.

Available In Hardcover from Pocket Books In April

POCKET
B O O K S